DEATH COMES
FOR PETER PAN

JOAN BRADY

Death Comes for Peter Pan

Secker & Warburg
London

First published in Great Britain in 1996
by Martin Secker & Warburg Limited
an imprint of Reed International Books Limited
Michelin House, 81 Fulham Road, London SW3 6RB
and Auckland, Melbourne, Singapore and Toronto

A CIP catalogue record for this book
is available from the British Library

ISBN 0 436 20261 1

Phototypeset by Intype London Ltd
Printed and bound in Great Britain
by Clays Ltd, St Ives plc

for
Hillary Rodham Clinton
who did her damndest to help

Acknowledgements

I could never have managed to write about the consequences of Medicare in the United States without the help of a remarkable library called the Data Centre in Oakland, California. The sources they supplied me with are too numerous to quote; there are literally hundreds of them. I am also grateful to the library at Torbay Hospital in Torquay, which supplied me with hundreds more.

The exchanges between Army Counsel Joseph Welch and Senator Joseph McCarthy on pages 132–135 are taken almost verbatim from the record as quoted in Michael Straight's book *Trial by Television*. Much additional information on McCarthy comes from this book and also from Anderson and May's *McCarthy, The Man, The Senator, the 'Ism'*. I also consulted Lillian Hellman's *Scoundrel Time* and Jane Foster's *An Unamerican Lady*. I owe – plainly – a great deal to J. M. Barrie's *Peter Pan* and to Lewis Carroll's *Alice in Wonderland*. I have quoted from both, adapted scenes and character traits from both and hereby acknowledge my debt and my gratitude to both. For the idea of Medicare as a Wonderland of a place, I thank Robert L. Kane, Dean of the School of Public Health at the University of Minnesota, who wrote of it in *Lessons from the First Twenty Years of Medicare*.

Beyond this, I also owe many thanks to many individuals: to Al and Jo Hart, who suggested years ago that I write the novel; to Jim Lee Yates, who gave me the first real grasp of what goes on in an American nursing-home; to Alexandra Pringle, who sold the book so wonderfully well; to Mary Siepmann, for encouraging me to go on, for suggesting the dedication and (perhaps most of all) for letting me cry on her shoulder; to Geoffrey Mulligan for his deft and sensitive editing job; to Diana Athill, Laura Morris and Alexandra again for many helpful suggestions; and to Gerald Parkes, MD, who was the first person to read the ms., for his enthusiasm as well as for his advice on the medical aspects.

I also want to thank my brother Michael Brady, just for being there (to say nothing of his many and various contributions to the text), my sister-in-law Mary Jane Masters and my friend Kira Strakhova, who helped me through the troubles of heart that the writing of this book caused me. Finally, I owe much on many levels to my son Alexander, for things he and I alone know (and some that only I know).

Part One

CHAPTER 1

i

The dogs lay in the laundry-room. Alice Kessler had to go past them because the laundry-room was the only way out of the apartment — a funny way to construct an apartment.

There were only four dogs left: the huge yellow one, the shapeless white one, the nondescript one and the little yappy one with a scraggled coat. The black dog was dead. Mud stuck in clots beneath the little one's belly. Was it a terrier? She didn't know; she didn't care. She hated the four of them equally, impartially — no favouritism — and each time she passed them the nausea in her spread out and deepened. Nausea is a finely-tuned gauge of fear; you can use it to calculate the subtlest changes in the substrate. They say dogs can smell such things. Maybe so. If these did, they never let on, although their eyes swivelled in their eye sockets, marking her progress across the room from inside door to outside door.

The dogs ran as a pack. This was supposed to be a secret, but in a moment of weakness Cordelia Macher-Daly had told her about it. Cordelia was her landlady. The dogs attacked a neighbour not all that long ago, and Cordelia had to bribe an official to keep them out of the dog crematorium, which puffed smoke from a vast, red chimney out on the edge of this ugly Middle Western town. In the end, only the black dog ended up there. The chimney was the centre-piece of the room Peter lay in.

But it wasn't dogs that scared Alice. After all, if they tore her to pieces, the whole mess would become somebody else's responsibility. For some time now, a year maybe, she'd wakened in the night with a start, her hands suspended above the sheets like some retired gun-fighter snapping to attention even in the safety of his bed, unable to let go of a past that had long since let go of him. But she was no retired gun-fighter: she was only thirty-five years old. Even so, each waking was the same. What was that? Hear it? Hold still. Don't breathe. Then recognition comes flooding in. Oh, what the hell, it's just yesterday's tedium clamouring to get itself born again today.

So she figured it was the tedium of crossing the laundry-room, dogs or no dogs – the grinding boredom of it – that intensified the nausea in her. Black porthole-face of washing-machine and faceless drier (both humming with homely warmth and efficiency), high window, dirty panes of glass, dog bowls, dog blankets, smell of dog hair and dog saliva. Why does this getting from one place to the next have to be gone through again and again? Forward and back this morning. Twice yesterday. Twice the day before. Twice every day for weeks. Why not edit it out this last time? Just clip a meaningless frame from the picture? Isn't enough ever enough?

Unlock the outside door, open it, walk through, shut the dogs in.

'They're sneaky,' Cordelia had said. 'They don't really want to get out, but they'll try to fool you, just for the fun of it. They have a sense of humour, these dogs do. They'll never let you win.'

The cold outside was fierce. Alice's feet crunched on the salt that covered the path from the back door of the house to the

4

stone-paved turnaround where the rented car stood. In Russian winters, when a man pees in the snow, it's so cold that his pee freezes from the ground up – shoots towards him in a frozen arc. 'The Middle West is Dostoevsky country,' Peter used to say. There were twenty-three steps between house and car. Her mouth moved as she counted them off. Seventeen to go. Despite the cold, the palms of her hands were greasy with sweat.

If only I didn't blabber on like this, she said to herself. Other people have silence in their heads. Why can't I? Same thoughts today as yesterday. Same thoughts yesterday as the day before. Wouldn't you think there'd be some variation? Maybe not other days – who would ask it? – but today? For God's sake, today?

Because today was different.

This day, at this very moment, she was on her way to kill Peter Kessler, who was dying anyway. Which she knew. Could anything be more absurd?

ii

Peter Kessler had been a beautiful man to look at once – not the kind of looks that diminish with age, either. Some people are disgustingly lucky. I'm talking about him as of a few years before all this happened, you understand, although fewer than you might guess. Sometimes when he was asleep, Alice had stared down at him and wondered how anybody so beautiful could be real – and this despite the fact that he was thirty years older than she.

But it's queer how you remember people, snapshot-like, out of context, a sideways glance or a sudden movement, a quirk here, a detail there. For her it was the tension in him. He'd always been tense, always uncomfortable as he sat or stood or walked, somehow unresolved, as though there were some dissonance deep inside: an elegant awkwardness of the hands, long, slender fingers that clenched and unclenched like a child's even while he slept.

This tawdry Middle-Western town in this dreary Midwestern winter: what a place for such a man to die. She concentrated on manoeuvring the rented car along the frozen streets and through the dirty snow in ridges along both sides of the tarmac. It was a large, soft car – too soft, no feel of the road. At night, towns like Overton glow under arc lights, an eerie, ugly orange, thicker in this town on this night because of the burning fields on all sides; this was the Night of the Corn Scorch.

Less than an hour ago, the good burghers here had torn themselves away from their television screens and started off the ceremony by setting alight a fifteen-foot-tall Corn King made of papier mâché. At least he was supposed to be papier mâché; Alice knew for a fact that his right hand was only chicken-wire. This late November funeral pyre was old as Middle-Western customs go, more than a hundred years old, once a rag-tag affair, now gaudily and seamlessly packaged for the tourist trade: the celebrating, as you'd expect, took place in the business district, well away from Alice's route. She drove from the best residential section of town through the poorest, where there was a deep sense of quiet. Only the occasional neon splutter of a supermarket sign or a gas station punctuated the haze.

Neon's no good unless it's frenzied. It needs to burst and spume, and yet she didn't really like big city lights either. The first time she saw Broadway at night, she'd stared at it aghast and said, 'My God, I had no idea. It's hideous.'

She'd been with Peter at the time. 'I love it,' he'd said with that quick smile of his. For all the time she knew him the speed and depth of his smile took her by surprise.

'I mean the lights.'

'So do I.'

'But all these colours – they're – ' She hadn't found any word other than 'hideous' and so let her sentence trail off. Then she said, 'You're teasing me, aren't you? You don't mean it. You can't. Nobody could love these things.'

'*I* do. I think – '

'It isn't fair. You're bigger than I am.'

Then he'd said with that self-conscious wonderment so characteristic of him, 'They could be in Chinese or Greek or Russian. You don't have to know what they mean or what they're for or even if they have meaning. Just look at them, Allie. It's exciting just to look at them.'

What was it about his voice? The unexpected stops and starts in it? Or was it the way his sentences ran? Trying then to figure out this now familiar mystery, straining to see as he saw and still finding the lights hideous, she caught the edge of his excitement and laughed with the simple pleasure of it.

But that was long ago.

In Overton – in this suffocating present – she found a parking-place in the lot nearest the entrance to the hospital annexe that housed Overton's only hospice, a squat pile of bricks, square, raw, desolate, unadorned by trees or grass.

She'd counted the number of steps from the doorway of the annexe to the elevator just as she'd counted the steps along the frozen path outside the apartment she rented from Cordelia. This number was eighty-nine. Eighty-nine is prime, she said to herself, as she'd said every day for the past few weeks while she walked this walk. Eight is two cubed and nine is three squared. Such a neat exchange of information. But eighty-nine is prime. How can such things be? She pressed the up button, hoping the elevator was stuck somewhere else on some remote floor, but the doors opened at once. The damned thing had been waiting for her. Look at it, she went on to herself, riding out her contempt on another wave of nausea: linoleum on the floor as worn and pitted as an old subway floor from the days when women wore stiletto heels. A stiletto heel comes down with a pressure of a ton per square inch. That's a scientific fact. No kidding.

An ancient, weary mechanism, this Otis elevator, that clanked in its shaft as she rode. Her heart clanked with it, so loud that when she stepped out on the fifth floor, the hospice floor, she was half afraid the nurse who faced her could hear it too.

'Hello again, Mrs Kessler,' the nurse said. 'I didn't expect you back until tomorrow morning.'

'No, I – They're still coming for him at ten?'

The nurse nodded. 'Best to get here a little before that, though. They tend to come early.'

'Eager, aren't they?'

'I expect it's just the traffic.'

'On the day after the Corn Scorch? Isn't that supposed to be a day of rest?'

'You ought to get some sleep.'

'I wanted to be here for this last – ' Alice began and then stopped, disconcerted as she had been before by the nurse's hugely pregnant belly. All the nurses in this hospice were pregnant: all the patients dying, all the nurses pregnant. She'd meant to ask why, but had never quite figured out how to phrase the question. Did they get pregnant the moment they arrived? Was it a way of coping with death? A defence against it? Or were they just transferred because of their condition from more desirable jobs in the hospital proper?

'I understand,' the nurse said.

'Is he awake?'

'I can't tell. Not really. Does it matter?'

Alice shook her head.

When she was a child she'd been in an explosion once. Somebody (they never knew who or why) had planted a bomb in the school she went to; she was eight years old, and three of her classmates had been killed, even little Dickie Lepplevine. Afterwards, she'd rocked back and forth on the floor of the

8

hospital emergency ward, her arms clasped around her knees, and tried to explain to her mother – to Angela – what it had been like. She'd heard no noise. How could that be? An explosion and no noise? None at all? Angela had always said she was a liar. But it was true even so. All of a sudden the air had just swollen and burst. Just like that. All of a sudden she'd been lying curled up in the field behind the school.

This time the moment of swelling was drawn out; the field in which she'd be lying only a few minutes hence was wholly visible to her. After all, this time she had a choice. She could stop right here. Right now. Who would blame her? Who would even know? It wasn't a long hallway. Peter's room was the third room down. Her steps dragged some, but when the moment came she crossed the threshold without hesitation and shut the door behind her.

CHAPTER 2

The hospice where Peter Kessler lay was in his home town. I'm not going to say exactly where this was for the simple reason that Alice promised Dutch Hashman I wouldn't. Myself, I can't see the point in secrecy now. Everybody's dead. But what the hell: a promise is a promise. An old friend of Peter's suggested I call the place Overton, which (if nothing else) is certainly depressing enough to suggest the Middle West. Anyhow, it was in Overton, years ago – years before my story started – that Alice first talked to Peter's mother about him.

'From the moment he was born, I knew he was extraordinary,' his mother said. Alice was barely twenty when this conversation took place. His mother was an old woman, very old, eighty-six or eighty-seven, skin slipsliding in folds over her forearms, and eyes the smeary pools of blue that pebble glasses make: she had glaucoma.

'He was different from my other children,' she went on, handing Alice a photograph. 'He was different from my friends' children.' In the time-honoured fashion she was showing baby pictures to a new daughter-in-law, but she wasn't enjoying it.

A battered suitcase full of family photographs lay open on the low coffee-table beside them. Peter's mother sat stiffly in a damask-covered chair. She was doing her damnedest, but her damnedest wasn't enough. This situation – this ridiculous marriage – was more than mortal woman could bear. How could Peter have done this to her? to the family? If he had to chase around after young flesh, why couldn't he find himself a nice whore? She looked in despair at twenty-year-old Alice, who sat at her feet. How could anybody be as impossibly young as this girl? Long, downy legs (folded up, tailor-fashion), flushed pink cheeks, freckles on her nose: viciously, ferociously young.

'In those days, as soon as the baby was born, they put it on the mother's stomach, and this baby – '

'Who did?' Alice interrupted.

'Percy did,' Peter's mother snapped. She hadn't meant to snap, but how could she help it? 'Percy Forthwright, our doctor. Who else?' She stuck an aged finger into the picture Alice held. 'He's six weeks old here.'

Alice pretended not to notice the tone of her voice. 'Didn't Peter's father deliver him?' Peter's father and most other Kesslers – men and women alike – had been doctors.

'Of course not.'

'I thought – '

'You didn't think at all. Doctors don't deliver their own babies. You should know that.'

'It's not an invariable rule,' Alice said, a little tartly despite her good intentions. 'My father delivered me.'

'That's different. You were in a hurry. As usual.'

'Why put him on your stomach? Isn't that an odd thing to do?'

'To help the afterbirth come out. That's obvious, I'd say.'

Alice tried shifting the ground. 'Was Memorial Hospital built by then?'

'What difference does that make? I don't remember.'

'I thought he might have been born there.'

'Peter was born right in that bedroom there, he – '

'He was born at home? I didn't know that. Right here? In this house?'

'Of course he was. A lot of babies were then. You interrupt too much. Your mother was a pretty thing, but she had such funny ideas about bringing up children. No discipline. None at all. Not that she had all that much herself. In fact, she – ' The old woman sucked in her breath, pursed her lips and then went on, 'I was very fond of her to begin with. I was the one who cut her hair. Did you know that?'

There were few things that interested Alice less than her mother's hair, but she said politely, 'Did you really? I thought she always had short hair.'

'She hadn't married your father yet. She had that elfin look to her: such a pretty girl. I said to her, "Angela, let me cut your hair for you." And she said, "Go ahead. Hair bores me to death." You're very alike, the two of you. Why don't you cut your hair too? I don't like it this way. Not one bit. You look like a schoolgirl.'

Alice had been prepared for the hostility Peter's mother was unable to hide. It wasn't only the thirty-year age gap between her and Peter; on top of that, they were cousins – technically speaking, anyway – both of them born with the name Kessler. There hadn't been much contact between his branch of the family and hers; she'd never met his mother before. His family (except for Peter himself) had stayed in Overton as the town's leading citizens; hers had wandered like nomads, the West coast, the East coast, England, Switzerland, Australia, following her father's peripatetic career. This was the official explanation, anyway, and Alice believed it, even though from the time she was small she'd sensed skeletons in the cupboard: unexpected tensions in unexpected places.

The old woman handed her another baby picture. Alice

turned it this way and that: chubby body, chubby face – no feature she could identify with the man she'd married. Several more pictures changed hands in silence. Sometimes the baby was sleeping; sometimes he was laughing. This is just any old baby, she thought, disappointed. 'You were going to tell me about Peter being different from other kids,' she said.

His mother took off her heavy glasses, sighed and put them back. 'When Percy put him on my stomach, I reached down to touch him, and he pushed my hand away. Just like that. Tiny little thing that he was: he pushed my hand away! I said to myself, "Maude, this is going to be an extraordinary child: three minutes old and already demanding his rights." '

Alice smiled up a the old woman. 'That certainly sounds like Peter,' she said, trying to sound enthusiastic. How could so trivial an incident take on any meaning to anybody?

'Here he is at two.'

Alice squinted at the picture and burst out laughing. 'I can see him at last,' she cried delightedly. 'That's his nose, and that's his smile. How old did you say? Two? It's magical, isn't it? Like disappearing ink: picture after picture of just a baby, and then – hey, presto! – Peter Kessler appears. Something must have been going on underneath all that time and nobody could see. He was very cute, wasn't he?'

Peter's mother harrumphed. 'He should have been a doctor. It would have meant so much to his father. Why aren't you in medical school yourself? It's a family tradition worth following.'

'I think I'll have a baby instead.' Alice was majoring in mathematics at Barnard then. 'One just like this.'

'Cousins shouldn't have children,' the old lady said petulantly. 'The genes get weak.'

'Oh, come on, Aunt Maude. My father's adopted.'

'You don't know what you're talking about.'

'There's nothing to know.' Alice reached into the suitcase and chose a picture herself. 'How old is he here?' she said.

'Besides, you're too young to devote your life to Peter. What are you going to do when he's dead? You're going to make an awfully young widow. He's not going to like being an old man, either. You wait and see. When he was little – ' She broke off. 'He is not without his limitations,' she went on, taking the picture from Alice and turning it to the light. The small boy in this one was a somewhat bigger small boy – five years old maybe – with bright, eager eyes that looked enchanted by whatever it was that he could see beyond the camera.

'Were you there with him?' Alice asked. 'I mean, when this picture was taken? Is it you he's so happy with?'

'How can you expect me to remember a thing like that? It's too long ago.'

Alice sighed inwardly. 'Tell me about when he was little – about not wanting to get old.'

Peter's mother replaced the picture in the suitcase. 'He was only five – ' She stopped again.

'Go on,' Alice said. 'Tell me. I want to hear.'

One day when Peter was five years old his mother took him to see his great-grandmother. Speak of old! His great-grandmother was born in 1837, the year Queen Victoria began her long-ago reign. Peter's great-grandmother was practically a hundred years old on the day of that visit, but she still controlled the Kessler fortune as well as the social life of Overton. A parlour-maid who wore a frilly apron served coffee and cakes – there was lemonade for Peter – on a silver platter with a pattern of rosebuds round the edge. Little Peter ate in a desultory way, studying this ancient personage, his legs adangle from a velvet-cushioned chair. Afterwards, out in the sunshine, he skipped alongside his mother down the street.

'What an old, old lady,' he sang, swinging her hand as he skipped. 'How rickety-pickety old she is! She's going to die soon, isn't she, mommy? How soon is she going to die?'

Alice could see it as his mother told it. Skip. Skip. That queer look on his face that children have: great intensity combined somehow with a manic scattiness, mind here, body there, no centre but no limits, either; the whole world at one, without seams or rifts. Skip. Skip.

'Will I live a million days, mommy?' he cried then. 'A million days? a million days?'

'Oh, no,' she said, laughing, 'you won't live anywhere near as long as that.'

She might as well have slapped his face. He dropped her hand. He stood stock still. Then he turned and dashed away from her. She ran after him; she was a big, strong woman then, and she caught him, drew him into her arms and tried to comfort him. He kicked and screamed all the way home.

'After that,' his mother said to Alice, 'for years and years — oh, I don't know how long — if anybody mentioned death, he'd make a bolt for the door: just turn around and run right out of the room. I warn you: he's not going to like being old at all. I'm glad I won't be around to see it.'

CHAPTER 3

i

A million days! Whatever was the child thinking of? It took him less than twenty-five thousand to reach a hospice bed in Overton, a tiny snippet of a million, a fortieth part. Besides, going to America made no sense. Absolutely none. He should have stayed in Devon. He and Alice had lived there for years – after all, a writer can live where he wants – and he was as much at home there as anywhere else. Their little boy had been born there, right in the Royal Devon Hospital; they felt half-English in a comfortable, comforting sort of way. The three of them lived in an ancient house with a walled garden and windows that looked out on Dartmoor pastures as pretty and green as Neverland itself.

I can no longer remember what I'd expected Dartmoor to be like before I saw it myself; I remember only that it was not what I'd expected. I certainly hadn't realized what a wonderful place it is for picnics. Peter loved picnics. He bought a wicker basket that held plates, glasses and a bottle of wine – and belonged really to another time and perhaps another country. He and Alice had their last picnic out on the moor on a freak day in early April when the sun shone as warm as July.

16

It was a Friday. Their little boy – they called him Tad – was going on a school trip to Paignton Zoo that afternoon; weeks before he'd started pleading to spend the night with his friend Jamie. Alice had given in reluctantly; she didn't like Jamie, and she knew the feeling was mutual. But Tad enlisted Peter in his cause, and Peter teased her about being over-protective. She hated that.

Anyhow, because of Jamie, Alice and Peter had the whole day to themselves. She packed the wicker basket to the brim: marinated chicken to cook over the Japanese hibachi, salads, wine, bread, fruit, real china, stem-glasses, knives and forks, a red tablecloth to spread on the grass that moorland sheep and rabbits – especially the rabbits, I gather – keep trim. She and Peter drove up through the thatched village of Holne, into the rounded hills past the reservoir: fresh buds everywhere and gnarled trees just beginning to bloom – up along the tiny, exposed roads that curl around those strange outcroppings of rock called tors.

'Let's stop here,' she said, seeing a grassy recess ringed with yellow gorse and sheltered from the wind.

Peter didn't even slow the car.

'What's wrong with it?' she said.

He shivered a little. 'I don't like it there.'

She turned to watch the spot disappear from the rear window. Behind and beyond lay a moonscape of barren lands, a purple-brown expanse, dead and cold – the touch of Utah that gives Dartmoor its alien threat.

'Besides, today I want a running stream with dapples on the water,' he went on. 'What I really want is a dappled stream *and* a river for the stream to run into.'

She laughed. 'You're never going to find anything like that.'

'Who says so?'

'I do.'

'You just wait. It'll be here somewhere.'

17

'We don't even have a map.'

'I don't need a map.'

At sixty-three – which is what he was then – Peter still looked on the right side of fifty. There were white streaks in his hair, but that's about all. The skin was still smooth, boyish even. He was nearly six foot four, eyebrows arched, face amused, body tense – a mercurial man and as much a mystery as ever to Alice, who could not yet decide just where his attention lay at any time, or his commitments either. Despite all the years they'd lived together, she was never wholly certain when she went to sleep at night that he'd be there beside her when she woke up.

'You're starving me to death,' she said. 'It's almost one-thirty already. Hey, look, there's a stream. Won't that do? Pull over.'

'Where?' he said with abrupt delight. 'Show me.'

'Over there. See? Well, a sort of stream anyway.'

'Oh, that.' He dismissed it with only the slightest turn of his head.

Alice sighed and felt put upon. She could see herself that evening, back in the old stone house, with over-marinated chicken abroil in the gas range and a sticky plastic container skulking in the sink. They drove on for fifteen minutes. Then Peter pulled the car to a sudden stop.

'There!' he cried in triumph. 'You see? I told you so. That's precisely it, isn't it?'

And so it was.

In the middle reaches of a river, the flow pattern absorbs the turbulence of any rock-interrupted stream that chooses to join it – and flows on. It's an awesome, magical sight. Peter and Alice laid their picnic on the moss at such a join, this one beside the overhang of a tree that trailed some of its fresh spring buds in the stream and some of them in the river. There wasn't a soul around but themselves. They lit a fire in the hibachi; they opened the wine; the chicken browned without burning.

The day stayed warm until evening. Try as she might in later years, even with the aid of maps and old friends who were experienced Dartmoor walkers, Alice could never locate the spot again.

Only a month later it was all over: only a month later the dizziness came.

'Not "dizziness" ,' Peter said irritably when she pressed him for details. They sat, looking out through french windows into the garden, where a white clematis tumbled over the stone walls that enclosed them on all sides. It was May.

'Isn't that what you said?'

' "Dizziness" doesn't begin to describe it.'

'What about vertigo?' she asked. 'Is that closer?'

'No.'

'What then?'

He turned away. She could see the ever-present tension rising in him. 'I don't know.'

'Describe it to me.'

'I can't.'

'You're a writer. It's your business to describe things.'

'Why do you torment me?' he burst out. 'What do you want from me? Why can't you leave me alone?'

Only then did she realize it was more serious than anything that had been wrong before.

Not that he'd had much wrong. He'd hurt his back several times; once he'd spent a month in traction. He slept badly; he always had. He took diuretics to control his blood pressure. Nobody likes such frailties, but they don't stand up and stare you in the face — at least not for long. And yet there *was* something else: his last book dragged on and on, which puzzled Alice — and worried her. It didn't sound so bad when she said it, even to herself, and she wasn't concerned about the money. Royalties from his earlier books were enough to keep them, if modestly. And he was a slow writer; she knew that. He always had been. But six years to write only six chapters? only a chapter a year?

The book was to be the final novel in a quartet that he'd worked on throughout his entire life as a novelist. *The Old Age of Pan*: that's what he was going to call it. A sad title, especially for him – especially now. Ironic too, of course. He was wholly aware of both elements, although when he'd planned this culmination to his *magnum opus* he'd been young enough to be untouched, personally anyway, by either. She couldn't find out what was in his mind about it – why he couldn't get on with writing it. Maybe he was afraid he'd have said it all, so maybe he was afraid he'd have to stop writing if he finished the book. Maybe he was afraid that if he finished the book, he himself would finish with it, disappear like some summer mist, never to be seen again. But could it really be? Hardly anything frightened Peter.

Except the dizziness. She knew he was afraid of that because she had such a hard time prevailing on him to go and see Dr Edgecombe about it. Dr Edgecombe suggested a CAT scan. Early in summer she and Peter went to Plymouth for it, to the grey Victorian workhouse of a hospital, where Peter stuck his head in a metal tube. It racketed at him – clap, clap, clap like a loose shingle in the wind – and revealed some atrophy of the cerebellum. When these results came in a month later they talked to Dr Edgecombe again. Dr Edgecombe wore a moustache to make himself look older, but the moustache only made him look younger still; he said a cerebellum looks like a ball of yarn and a little atrophy wasn't wholly out of keeping with Peter's age.

'Sixty's a bit early though,' Dr Edgecombe said. 'Are you really sixty? I find it hard to believe you're as old as that.'

'Sixty-three,' said Alice.

'These things have a wide range.'

Peter sat silent beside her.

'What does it do?' she asked Dr Edgecombe.

'What does what do?'

'The cerebellum.'

'Posture. Balance.'

'What does that mean for the dizziness?'

She'd asked the question, but Dr Edgecombe addressed himself to Peter. 'I'm afraid the dizziness will get worse. You'll stay for a while on a plateau. Then there's a drop, from which you'll recover – a plateau again but not quite up to where you were before. Then another drop.' With his hand he traced out a bumpy, downward path. 'Like that,' he said.

There was a pause. 'How long?' Peter said then.

'That's hard to say.'

'You can do better than that.'

'I'm sorry?'

Peter had a cold, angry side; to put it at its simplest, he did not believe the rules applied to him – not any rules – and he was always outraged when anybody dared suggest otherwise. 'The. Length. Of. Time,' he said, cutting the words up and tossing them at Dr Edgecombe like so many chunks of meat to an inmate of Paignton Zoo.

'These things vary immensely from one person to another,' Dr Edgecombe said. 'I really don't know.'

'I'm not asking you to *know*. I'm asking you to make an informed guess. Surely you can manage that.'

Dr Edgecombe always allowed extra time for Peter Kessler's appointments (Americans are so preoccupied with their health); but this morning was Monday, and Mondays are always hard on doctors. He leaned forward on his elbows.

'Well, er, let me put it like this. If you want to do any travelling – go anywhere where you have to be able to get about on your own – I'd do it in the next year or so if I were you. After that – ' He spread his hands. 'Well, after that, it will be more difficult.'

When Peter and Alice got back to their ancient house, she
fixed a drink even though it was only eleven in the morning.
They sat looking out of the open french windows onto the
walled garden, now in the bloom of early summer – huge,
purple clematis (planted to succeed the spring's white) inter-
twined with weird, delicate passion flower – bobbing and shim-
mering in the light rain so common to summer mornings in
Devon. Half an hour later, she got up to make a second drink.

'We haven't finished the first drink,' Peter said as she
returned, glasses in hand.

'I know.'

'Then why the hell fix another one?'

'Let's go to Overton.'

He shook his head.

'Why not?' she said. 'We can get a second opinion there.'

'We can get a second opinion here.'

'We could visit Pop.'

By this time the peripatetic life Alice's father had lived
throughout her girlhood was as much in the past as her girlhood
itself; he'd retired to Overton and returned to the bosom of
his family.

'You could see Skip Seago and Chuck – all your old friends,'
Alice said. 'It's been ages since you've been back. Tad would
love it – and the plane trip. Just think of it. He'd be flying at
last. Besides, he and Pop are so mad about each other.'

Peter shook his head again. 'What's the point? There's
nothing anybody can do.'

The rain increased. Alice got up and shut the french
windows.

'Don't!' he cried.

'It's going to get wet inside.'

'I don't care. Leave them open.'

22

She opened them a little.

'All the way,' he said, and the intensity in his voice was unlike any she'd heard there before.

'But – '

'What difference does it make in the overall scheme of things if a floor gets wet?'

Alice opened the windows all the way and sat down again. 'If there's nothing anybody can do,' she said then, 'we don't have anything to lose by going to Overton.'

He stared out at the rain. 'If there's nothing anybody can do, we don't have anything to gain.'

In the single week that followed, the Peter whom Alice had known ceased to exist.

She went to see Dr Edgecombe by herself.

'I don't think he can handle what you've told him,' she said.

Dr Edgecombe frowned. 'Badly upset, is he?'

She nodded.

'Every way you say this sort of thing, you never get it right. I thought – He always wants to know everything – far more than I can tell him most of the time. Usually I have the feeling he's playing games with me – setting traps. Is he working at all?'

'He sits at his desk.'

'How long since he published anything?'

'Maybe seven years.'

'You must see how slowed down he is.'

'Is he? Have I noticed that? I've certainly noticed something, but – Are you sure? Since when?'

'You mind if I smoke?' Dr Edgecombe fumbled in his pockets, pulled out a squashed package of cigarettes, put one in his mouth, took it out again. 'This is the worst sort of illness. Even cancer is better.' Outside the window of this small office the summer rain of Devon was falling as it had been for the whole of the week. 'If it's cancer, either we can do something or it's all over in a year or so. But this – I knew a man once, a university don. It took him ten years to die, and the whole time he knew what was happening. He just sat there and watched his own mind crumble.'

Alice studied the contours of Dr Edgecombe's face, the cheeks hollowing – bellows-like – as he sucked fire from the match into the cigarette. 'What happens in the end?'

'If you're lucky he'll lose insight.' He shook the match and put it back into the matchbox. 'Senile dementia is merciful in its way.'

iii

When Peter was little, he raged (just as Tad had come to) if his shoe refused to do its duty and get itself over his heel. Was he not in the right? Was he not smarter than anybody else? braver? more charming? How dare a mere shoe not do as he command? He stamped his foot if his pencil-box rebelled and wouldn't open. How could this – this *thing* – defy him? When he got older, he turned his fury on badly-made gear-shifts, recalcitrant locks, pens that ran out of ink. Most of the time – man and boy – he won. Most of the time, the terrorized object (whatever it was) went back to working properly. Peter loved to win, and his delight in victory was so infectious that nobody around him could fail to take pleasure in it.

After Alice's visit to Dr Edgecombe the balance of power began to tilt. Skirmishes became more frequent, fighting more fierce, victory less certain. Just out of bed, Peter faced insolent razors, idle toothpaste-tubes, stupid shoe-laces. Downstairs there were rebellious milk-cartons, jam-jars, pepper-grinders. At night: soap-trays, bath-towels, pill-bottles.

He owned an old manual typewriter, one of those heavy office machines, good in its day, but its day was already over when he bought it – and that was a quarter of a century ago.

He'd used it ever since, a hunt-and-peck typist, fast and accurate, an accomplishment he was proud of. His fingers began to slip between the keys. He shouted at the machine; he damned its designer, its manufacturer, the idiot who'd sold it to him in the first place. Listening to him rail, Alice thought she heard an unknown something in his voice. She puzzled over it for days before she realized that what she was hearing was panic. In a panic herself, she took the typewriter away and substituted a word-processor; fingers can't slip between the keys of those.

But a word-processor! The woman was out of her mind. For a man besieged by things, what greater reinforcement can the enemy hope for? It had a curious effect, though, at least for a while. The toothpaste-tube got a reprieve. So did the pepper-grinder. Peter reconnoitred. He surveyed his options. He pecked at the sleek, plastic keyboard. He studied the beep and glow. Then he called Alice into his study and announced the result of his findings.

'I hate it.'

'What's the matter?' Alice said.

'It doesn't work. It won't work.'

'Let me see,' she said.

'I did precisely what *you* told me to. Either it's broken or you're wrong.' She sat down to his machine. 'It keeps repeating this *M* all the time,' he said, pointing angrily at the screen.

'But we – ' she began and broke off.

'We what?' She looked away uncomfortably. 'What are you trying to say?' Then he added, sensing triumph (after all she was the one who looked uncomfortable), 'Why won't people ever say what they mean?'

'You've just mixed up one of the commands,' she said, more uncomfortable still and careful – oh, so careful – not to add 'again'.

'I didn't.'

'It's all in the manual.'

'To hell with the manual. You bought the damned thing. Why can't you explain it to me?'

'I did my best,' she said, nettled despite herself.

He was at once on guard. 'What best?'

'Don't you remember – '

'I hate that manual,' he burst out. 'I defy you to explain – wait a minute – just wait a minute.' He thrust the booklet in front of her. 'What could this garbled excuse for English possibly mean to anybody?'

Does she shout back? Battle him as he devoutly wishes she would? As even a self respecting toothpaste-tube does? No, she sits down at this machine – this word-processor that out of sheer love of injustice resists him but not her – she fiddles a minute, and then says with that maddening woman's patience of hers, 'See? You've just pressed *control* instead of *shift*.'

Nobody understands. Nobody can. The more she tries to forestall his terrors by anticipating them, the more terrified he becomes. He could not remember what he could not remember (he who'd always remembered more, better, faster than anybody else), but he read it all in her manner. Alice was a good girl. She was kind to people who weren't as smart as she was, to little Tad and his friends, to irritable sick people, boring people. How cute, he'd thought – fondly, indulgently – watching her at the breakfast-table or catching glimpses from across the room at parties. She wasn't like that with him. Never. With him, her face moved a little faster; her hands had a heightened nervousness. The fact is, she was in awe of him, which he knew and which he thought enchanting.

So it was with real horror that he watched her turn her kindliness in his direction.

She drew up a table of simplified instructions for his word-processor. She made graphs. When he faltered, she simplified further. She programmed the machine to make it easier to operate. And after a few months he came to take a half-terrified pleasure in it, like a man on a roller-coaster; he got a kick out of writing letters to her father, who was an old man and wouldn't dream of using such a thing as a word-processor. But techniques for this and that kept slipping out of mind, and Peter (who had never before needed anybody's help for anything) could not get them back without her.

One afternoon about six months after the CAT scan – he was wedged under his desk trying to tidy up some electrical connections – something happened, something in his brain, something critical. He took to his bed at once. He refused to let Alice call in Dr Edgecombe. He said it was hopeless; he said he was paralysed; he said, as he'd said before, that there was nothing anyone could do. Gloom hung over the house. Tad cried out in his sleep that night, and Alice ran back and forth in her bathrobe between him and Peter, who slept not at all.

Up to this point, Alice figured she'd succeeded pretty well in keeping Peter's deterioration from Tad. 'Daddy's working too hard,' she'd said to him. 'People get irritable when they have too much to do. They forget things.'

But she hadn't been wholly successful. How could she be? There was the afternoon a week or so before when Tad had run into Peter's study, as he often did after school, with news of some excitement or other, only to find his father not at work at all, but slumped over his desk, head buried in his arms, despair incarnate.

'Daddy?' Tad said, tentative, balancing on one foot, swinging a little forward, a little back, unsure what to do. No answer. He was a courageous little boy. He went over and gently shook Peter's shoulder. 'Daddy? Speak to me. Daddy?' He shook the shoulder again. 'Daddy!'

Fortunately Alice had come in then. 'Daddy's been working too – ' she began. She couldn't even finish. The expression on

Tad's face: was it anger? fear? simple mistrust? 'He's just not feeling very well today.'

She drew Tad into her arms and steered him towards the kitchen; but he wriggled loose and faced her sternly, legs apart, arms akimbo. He frowned. He started to say something. Then turned and ran out of the house.

The morning after the inexplicable happening under the desk, Tad wouldn't speak to her at the breakfast-table. As for Peter, he wouldn't even get out of bed. He wouldn't eat the breakfast she brought him on a tray. As soon as Tad was off to school, Alice telephoned Dr Edgecombe, and that evening a neurologist by the name of Dr Fearling arrived at the house.

She took him upstairs. From the doorway he studied Peter's angry back. 'Good evening, Mr Kessler,' he said.

'Go away,' Peter said.

'I'm just going to examine you.'

'Go away.'

'Come, come, Mr Kessler. Let me do my job.' Peter sighed a ragged sigh; but to Alice's surprise, he relented almost at once. Dr Fearling tested reflexes. He made notes. Then he said, 'Stand, please.'

'What for?'

'Come now, Mr Kessler, have a go at it.'

Peter dragged himself out of bed. Dr Fearling was a sparrow of a man with sharp features and tiny, fastidious hands; Peter towered over him.

'Good,' said Dr Fearling. 'Now walk a straight line.'

'I can hardly stagger my way to the bathroom.'

'Try.'

Peter walked a straight line.

'Now run,' said Dr Fearling.

'You're mad,' said Peter.

'Try.'

He managed a trot and turned a happy, half-baffled smile on the doctor. 'Is it going to be all right?'

'I've seen a lot worse,' said Dr Fearling. 'Now I want you to go downstairs and have dinner with your wife. Tomorrow, get up and go for a walk with her. Walk with her every day for a week. The next week, go by yourself.'

It was early spring. Alice and Peter walked in the garden first, where the remains of frost glittered on the stone walls. By the end of the week, they were walking down the High Street.

Outside the house (where there was danger) he walked well enough; inside it (where he felt safe) he lurched wildly. A body is just a thing. So is a brain. Show 'em who's master. Show 'em what'll happen if they go on like this. Frighten the bastards into behaving properly. By summer, he was walking regularly in the town by himself, just as Dr Fearling had insisted. But it was a tentative, slow, invalid's gait, easily upset by Tad on his skateboard. Which is to say, he was better but not as good as he had been before: which is to say he was showing that bumpy downward path Dr Edgecombe had predicted.

iv

How can you explain such things to a child? There isn't any explanation, not for anybody. Alice watched Tad's confusion grow. He often cried in his sleep now. Often Alice couldn't separate him from his dreams. She took him out of bed, held him in her lap, soothed him; when he grew calmer she put him back to bed before he woke because if he woke and found she'd seen him crying like that, he'd feel ashamed. He no longer ran to Peter's study after school with tales of adventure. He no longer pleaded for stories of Peter's childhood or reminisced about the walks they used to take together, collecting beetles and moths in mayonnaise jars to bring home for Alice.

29

Nothing was as it used to be. Peter, who'd always been first downstairs, didn't come down to breakfast any more. Dinner had once been a major event of the day, a time when the three of them talked and laughed and played word-games. Now Peter sat at his end of the table, silent, unmoving, almost inert. What conversation there was went on between Tad and Alice, who spoke with more and more animation as she saw her son's eyes stray towards his father, which they did again and again, half-worried, half-frightened, deeply puzzled, during the course of a meal. She was the one who told stories now. She worked hard at the craft; she heard herself acting out all the parts.

For Christmas she redoubled her efforts. Over a roast turkey with stuffing and chestnuts, while Peter sat silent, she told Tad about the time she'd visited Peter's mother and looked through the box of baby pictures. She watched her own hands flying here and there, describing this picture, then that, her own reaction, the old woman's annoyance; she told about how she'd decided then and there to have a baby just like Peter, and how – lo and behold! – here was Tad, the precise replica of those old pictures of his father, down to the arched eyebrows, the eyes that were both dark and light at the same time – and that so often looked a little baffled, as though somehow by accident they'd caught an unshielded glimpse of the sun.

Tad laughed delightedly, more at the telling than at the tale; Peter brooded at the end of the table as before. Still laughing, Tad turned to him and said, 'Why don't you laugh, daddy? Isn't it funny? Doesn't she say it just as good as television?'

There was no reaction.

'Well, doesn't she?' Tad demanded.

Peter took a shuddering breath. He pushed out his chair and struggled to his feet; he supported himself on the table, arms straight, head bowed; he leaned forward, drew back, leaned forward again. Then he turned towards the hallway and the stairs.

30

'Say something,' Tad shouted after him, his puzzlement dissolving into the comfort of anger, order at last in a battle to protect his mother, no longer afraid, his mind made up, indignant, self-righteous. 'It's not nice to say nothing.'

Peter stopped. Even though he didn't turn his head Alice saw that tears ran down his cheeks. 'Oh, God,' he said, 'even *this* bores me.'

Alice had spent her last pre-university year in Switzerland, high up in the Alps, at a friendly school with pupils of all ages from all over the world; she called the headmaster, who'd been new to the job then, a young man, bearded and beaded. It was no time of the year to accept new pupils, but Alice is very persuasive when she has to be; they made the arrangements then and there. Tad left England after the Christmas holidays. A week later, sitting in pale winter sun through the french windows, Peter had a flurry of strokes.

v

Ladies and gentlemen, do not believe what they tell you. They lie. This dying is a cruel, evil business. This is when things master a man at last – any man, even Peter Jordan Kessler – when the toothpaste-tube and the pepper-grinder take their final revenge. At his desk, the word-processor (field-marshal to the enemy) squatted in wait and scanned him with its hard eye. He fought back. Of course he did. He was Peter Kessler, wasn't he? He defied it. He took pen and paper and wrote

What a writer must do

then drew a long, meandering line to the bottom of the page, where there was nothing: this was the opening of his two new manuscripts. He decided to call the first *The Temple of Addresses*;

it was an authoritative list of the sensations in his hands, his arms and legs. The second was *The TV Guide to Strokes*, where he listed contortions, obsessions and lunacies.

'It's a doozy,' he said to Alice. 'I can't explain it. It's a doozy.'

After lunch, he took a nap; when he woke she drove him through the countryside. Then he sat at his desk again and added his lists together – the ones in *The Temple of Addresses* and *The TV Guide to Strokes* as well as any others he could find: shopping lists, laundry lists – and totalled up the result, which was always the same: everything is meaningless, even his own suffering.

When Tad came home for the Easter holidays, Dr Edge-combe arranged a room for Peter in a small private hospital so that the little boy saw him only for brief visits, never long enough to make out the ferocity of his condition. Peter didn't come home until after Tad went back to school abroad.

During this second springtime of illness, Peter walked with two canes and a posture so curled over that he was no taller than Alice, although he was still several inches over six feet and she was five foot eight. He could no longer dial a telephone number. He couldn't get up off the floor by himself if he fell, and he fell often. There were crush fractures of the spine where his old injuries had weakened it. Pain was constant. Soon he was crapping the bed at night. He pissed the bed too – until June, that is, when he couldn't piss at all, so they catheterized him, which brought on bladder spasms and more pain. One evening, sunk into a chair from which he could no longer get up without help, he said, 'Oh, Allie, just let me be comfortable.'

You'd think she'd see what was happening, wouldn't you? Oh, she saw the day-by-day decline, all right. What else had she been hiding from Tad? Why else did she send the little boy to Overton and his grandfather for the summer holidays when summer came? But the full extent of the matter? That's what she managed to hide from herself. Perhaps it's a protective

32

mechanism. Perhaps when the world narrows down around you, you narrow down your vision to fit. And Alice made things worse for herself by being one of those people who just don't know when to quit.

On the other hand, if you'd talked to Peter yourself for a few minutes, you'd have seen in him something of what she saw. He could still sound rational and perceptive, interesting – I kid you not – even charming. He could talk politics. He could talk literature. He could talk about crapping the bed too; and he could talk about what it was like 'down here', as he put it, as opposed to 'up there' where Alice and the rest of us live. The very sick tend to jettison their personalities this way, piece by piece.

But Alice, being Alice, refused to let go of what was gone. She arranged for a vascular surgeon, a cardiologist, a new neurologist. She found physiotherapists, occupational therapists, dietitians, even an osteopath from Korea. She bought a hospital bed, fitted the house with hand-rails, studied medical journals, monitored liquid intake and liquid outgo – and charted it all as though it were the path of some new comet. She read about Pasteur, who had had a stroke, too, and whose great discovery was made after it; when they did an autopsy on him, they found only jelly in the right side of his cranium. If Pasteur could do it, so could Peter.

She decided he had to have a prostate resection. Maybe there wasn't anything anybody could do about the dizziness – all right, she'd accept that (for the moment anyway) – but if he got the prostate resected, at least he'd be more comfortable, and a prostate is so eminently fixable: such a neat, discrete piece of tissue and one of those fine, simple operations that really works. How could it not help? She made an appointment with a urologist called Mr Hook. A week after the examination, she went to talk to Dr Edgecombe about the results.

'It's a pity your husband didn't let us deal with this situation when he was fitter,' Dr Edgecombe said.

'Well, he wouldn't, and now we've got to. He's in pain all the time.'

'What about the pills I prescribed?'

'They hardly touch it.'

Dr Edgecombe reached for his prescription pad. 'I'll give you something stronger.'

'What does Hook say?'

'He, er – He thinks that this is not the right time for surgery.'

'Nothing else will deal with the pain. Isn't that what you told me?'

'Well, yes and no. There are balances in these things.'

'What balances? A man's in pain. You can help. What can balance that?'

'You have to weigh – Mrs Kessler, Mr Hook doesn't want to operate.'

Alice had become almost as impatient as Peter himself used to be. 'Then let's call in somebody else.'

'There's no point in that.'

'Whyever not? If Hook isn't happy with what needs to be done, let's find somebody who is.'

Dr Edgecombe studied her a moment. 'You are not taking on board what I'm trying to say to you.'

'What about that vascular guy?' she rushed on. 'What's his name? Northgate? What's his opinion? He must know somebody who can step in the breach.'

Dr Edgecombe stared down at the tattered manila file on his desk. 'You really want to hear his opinion?'

'Of course I do.'

He opened the file, shuffled in it, pulled out a letter, read it through, then put it down. 'Your husband – ' He broke off, looked up at her, back at the letter in the open file. Then he sighed. 'Leave the poor man alone, Mrs Kessler. He's not going

34

to make it past Christmas. We may not understand why his condition is as serious as it is – or how it got that way so quickly – but we all agree on this one point. There's nothing more any of us can do.'

vi

Alice remembered the white flowers in the garden before the CAT scan and the purple ones of summer when she and Peter learned the results, but after that the seasons had come and gone for the entire time of Peter's illness, and she hadn't noticed them. Flowers were sometimes one colour, sometimes another. Sometimes Tad was at home; sometimes not. Sometimes it was cold, sometimes it wasn't.

Hearing Dr Edgecombe speak out his judgement, she suddenly saw the washed-clean day outside the window behind him and realized that the summer was long gone, that the fresh cob nuts Peter had once loved were probably no longer in the town market on Fridays, that even the red of the Virginia creepers was probably past its best. How could she not have realized? It was more than a month since her father had put Tad back on the plane to Switzerland for the autumn term in the Alps.

A walled garden not unlike her own lay outside Dr Edgecombe's window. It had an oak tree in it, one of those huge forest oaks, Gulliver-like – asquat, absurd – in its Lilliputian surroundings.

'The leaves must make an awful mess,' she said, nodding in the oak's direction. It was brown and gold coloured because of the frost.

Dr Edgecombe swung around in his chair to look at it. 'I don't know why the Council doesn't cut it down,' he said. 'I feel like I'm underwater in the summer.'

'You'll have to go out one dark night and throw a bag of salt on it.'

He laughed. 'Besides, this is clay soil. I don't know what's the matter with them. By now the damage has to be irreparable.'

'Then most assuredly they won't bother to cut it down,' she said. She stood up and offered him her hand across the desk. 'Thanks for talking to me.'

'I'm sorry, Mrs Kessler.'

'I guess it was time I knew.'

She walked back up the High Street in the bright, crisp morning. She fixed Peter's lunch, fed him, helped him undress for his nap. By the time he awoke, there was a shimmery edge to her thoughts, an uneasy, unfamiliar nervousness to things. She helped him dress, helped him down the garden path to the garage and into the car. As usual they set out into the countryside.

Not far from the tiny village of Lamerton, where there's a three-pronged bridge, she blacked out behind the wheel.

Just blacked out.

One moment she was driving along where she belonged, with Peter beside her, and the next – without any interstice at all – she was sideways across the road, the bumper of her car crumpled up against one of those pretty red post-boxes that still looked to her, despite her years in England, like pop-ups in a children's book. No other cars were about, so there'd been no collision. She'd been going slowly; the damage was minimal. But she was shaken. Nothing like this had ever happened to her before. She'd never even fainted.

To be sure, she wasn't at her best. She knew it. No disease or anything, but she could see for herself that her face had taken on a pinched look; she could hear the measured care in the way she spoke and see it in the way she moved. Nobody on twenty-four-hour duty sleeps much, and nights were as bad as days – sometimes worse. Her hands trembled. Her ears rang.

36

She had night sweats. She gagged when she brushed her teeth. But a blackout? What did it mean? Brain cells on strike? What *could* it mean?

You give up continuum when you take care of somebody as sick as Peter for as long as Alice had. You don't see the railway sleepers retreating into the distance anymore; you're a beetle scuttling along the track, one hurdle at a time. It makes you suspicious, insular, combative. Lying awake that night, asweat in her sheets, Alice was abruptly outraged. Who the hell did Edgecombe think he was? So he and a couple of English consultants said Peter was dying. Well, what do you expect? The English are a rag-tag people, a left-over people, elegant in their faded way perhaps, sort of like good china that's been through the dishwasher too many times. Who are they to judge the life prospects of an American? She'd show them. She'd take her Peter home. She should have done it long ago, despite his protests. The Americans would make him whole again.

At three in the morning she got up and dressed. Before dawn she had the suitcases packed. She bought the airline tickets as soon as the travel agent opened. She cancelled the papers, paid the bills, turned off the water, gas, electricity, arranged for a taxi to take her and Peter the two hundred miles to Heathrow. At two o'clock, just after lunch in Devon, half an hour before the taxi was due to pick them up, she made a telephone call to her father in Overton.

It was seven o'clock in the morning there. Her father was still in bed.

'If I can get Peter home,' she said, 'can you get him into a hospital?'

'Ah, come on Alice – ' her father began. His name was Christie Kessler. (One virtue of marrying a cousin, as Alice had, is that a woman can keep her own name without making an issue of it.)

'Come on what?' she interrupted.

37

'You're not making sense, honey.'

'I don't know what that means.'

'Don't you think you're being just a little impetuous?'

'Are you saying you won't help me?'

'No, I – '

'You can't? Is that it?'

'Of course I can,' he protested. Christie had his vanities, which Alice knew – and which she was counting on. The family was so old, the tradition of Kesslers doctoring the populace of Overton so enduring, that Christie could not bring himself to deny her even though he was nearly eighty years old. He loved medicine. He loved being a doctor. He'd been seeing patients on a part-time basis as recently as a year ago – to the terror of his partners, not a one of whom hadn't had nightmares about malpractice.

'Thank God,' Alice said.

'I haven't said – '

'We can make Heathrow by evening. We should be on the morning flight tomorrow. Can you meet us at the airport?' There was a pause. 'Pop? Are you still there?'

'Look, Alice, Peter is a very sick man.'

'Yes.'

'It's such an awful long trip. I mean, how far is Heathrow, anyway? Three hours? Four? Then you've got, I don't know, eight hours to Chicago. Then the connecting flight. It's an ordeal for anybody, and for – '

'They won't help him here. They've washed their hands of him. I can't just let him slip away like this. I've got to take him somewhere where somebody's willing to make an effort.'

'Allie, honey, he may not survive the trip. In fact, if he's lucky – '

'If he dies, he'll die with some hope. There's no hope here.'

Christie sighed. 'Okay, okay. I'll be there. Felicity'll get the spare room ready for you.' Felicity was Christie's second wife,

Alice's step-mother. (She'd gone to that fancy East Coast university, Vassar.) 'Call me with the flight number and the – '

'I've got the number and the arrival time right here. Do you have a pencil? Is there anything special I should plan to do?'

He laughed. 'Good Lord, you do move fast. Suppose I'd refused outright?' Alice made no answer. He sighed again. 'Do about what?'

'For the flight.'

'I'd take morphine with me if I were you.'

'I'll call Dr Edgecombe as soon as we hang up. Anything else?'

'Hey, what about Tad?' Christie said with a sudden urgency. 'What are you going to do about him? He's going to miss a lot of school if you bring him. If you don't, who's going to take care of him? You can't hire just anybody. He's such a little boy.'

The urgency, and the questions, too, seemed so out of place that she didn't know how to answer. After all, Christie had put Tad on the plane to Switzerland himself; he was the one who paid the school fees (Peter's royalties wouldn't really stretch that far). She said tentatively, 'Is it the holidays you're worrying about?'

'Oh, come on, Allie, not just the – '

'If all goes well,' she rushed on, 'we might be back here for Christmas. If not, he can come to Overton.'

'He's so little – '

'Come on, Pop, he made the trip only six weeks ago. Besides, you know how he adores flying.'

There was a momentary pause. 'Aren't you even going to talk to him?'

'I'll write when I get there. Why are you asking these funny questions? I've got to write the school anyway. At the moment Tad is the least of my worries.'

'You ought to talk to him.'

'I'd only scare him, and he's scared enough about Peter already. Why make it worse?'

There was another pause. 'I don't think you should do this at all. I really don't.' She didn't respond, not even to protest. Christie figured she was probably holding her breath, and he went on, defeated. 'Well, I don't know, make sure Peter drinks something every half hour or so. For the whole time, to Heathrow, at Heathrow, on the flight – especially on the flight.'

'Why?'

'Sick people get dehydrated more easily than well ones. Don't forget, huh?'

vii

On the ride to Heathrow airport (the taxi company was a local firm that prided itself on its fake sheepskin covers), the fool of a driver got lost, this fool with golden curls and a single earring, this young fool to whom such things as were happening to Alice were never going to happen, just as – five years before – they'd never been going to happen to her. What with that extra hour on the road, it was only because of the catheter that Peter didn't piss his pants. As for a crap, well, sometimes people are lucky. Sometimes Murphy's Law isn't absolute. Or is it Sod's Law? Not that it matters. But on the approach to Reading, Peter's exhaustion was terrible to see.

They spent the night at an airport hotel. The next morning, she hired another taxi and ferried him to Terminal 4, where a wheelchair porter took charge of him and, when the plane was ready for boarding, transferred him to a special device, half-chair, half-dolly, that carted him down the aisle on wheels like a piece of excess baggage to four seats at the back of standard class (gift of a sympathetic check-in clerk), arm rests down – an in-flight bed as narrow as a stretcher. Alice settled his head

40

in her lap. His shoulders cantilevered out over the edge; he was still a big man, barrel-chested despite his years of illness.

For the entire flight she forced him to drink every half hour as her father had directed, and it was probably her liquids – or such was the charge she was to bring against herself in later years – that accounted for his surviving it.

CHAPTER 4

i

In his day, Alice's father Christie had been nearly as good to look at as Peter himself – cat-in-the-sun handsome, though, not like Peter's quick, tense beauty. It's one of the wonders of the world that rotting hulks like these, like Peter and Christie, were so beautiful once – that Christie, who had walked with a roll to him (the cat up from its nap and about to spray a garden wall), rolled no more, tottered instead through the airport lounge, a rabbit now rather than a cat, nothing left of what he had been but the Cheshire cat's smile – and that visible only if you knew, as Alice did, where to look for it. He wore a beige summer suit on this unexpectedly warm fall day.

She hadn't embraced him to start with; she didn't know why, and he, noting her reticence, held back too. But in the press of the crowd, she stopped and threw her arms around him. She buried her face in the crook of his neck where she used to bury it when she was a small girl (she'd always been his favourite). His once-solid frame half-collapsed in her arms as though it were no more durable than those Chinese lanterns made of rice paper and matchwood struts.

'Hey,' he said, 'you're squeezing the life out of me.'

'How are you, Pop?'

'Not too bad for an old man,' he said, patting her gently on the back from within the confines of her arms. 'Where's Peter?'

'They said I should get the bags. They said they'd get him off the plane for me.'

Christie disengaged himself and held her out at arms' length, his hands on her shoulders. 'He can't walk at all?'

'Not so's you'd notice. We'll get some sort of priority – so they say, anyhow. How's Felicity?'

Airlines are at their best with wheelchair cases. Only fifteen minutes after landing, they'd unloaded Peter and his luggage from the plane and into Christie's car. Because Christie was a doctor and because she'd warned him, he showed nothing; but he was deeply shocked. Peter was his nephew, his older brother's boy, the glory of the family, fifteen years younger than he. How could somebody fifteen years younger have come to this? He looked dead already. Grey face, bowed head. He had barely the strength to take the hand Christie offered him, and no strength at all for the small talk that such greetings are made of.

Alice didn't remember much of the ride that followed, although the trip seemed to her, when she thought about it later, to have taken longer than it should have. Her father crept along, body scrunched over the wheel, face jammed up against the windscreen.

'They keep changing the roads around,' he grumbled. 'What do they need a junction here for?'

The junction looked to Alice as though it had been there for years, but she couldn't say for sure. She hadn't been to Overton often enough to know it well. Christie hesitated in the middle of the cross-roads and again half-way down the block, hesitantly starting again, cornering, pausing. If she hadn't been so tired, she'd have asked him if he needed new glasses. Or sunglasses maybe. The day was painfully bright. Wide stretches of highway, faceless buildings sprouting from weed-infested lots, empty fields scratched out here and there like mange on a dog, everything flat under a flat overhang of sky: raw, flat planes of light that hurt her eyes. Probably they hurt his eyes too.

He stopped the car, struggled out and disappeared. They'd parked in one of those wasteland lots that seem to begin nowhere and end nowhere. Large grey backs of buildings closed in the space on two sides. There were no other cars. Christie returned with a wheelchair.

'Where's the hospital?' she asked.

'Special way in,' he said. 'You need any help?'

She shook her head. She'd worked out a lift for getting Peter out of cars by herself, and Christie was so frail.

'Follow me,' he said then. She wheeled Peter behind him down a concrete ramp to an underground entrance. Christie pushed open a glass door for her.

It was eerily silent inside and eerily dim; a neon glow flickered, power maybe a quarter strength. No nurses, no secretaries, no porters, no doctors, no other patients. Nobody at all. The glass enclave of an office off to one side was unoccupied and dark.

'Pop, are you sure – ' Alice swung around to see him lurching off down the corridor that led away from her. If your name is Alice you get teased about *Alice in Wonderland*, but you don't expect to end up in Wonderland yourself; and yet the dark of the place and her own dream-like state gave the corridor the claustrophobic look of a rabbit-hole, and her rabbit of a father – scurrying away down it in his pale suit – looked precisely like the White Rabbit on his way to play croquet with the Queen of Hearts.

'Hey, where are you going?' she called after him.

' – get somebody – '

'Pop, come back a minute. Wait! Hey!'

44

' – admissions – '

She couldn't make out the rest, and he was gone.

She leaned against the wall beside Peter, who sank lower in the wheelchair. Her muscles trembled beneath her skin as she stood – the rhythm of the flight still with her – and she checked her watch again and again to find that only a few seconds had gone by since she'd checked it the time before. She sat down on the floor; there were no chairs. Ten minutes passed.

'I can't stand this,' Peter said. He'd hardly spoken on the flight. He'd hardly spoken since landing.

'I don't know what to do.'

'Go find him.'

'And leave you here? He can't have gone far. He can't have just deserted us. It doesn't make sense.'

'Go find him.'

She was afraid to leave Peter, afraid not to. Hospitals are so vast, so Byzantine. But what choice was there? She set off down the corridor just like Alice down the rabbit-hole. This Alice, though, can't tell right from left. Both Christie Kessler's girls (Alice is the younger) are a little dyslexic. She has to think, 'Turn towards the hand I write with.' 'Turn away.' To make sure she's got it, she has to pretend she'd holding a pencil; even so, she's often wrong.

She broke into a trot as the route began to get lost in her head; she passed a deserted section with a sign that said 'Out-patient Dialysis', then a deserted X-ray department. Suddenly it was dark. What kind of a hospital was this anyway? If it wasn't a hospital, what was it? The corridor was so dark she could barely make out her hands in front of her.

'There was another time,' Peter's mother had said when she and Alice first met and sat together over the heap of Peter's baby pictures – when Alice was a bare snip of a girl, only twenty, a lifetime ago.

45

'Tell me,' Alice had said, hugging her knees to her chest. 'Tell me. How old was he when this one happened?'

'I don't know. Six maybe. It was a year or so after the visit to his great-grandmother. He'd done something naughty. I can't remember what. I locked him in my clothes closet.'

'Oh, dear,' Alice cried in distress.

'You think I did wrong?'

'I'm scared of the dark. I have to have a light on when I go to bed.'

'Really? At your age? Aren't you a bit – '

'Wasn't he terrified? He was so little.'

'Of course not,' the old lady said irritably. 'He's never been afraid of silly things like that. My Peter was not like other boys.'

'So what happened? Did he cry?'

'That's what I expected him to do.' Peter's mother ran her hands over the skirt of her dress, one of those ugly dresses with big ugly flowers in ugly pastel colours. Are they stigmata of age, these dresses? Why do old women wear them? 'I thought he'd kick and scream, but there was no noise. Not a peep. After a while I got worried. I listened hard. Still not a peep. So I opened the closet door.' The old lady laughed, so pleased with her memory that she forgot her irritation at Alice. 'Oh, that child! He *tingled* with life. That's what he did. He just plain tingled. There he stood in that doorway – cocky as anything – with his little legs apart and his hands on his hips.

' "Go away," ' he said.

'I was so taken aback that all I could think to say was, "Will you behave now?"

' "I am being have," he said.

' "You are not."

' "Yes, I be. Go away."

'I didn't know what to say to this, and so I said (even though it didn't make any sense), "I can't let you out unless you promise to behave."

46

' "Don't want to get out."

' "Of course you do."

' "Don't. Won't."

' "Why not?"

' "This is my closet. I'm not done yet."

She laughed again. ' "Not done yet? You are a funny child. What can you be thinking of?"

'I could see his face light up and his eyes sparkle – this was the very question he wanted me to ask – and he said, "I've spat on your shoes and I've spat on your underwear and I've spat on your dresses, and I just waiting for more spit to come so I can spit on your coat." '

Of all the qualities Alice admired in Peter, she'd admired his fearlessness most. How can anybody be unafraid of the dark at only six years old? In the dark, menace is everywhere; there's nowhere to put your back. Her heart jolted in her chest as she saw a thin vertical strip of light between what had to be two doors. She stumbled through them. Beyond lay a sunlit space with rooms on either side – a wing for semi-private patients, she figured. But there were no patients. She passed a nurses' station with telephones and dark computer screens. No nurses. A row of intravenous drip pumps stood on guard at another set of doors.

Then another corridor, properly lit this time, with a proper hospital smell of disinfectant and institutional cooking. This final corridor opened out into the place where – it was obvious at once – she and Peter should have been all along.

Here was an entrance-hall large enough to hush people's voices; here was just the right mix of people to be hushed in such a place – patients, relatives, visitors, an administrator with a clip-board, a brace of children dangling from a grown-up arm. Alice's relief was so great that at first she could only stand and stare. It was all so normal. Here were plastic ornamental ferns, plastic chairs in red, a café behind a screen of plastic flowers, a glassed-off gift shop with real flowers and magazines, glass window-walls looking out on the sunny day and cars drawing up outside. Here was an information desk studded with computer terminals, all lit up as they should be. There was no sign of Christie.

Alice approached the desk. No people were visible behind the terminals. She wasn't quite sure what to do. 'I have a patient for admission,' she said, a little tentatively, to one of the terminals. After all, it might have been one of those voice-activated machines. 'What do I do about it?'

From behind this barrier a frizz of hair emerged surrounding a smile so bright that Alice recoiled. On the woman's breast there was a label that read

My name is Maybelle
It is my pleasure to serve you
in any way I can

'Listen, you've come to the right place,' Maybelle herself said, her smile blooming like a catherine wheel. 'Are you the patient?'

'No, no. It's my husband.'

'Oh?' Maybelle leaned out over the vast desk to scan the area at the base of it. 'Where is he?'

'He's – ' But what could she say? That she'd lost her own husband in some dark, silent corridor? So she settled for. 'He's Dr Kessler's patient.'

Maybelle frowned. 'Dr Kessler? Dr Christian Kessler? He's retired. Are you sure you mean Dr Kessler?'

'He just drove us in from the airport.'

'Poor you!' Maybelle stifled a giggle.

'He's my father,' Alice said.

'Listen, I'm sorry. I didn't mean – '

'Don't apologize,' Alice said through her teeth. Anger at

48

Christie flushed her cheeks. How could her beloved father have done this to her? To Peter?

Maybelle let her smile fizzle into a mock frown. 'Causing problems, is he?'

'Can you page him?' Alice said. She had to struggle to keep her voice calm.

'No point. He didn't wear his bleeper even before he retired. Couldn't work it. He'll show up sooner or later – always does. He must have arranged for somebody to act as admitting physician. You got your card?'

Alice had no idea what card Maybelle might want; she'd scooped up all she could find from Peter's desk just before they left. She emptied out her wallet: insurance cards, employment cards, credit cards, driver's licence, passport. Maybelle picked out one that read:

Health ⬤ Insurance

SOCIAL SECURITY ACT

NAME OF BENEFICIARY
PETER JORDAN KESSLER

CLAIM NUMBER
066-03-6731-A

SEX
MALE

SOCIAL SECURITY NUMBER
043-50-4748

BLOOD TYPE
AB NEGATIVE

SIGN HERE ◊ *Peter J. Kessler*

'Kessler? Is he one of *the* Kesslers too?' Alice nodded. 'Well, whaddya know?' She tapped the keyboard in front of her, paused, sighed and leaned back. 'Nope. No record of him. Listen, are you sure he's due in today? Maybe he's – '

'He's at some underground entrance,' Alice interrupted. The trembling left over from the flight suddenly increased and she longed to sit down.

'Underground entrance?'

'It's dark there. Nobody around. Isn't there a porter or somebody?'

Maybelle called a security guard with a gun and a billy stick, who set off and returned in less than five minutes pushing Peter's wheelchair with Peter slumped in it even deeper than before. Alice checked the time on her watch. All those twists and turns she'd taken – how could they have been reduced to less than five minutes? going and coming both?

'Now the question is,' said Maybelle, 'can we find a bed for him?'

Alice stared at her. 'You're loaded with beds,' she said. 'There's a whole wing full of them back there.'

'Those are not beds.'

'Of course they're beds,' Alice said indignantly.

'A bed,' said Maybelle with a terrifying grin, 'is a bed you can sell.'

'That's the silliest thing I ever heard.'

Maybelle shrugged. 'Listen, you ain't heard nothing yet.'

'I suppose that's not an X-ray department out there either? and not a dialysis place for out-patients?'

'Mrs Kessler, you're gonna be lucky if I can find a bed for you at all. Kessler or no Kessler, you can't come in out of the blue like this and just expect a bed to appear. You just may have to make do with a motel room tonight.' The idea so horrified Alice that she couldn't think of anything to say. Maybelle turned in triumph to study her screen, but softened almost at once and turned back. 'Listen, I'll give you a voucher so you and your husband can have dinner in the hospital restaurant – '

'Dinner?' cried Alice. 'Look at him! Dinner? How can he? Besides, it's only four o'clock. What do you expect him to do until dinnertime? Take a walk? Play football?'

'Hey, listen, there's no need to get excited.'

50

'There's *every* need to get excited, Maybelle. You get this man into a bed instantly – '

'Calm down, Mrs Kessler.'

' – or I'll sit down here on the floor and – '

'Listen here, lady – '

' – and scream until you do find one. Do you understand me?'

Maybelle's smile had dimmed enough for Alice to stare into it without wincing. 'All right. All right,' Maybelle said, turning again to her screen.

Alice waited impatiently. Five minutes passed. Maybelle turned back. 'Okay, I've got him a bed – '

'Thank God.'

' – but the only one available in this whole hospital is in Labour and Delivery.'

'Labour and delivery? Babies? What about all those empty beds I saw?'

'Take it or leave it,' Maybelle said.

Alice took it.

ii

Peter lay on the hospital bed as inert as a dead man, and even so Alice felt safe.

It was going to be all right.

This was America. They'd made it. They'd got here. So the start was a little rough. So what? Think of all those babies getting themselves born in this ward. That's pretty rough too. Just look at the nurse: middle-aged, blonde, white nylon pants and a white nylon shirt that rustled as she moved. Who wouldn't feel safe with a nurse like that? Tad had been a Caesarean birth, and the clipped accents of the English nurses as Alice went under the anaesthetic had frightened her more than the prospect of the knife. Not like this. This was America.

51

This was an American nurse with an open, uncomplicated American face and a warm American voice. Temperature. Heart rate.

It was going to be all right.

The nurse undressed Peter and clothed him in a hospital gown, reaching her arms into the sleeves to pull his hands through (not a dignified garment, open down the back, bows untied) just as she did with the new-born babies that lay in rows of cribs down the hallway, just as (in a few hours) she'd dress the baby getting born in the room next door. When she was nearly finished, Christie walked through the door.

Alice made up her mind at once – the moment she saw her father – that no apology was good enough. She reached him before he was more than a step beyond the threshold. 'Get out,' she said.

His face collapsed in puzzlement. 'What's the matter? Are you mad at me or something?'

'Mad at – ? Get out.'

'Felicity's going to have dinner ready in an hour or so. You must want a drink.' When she only glared at him, he shrugged. 'Well, if you won't tell me what's wrong there isn't much I can do about it, is there? Why don't I take the bags now and come back for you later? Where are they?'

'None of your business.'

'So where are you going to sleep tonight? You can't sleep here.'

Alice opened her mouth, then shut it. The desertion itself was unpardonable. But to pretend it hadn't happened – and barely half an hour later at that? She was appalled. 'Where I sleep is my affair,' she said furiously.

In the background the nurse was taking Peter's blood pressure: rip of Velcro, puff-puff of the sleeve. 'I'll just have a word with Peter,' Christie said.

'He doesn't want to speak to you.'

Christie looked down at his feet, then back up at her. 'How do you know that, honey?' She didn't answer. He sighed, put his hands in his pockets, half-turned, turned back. 'The physician of record is Morgenstern,' he said. 'Never liked him much myself – a stuffed shirt, I always thought. Not that that's going to bother you much.' He slipped her an impish smile, another relic of the cat he'd once been. 'He's a good man in his field. Felicity says – '

'So when do I have the pleasure of meeting this Morgenstern you've got to practise on your nephew even though you don't like him yourself?'

'Dunno. Not tonight.'

'When did you call him?'

'I just talked to him.'

'What about yesterday? Did you talk to him then? Or was this your first chat in weeks?'

Christie sighed again. 'Well, um, tell Peter I'll see him tomorrow, okay?'

'No.'

'What does that mean?'

'It means no.'

'Are you banning me from the hospital, Allie?'

'You bastard. I trusted you.'

But she wasn't going to let him spoil the promise that lay ahead. She didn't even watch him walk away, and it wasn't until the next morning that she realized he hadn't attempted any apology for her to thrust aside. She turned back to Peter and his warm American nurse.

It was going to be all right.

Alice slept that night in a lounge chair beside Peter, and in the morning he had a little colour in his face. He seemed rested. He seemed almost interested — a little bit, anyway. At just after nine o'clock, another nurse and an orderly pushed his bed out of Labour and Delivery, into the elevator and out again at Oncology, one floor down. Nobody thought he had cancer, so the nurse said to Alice, who trotted alongside, carrying his toiletries, but there were still no beds in Urology where (so she said) he belonged.

The new room was light and airy. It had its own bathroom and a view out over the ambulance heliport site, where there was a huge red cross on the tarmac; to one side stood a row of maple trees, beyond stretched the cornfields, now brown in the approach of winter. The colour made Alice think of freshly baked bread. Bob Morgenstern appeared within the hour, and he too seemed to give off an air of homely things: good cotton maybe, fine weave, sheer finish, the best sort for sheets — which seemed precisely right in a Midwestern doctor. (Besides, she knew approval of him would irritate her father.) He had an odd bump on his forehead, rather like a billiard ball in bas-relief, and to her delight — and Peter's as well, tired though he was — the examination he conducted was the sort of examination the English doctors, one by one, had given up.

When it was over, Bob sat down in the chair beside the bed with his binder open on his lap. He'd known Peter years ago, not well, not socially, but in the easy way the medical fraternity has with people on its periphery, relatives, business acquaintances, that sort of thing.

'Just one more question,' he said. He glanced out at the helicopter landing-site and then glanced back. 'What day is it?'

Peter was lying back against the pillows. 'What?'

'Can you tell me what day it is?'

'I don't know what you're talking about.'

Bob looked down at his binder. 'I have to ask you. It's hospital policy.'

'You're out of your mind,' said Peter.

'Some regulations make sense. Some don't,' Bob said. Peter said nothing. 'I gather you aren't wholly certain. Am I right?'

'Do you know Yiminez?' Peter said then.

'Who?'

'He said: "If they give you ruled paper, write the other way." '

Bob shifted the papers in his binder, sighed, shrugged. 'You know, Peter, some things are worth fighting for and some aren't. This is one that isn't worth it.'

Peter turned his head and looked out of the window.

'Please, Peter,' Alice said urgently.

He turned back at once. 'Wednesday the eighth of October,' he said.

'Isn't it the ninth?' Alice asked, apprehensive.

Bob shook his head. 'Nope, he's right. And the year, Peter?'

'Go fuck yourself.'

Bob laughed. 'It's good. It's good. I'll just take it that you've answered correctly.' He closed the binder and leaned forward over it. 'There's a lot of work to do here.'

'How wonderful to hear an American doctor again,' cried Alice.

Bob laughed again. 'You haven't been back in quite a while, have you?'

'I'm so tired of the English. They give in too easily.'

'Giving in isn't always bad.'

'Yes, it is,' she said.

He looked away, embarrassed. 'We might try a brace for the back. I want that blood–pressure down. We'd better run some tests on him, but I think the prostate is where we can be most helpful.'

Beginning that very afternoon, there were X-rays, CAT scans, blood chemistries, electroencephalograms, electrocardiograms. The results were inconclusive. There were tests of the middle ear to see if the dizziness might come from somewhere other than the cerebellum; they strapped Peter into a chair and spun him like a top. For hours afterwards he looked electrified. The results were inconclusive. They injected dyes into his veins and took pictures; they investigated every orifice with lights and mirrors. The results were inconclusive.

Alice looked on with mounting excitement: as long as the tests proved nothing, Peter had a chance. That's what she figured. She figured such results left them free to fix the prostate. If they fixed the prostate, why shouldn't the rest follow?

All right? Of course it was going to be all right.

CHAPTER 5

i

For most of her married life Alice had studied Peter much as Tycho Brahe studied the planets, collecting and collating her findings so that they would be ready, as Tycho's had been, for Kepler's great insight when Kepler came along. She analysed the way Peter hung pictures on the wall and the way he arranged furniture to give that strange, rich Neverland texture to a room. She listened to his voice, how he used this word and that, where he put stress in a phrase, and how the tenor of it varied from gaiety with friends or family through a range to prickly and cold with people who didn't appreciate his worth.

She'd gauged her mood by his; she'd been buoyant when he was buoyant, moved when he was moved, angry when he was angry. She scrutinized his reactions to her, saw that he hated any habit that showed up her girlish insecurities — when she spoke with her hand over her mouth, when she didn't finish her sentences, when she tried too hard to please someone who wasn't pleasing her — and she fought to change herself accordingly. She exaggerated her lack of interest in clothes when she discovered that he loved buying clothes for her as much as she delighted in wearing anything he chose.

He said a book was good. She read it at once. He said he liked a picture, a symphony, a play, a part of town, a pudding his mother made. At once, she bent herself to the task. In the course of her study, she'd learned many important lessons: how to wire a plug, how to unplug a sink, how to switch sides in the middle of a conversation and not get caught, how to fight (never apologize, never argue the other guy's point of view) and how to win (always claim the moral high ground).

Sometimes she did not agree with Peter – sometimes she thought he was completely wrong – and she was subtle enough to know that when she did not agree, he would judge her adversely for pretending she did. But often, behind his back, she would redouble her efforts to bring her thought into line with his because, after all, he was perfect. She could not find a single flaw in him.

The years of his illness – when the balance of power had shifted, when she herself had become sovereign of moods – had been curiously like years of exile. And while she had hopes in this American town that she hadn't dared have in Devon, this place – this Overton where Peter had been born – could readily have stood in for the barren landscape she found inside herself these days, with only enough of his magic left to light up a remote corner here and there.

Take the streets around Memorial Hospital, for example. After that first night, she'd moved into a nearby motel, down a block, over two, a desolate, dreary walk that she walked each morning and evening: abandoned refrigerators in front yards where the grass was weeds and the weeds were yellow; where porches sagged and screen doors hung by a single hinge; where the houses were clapboard, peeling, askew, set on pillars above the ground like houses in a bog. There was little movement anywhere of any sort, human or vehicular, the pavement

58

was cracked, sidewalk and street alike, falling away in places. Stores were cased in electrified fencing like administration blocks in a high-security prison.

On the other hand, American motels – bland as they are – have much to recommend them. They're clean and comfortable: that reassuring strip of paper across the toilet bowl, the insulated walls, ice-machine, television, good bed, sheets changed every day. Alice was brushing her teeth in front of *Cagney and Lacey* when she got the telephone call from Cordelia Macher-Daly, who owned the whole of the middle of town as well as this derelict fringe and great tracts of land in the countryside beyond. Cordelia and Peter had grown up together.

'I hear you're not with your family,' she said to Alice. 'How long are you going to be in Overton? Weeks? Months?'

'It'll be a – '

'You can't have found anywhere to live for longer than a month – not with the Corn Scorch coming up.'

'Of course!' Alice cried, 'I'd forgotten. I – '

'The Corn Scorch brings us more tourists than all the rest of our charms put together,' said Cordelia, who had a portentous side to her. Then she laughed. She was also very shrewd. 'The pity of it is, they gawk and make a mess, but they absolutely refuse to buy. Anyhow, I think I can help. You don't mind eating with Schpiegal, do you? I mean, some people mind. Do you?'

'I've never met – '

'It's good for him to see people from time to time. We can talk afterwards. Are you sure you don't mind?'

Peter had told Alice that Cordelia's father, Schpiegal Macher-Daly, was the dullest man in Overton – no mean achievement, as he'd said, for a man in the dullest town in America. 'Well, I – ' she began.

'I'll pick you up at the hospital at noon.'

Alice had met Cordelia only once before and very briefly, but nobody could mistake that seagull look she had to her: grey-white hair, downy white skin, orange beak of a nose. She had a withered arm, which she held close to her chest, a thin, angular, alien limb, each joint sharply bent like the wing of a new-hatched bird. She'd taught business administration once; she was proud of this long-ago academic career, and she liked to say that her mind could still perform mental feats with all the skill of a gymnast on parallel bars. She could fly, she could swoop and dive. She loved to demonstrate these skills, talking without let-up and over everybody much as she'd talked over Alice on the telephone. The subject of conversation was immaterial.

Alice said, 'Oh, really?' and 'Hum,' as they sped through town. Nothing more was called for. Despite her bad arm, Cordelia manoeuvred her aluminium-coloured Mercedes with ease and dash; in less than fifteen minutes, she and Alice had arrived at the leafy and moneyed residential section where she lived. She turned onto a drive that twisted through a private forest.

'Do you really live in here somewhere?' Alice said.

But Cordelia was mid-flight and didn't answer. The house, when they reached it, rambled away into the foliage, one storey here, three storeys there, leaded windows and plate-glass windows side by side. Furious barking began at once, audible even from the stone turnaround in front of the house where Cordelia parked the car.

'They miss me when I go out,' she said to Alice, leading them up a wide flight of stairs to the porch. 'Stand clear.'

Cordelia opened the door, and Alice leapt backwards despite the warning. Dogs jumped, slavered, yapped, licked – an explosion of dogs, a frenzy of dogs – fur, paws, teeth, tongues, claws that screeched on the floor and smell of stagnant marsh welling up. The big black dog was still alive then.

'Down!' Cordelia cried, as delighted as the animals themselves, and flapped her little wing above the scramble. 'Do as I say. Lie down!' The dogs paid no attention. She turned and shouted to Alice. 'Do you mind if we eat as soon as we go in? Schpiegal is ravenous at noon.'

Alice followed in Cordelia's wake down a hallway, through a door and into a room so dark after the brightness of the day outside that at first she could make out only the lone bulb that flickered from beneath a heavily shaded floor-lamp in the dining-room. The dogs barked and scampered and growled. An ancient man — bent, frail, gape-jawed, with the lashless turtle-eyes of the very old — sat slumped in a chair at a dining-table laden with silverware, napkins and cut glass. It was cold.

'This is Alice, Schpiegal,' Cordelia shouted at the old man. He didn't move. Cordelia patted his shoulder and smiled at Alice. 'Sometimes he isn't all that responsive. Make yourself comfortable. Take that chair over there. I'll bring on the soup right away. Oh, and do be careful: the table wobbles a little.'

Alice sat down as carefully as she could; the table swayed as though it were on board ship. Schpiegal's glass teetered and fell. 'Oh, Lord,' she cried, 'I'm so sorry.'

The old man sat as unmoving as before while she righted the glass, but the dogs were abruptly silent, tails high, eyes on her, big black dog in front, his four courtiers ranged behind him. Cordelia talked on from the kitchen.

'. . . of a town like Overton which began as a veritable tower of Babel' — she appeared at the door with bowls of soup on a butler's tray crudely constructed from bamboo and the wheels of a baby carriage — 'which as a market analyst I . . .'

Schpiegal ate nothing. He hung motionless over his soup — a curious way for a hungry man to behave, Alice thought. Cordelia talked while they ate and while she restacked the bowls, including Schpiegal's untouched one, and ferried them back to the kitchen, where her voice got lost from time to time in the clatter of pans. Alice was beginning to feel sleepy; the barrage of words had taken on the feel of a single unending sentence played out yard by yard as though it were fishing-line instead of syntax. Cordelia emerged, still talking, with a casserole dish of stew and doled it out.

Schpiegal's attack on his plate was so sudden and so fierce that Alice jumped and the table swayed again.

Cordelia didn't seem to notice. '. . . England, Germany, Poland, Russia – bonfires and beerfests – and Thanksgiving too, so that all – '

'What's she doing here?' Schpiegal interrupted. Alice saw that his plate was already wiped clean.

' – all these nationalities – '

He slammed his fist on the table. 'What's she doing here?' he shouted.

Cordelia sighed. 'Who? Allie?' she said.

'Her! Her!' He pointed his fork at Alice.

'This is Allie, Schpiegal.'

'What's she doing here?'

'She's come to lunch with us.' She glanced at Alice with compassion. Alice smiled back.

'Hasn't she got anything to eat at home?'

'She's come to eat with us, Schpiegal. Have some more stew. I didn't tell you about the tourists' driving, did I, Allie?'

'Not yet,' said Alice, who hadn't the least idea.

Schpiegal drooped again over the table, and Cordelia removed the plates, talking from the kitchen as before. She returned with ice cream. '. . . arrive here and see a huge effigy on fire and fields on fire as well, and dancing in the streets, floats and bands. For some reason, everybody goes faster – '

'Why doesn't she go home?' Schpiegal said.

62

' – even good drivers, which is interesting to the market analyst – '

He slammed the table with his fist as he had before. 'Why doesn't she go home?' he shouted.

Cordelia sighed. 'She's come to lunch. That's why.'

'Lunch is over. Can't she go home now?'

'Lunch isn't over. Not yet. When it is, I'll drive her home.'

'Hasn't she got a car of her own?'

'No.'

'Then call her a taxi.'

'When the time comes, I'll drive her back.'

'Why is she making you do that? What right has she to make you drive her? Call a taxi. Can't she afford a taxi?'

'That's enough, Schpiegal. Be quiet.'

He looked balefully at the dish in front of him.

'Where was I?' Cordelia said.

Grasping at what little she'd caught out of Cordelia's monologue, knowing it wasn't quite right, Alice said cautiously, 'My mother was a careful driver.'

'Angela? That doesn't sound like her.'

'It doesn't, does it? She wasn't timid in anything else, but she took Mollie and me to see the Mardi Gras in New Orleans, and while we were there, she drove a hundred and ten miles an hour.'

Cordelia nodded happily. 'That's just exactly the sort of thing that is of interest to me as a – '

'I drove fast in Louisiana,' Schpiegal said, looking up.

' – a market analyst working on the petroleum – '

'I drove fast in Louisiana,' he shouted, banging the table.

'Did you?' Alice said.

'I was driving with my wife and two black Labrador dogs. We had a big station wagon – my wife and I in the front, the two black Labrador dogs in the back – and my wife said, "Pull over, Schpiegal, I don't feel well." So I pulled over, and she died.' He blinked his turtle eyes. 'I was behind the wheel and she was sitting in the passenger seat. So there I was all by myself in Louisiana with a dead wife and two black Labrador dogs.'

'Was it a heart attack?' said Alice, who was interested in anything medical these days.

'I drove as fast as I could to get out of there. I drove for miles and miles. The dogs were hungry.' He turned to Cordelia. 'I'm sleepy, little C.'

Cordelia got up at once and helped him out of his chair. 'Pour yourself a cognac,' she said to Alice. 'Go on into the living-room. I'll be back in a minute. Move anything that's in your way.' The dogs shook themselves, stretched, yawned and trotted after her out of the room.

The living-room was even colder than the dining-room, and the disarray was formidable. Piles of paper – old files from the look of them – filled the corners, lined the wall behind the sofa and covered the surfaces of the tables and the seats of all the chairs but one. On that one lay a crude paper cut-out of a hand – sausage fingers, balloon palm, a giant of a hand. Alice registered it in a distracted sort of way. She didn't really want a cognac, but the smell of dog was so strong that she poured herself some anyway, cleared one of the chairs and sat down.

'You could rent this apartment of mine,' Cordelia said when she got back, followed by the big black dog, who was followed (at a respectful distance) by the other four. 'It's very handsome. It's right here in – '

'That for the Corn King?' Alice said, pointing at the hand.

Cordelia shrugged. 'Not very good, is it? Schpiegal used to design wonderful ones. He hired Buddy Sam to make them up.' The Corn King was the mascot of the Corn Scorch festival; each of the prominent families of Overton was responsible for making some part of one of his limbs. The less prominent made the torso and the thighs, and each year the Corn King was one inch taller than the year before. 'He's reached fifteen feet this time – an inch or two over that, I think.'

'That's not big enough for a fifteen-footer,' said Alice.

'I know. That's just a model.' Cordelia cocked her head. 'Are you sure it's not big enough? It looks huge to me.'

'It'll have to be at least twice that size.'

Cordelia poured herself a glass of cognac and tossed it back in a single swallow while the dogs settled themselves in the middle of the floor. 'Could you make the Corn King's hand if you had to?'

'Probably not.'

'You're going to need somewhere to take Peter when he gets better, and that's going to take some time. You can't spend the Corn Scorch in the streets. Do you want to see the apartment? How much could you pay? The apartment isn't a mess like this. I don't allow the dogs down there. Only Wiffles.'

Two days ago Alice would have refused at once. But two days ago she'd forgotten the Corn Scorch. 'Wiffles?' she said.

'Cat.'

'I'm seeing a place tomorrow that belongs to a friend of Felicity's. It's in the range of two hundred a month, and it's out of town – out in the country somewhere.'

'This isn't the country. How about three fifty?'

'I ought to go and look at this one first.'

'What do you say to three hundred? including heat and electricity?'

'Why offer it to me?' Alice said, suddenly curious. 'Wouldn't a local tenant serve you better?'

Cordelia poured herself a second shot of cognac and tossed it back as she had the first. 'I like the idea of making the Corn King's hand out of useless paper from the past – old files, that sort of thing,' she said, waving at the paper that lined the room. 'You could do that, couldn't you? I'm going to have to sort them all first, but think of the money I'll save. Tell you what: I'll throw in a car.'

'What about Buddy Sam?' Buddy Sam had made parts of the Corn King for as long as anybody could remember.

'He insists on special paper, a totally unnecessary expense, which as a market analyst − '

'I don't know anything about making a hand,' Alice said, a little alarmed.

'You can have the apartment for two fifty. Car included. Come on. I'll show you.'

To Alice's dismay the dogs got up, too.

'No!' Cordelia said to them sharply; they growled but obeyed, and Cordelia took Alice through the kitchen, through the laundry-room (where smell of dog mixed uneasily with smell of detergent) and into the apartment.

iii

The apartment was newly built, light, different from the rest of the house. Windows, floor to ceiling on three walls, wall to wall, looked out into the woods; no other house was visible, and the trees were so close and so dense − and the windows so large − that the room seemed secreted away in them like a nest. Cordelia opened the cupboards in the kitchen alcove off to one side and turned on the taps of the shower in the bathroom. She led Alice across the room to a doll's house of a staircase, built on so tiny a scale that Alice had to wind herself sideways to climb it.

The bedroom above had paned windows, darkened even at noon by foliage, and so was even more nest-like than the downstairs. A door from the bedroom led into the main house; Cordelia explained that the apartment had no telephone of its own, that Alice could use the telephone through that door if she kept a record of her calls. Downstairs again, she told Alice she'd come in every day to feed the fish with lacy tails that swam in the tank in front of the windows and to continue sorting through the boxes of papers that lined the fourth wall of the main room. The empty box she pointed out was where, as soon as she got started, she planned to put any papers that could go into the making of the Corn King's hand.

Somewhat to her surprise, Alice realized that she was going to welcome these intrusions. She couldn't help liking Cordelia, although she couldn't for the life of her say why. Besides, she did need a car, even if she had no idea how to make a hand for a Corn King. She moved in at once. That afternoon she walked past the dogs alone for the first time; and for the first time, the dogs – bodies tense, eye swivelling in eye-sockets – marked her passage from door to door.

CHAPTER 6

i

From outside, the window walls of the apartment were opaque at night: that was why there were no curtains. So Cordelia said anyway. Macher-Daly Enterprises held a patent on the glass – not on the market yet. Alice didn't really believe her. Inside, the plates of glass reflected light back and forth in fractured, scattered regressions of dots; and that first night, studying the tropical fish in the fish-bowl, Alice couldn't shake the feeling that she was being watched the same way. She went out to look for herself. From the stone turnaround where the Mercedes stood, the apartment glowed – pulsated almost – but the glass walls were milky: impenetrable to the eye. Just as Cordelia said.

She was barely inside again when the call came – the one that ended up changing everything. The telephone was in Schpiegal's old study, which was on the opposite side of that door in the apartment bedroom. She heard Cordelia shouting for her, so she rushed up the tiny staircase, climbing it almost as though it were a tree, and turned the knob. The door opened a little, then met resistance.

'Cordelia?' she said.

'Can you push?' Cordelia said through the crack. 'The door's kind of, well, wedged from this side. I guess I'd better start sorting in here, hadn't I? Can't you push any harder?'

Alice pushed and the door gave way in a flurry of paper. Files, magazines, letters, newsprint lined all four walls, floor to ceiling; they covered the window and the floor except for a winding path to the telephone, which balanced uneasily atop its own pile of paper.

'All for the Corn King,' Cordelia whispered, waving her good arm, and left.

'Hello,' Alice said into the receiver.

'This is Dutch Hashman,' the voice said. 'We met once. I don't expect you to remember, but your daddy – '

'Of course I remember,' she said.

Who could forget a name like Dutch Hashman? You know the moment you hear it: yellow-haired kid, cow-lick, neighbourhood tough out of the *Saturday Evening Post* of long ago, jam on his face and a slingshot in his back pocket: eleven years old – something like that, never older.

A couple of years before he got sick, Peter said to Alice: 'The best of all possible ages is eleven.'

'Eleven years old? Why? Whoever wants to be eleven?'

'I do.' he said with that quick smile of his. They were lying in bed on a rainy afternoon, the sheets tousled around them; little Tad would be in school at the bottom of the hill for at least another hour.

She laughed happily. 'Why eleven? Why not seven? Eleven's such a dull age.' But what did she know? What does any *girl* know? 'Tell me about it.'

'About what?'

'About Dutch Hashman,' she said, picking the name out of earlier stories he'd told her. 'I want another story about him.'

'Like what?'

'I want an adventure. Tell me an adventure.'

Peter lay back on the pillows. 'Well, there was the time we found the beads that belonged to the lady with the beads that jangled.' He was one of those men who rarely look at the person they're speaking to, not even in bed, and he stared dreamily at the ceiling as he spoke. Alice – suspicious – scanned his face for the mischief that she knew was there somewhere. 'They were in a pretty little nest overhanging Sweetbrier Pond – '

'Damn you, Peter, this lady is a made-up lady, isn't she?'

'All ladies in stories are made up.'

'I want a real story,' she said.

'How about that day of days in summertime when Dutch went to sleep on a leaf – '

'Peter!'

He laughed. 'What you want is a boring story.'

'What kind of games did you play?'

'Same games all kids play.'

'Tell me.'

'Too boring.'

'Tell me!'

So he told her about Washington Avenue, where he'd lived when he was little, about the boulevard that ran down the centre of the street, the widest boulevard in Overton, shaded all along its length by elm trees – huge, old, arching – that on summer days made a canopy so dense the sky wasn't visible. This boulevard ran all the way to the woods around Macher-Daly House and even farther, to Sweetbrier Pond. Here he'd played Red Post and Kick the Can and all the other games American children used to play in the days before every house had a television. Here he'd staged his battles against (and occasional alliances with) Dutch Hashman, the toughest kid in town.

Alice strained to see it for herself. With her eyes shut tight, she could just glimpse Peter's mother watching over him from the tactful distance of a porch swing that creaked with every rock. She could almost hear in her own ears the little-boy yelp and clamour of the evening as it grew darker – almost feel in her own body the magic Peter felt as the street-lights came on and made yellow pools on the ground.

'Did nothing bad ever happen?' she asked. 'Was all of eleven perfect?'

'Um,' he said.

'I don't believe you. There must have been something bad.'

'My father gave me too much money.'

'That's bad? Why haven't you told me about this before?'

'Awful,' he said, his cheeks reddening a little against the white of the pillow. 'The neighbourhood had a going rate of twenty-five cents a week. My father seemed quite unaware of the proprieties of the matter: he gave me ten-dollar bills. I didn't know what to do with them.'

'Spend them?'

He shook his head. 'Out of the question: think of my reputation.'

'What did you do with them?'

'I hid most of them. That summer I devised a plan and managed to foist them off on Dutch, which was very clever of me, don't you think?'

'That sounds like a real adventure. Tell me it.' She knew how changeable his moods could be, but the tension she felt this time was more in herself than in him; the moment was so pleasant – the yearning so strong in her to prolong it. 'What happened?' she pressed when he fell silent beside her.

'It's a secret.'

'No, it isn't. Tell me.'

'I buried the money. Oh, Allie this is so – '

'Tell me!'

He shrugged. 'I made up a fanciful story.'

'What story?'

'I don't know. Buried treasure, I suppose.'

He was drifting away. She raised herself up over him to pin him back, force him to see her. 'How much money was there?'

'I don't remember.'

'Because of Dutch, the other kids assumed you'd stolen it. Isn't that right? You were free to spend it. What did you spend it on?'

He studied her face quickly, its almond-shaped blue eyes intent on him, her hair tumbling down over his naked chest, then turned his glance to the window and the rain. 'Oh, I couldn't tell you that,' he said, demeanour grave.

He was teasing and she knew it, but there was that half-bafflement on his face too, now turned away from her so that the long muscle in his neck, back of ear to base of throat – one of the most elegant lines in a man, steely and sensuous both – cast its shadow in the dim light. 'Why not?' she said.

He reached out, pushed the hair away from her forehead, watched it fall back again and again turned his glance away. 'The code,' he said.

'Code? What code?'

'*The Code*,' he repeated. He made no attempt to hide the smile he knew she was studying for hints and clues.

'Is this some deep male mystery?' She frowned – that look of bafflement always disconcerted her so – and he burst out laughing. 'Peter! Tell me. Now you've got to tell me.'

'Nope. It's against the code to – '

'Oh, come on, tell me. Please. Pretty please.'

He reached out to her face with both hands this time. 'You wouldn't want me to break – '

She caught at the hands before they touched her. 'Of course I would. I can't wait another minute. Tell me.'

Suddenly the wind changed, and Peter the will o'the wisp changed with it. 'This really is boring,' he said, relaxing his arms out of her grip and turning back to the window, where rain ran down the glass in rivulets. 'You don't want to hear any more about this.'

'Yes I do. I do.

'All stories come to an end.'

'Not before you find out what happens.'

'This one does. Nothing happens. There isn't any more.'

'But I want – '

'For Christ's sake, drop it.'

Sometimes she was just too much. He was by no means modest, but how could anybody find *anybody* as fascinating as she found him? He loved this fascination and hated it, was torn between struggling against it and giving into it body and soul; it bound him like a snake-charmer's music, far more potent than her young shoulders, her young neck, her firm young mouth. And yet sometimes it seemed to him that she was snake and snake-charmer both, that her aim was to suck the very substance out of him, to taste his being in her own mouth. Nothing sexual here, however it sounds. Her need, or so he thought of it, was alimentary in nature; he could feel her hunger, her desire to swallow him down – digest the meat of him.

Even after all the years they'd lived together, it was as though she had no soul of her own and was out to requisition his.

ii

Alice had met the real Dutch Hashman only once before his telephone call to her at Cordelia's; he'd been a disappointment – not at all what Peter's stories had led her to expect. Perhaps his hair had never been yellow. Perhaps he'd never had the cow-lick. The company she'd met him in had been polite, a cocktail party of the standard Overton variety, brittle conversation, too much booze, too much noise. He was middle-aged and looked it; he had a bug-eyed face and a plump body stuffed into white pants with little black horses printed on them — memorable to be sure, but not pleasantly so. She hated the way he held his thighs. She hated the fake hillbilly accent that he swung at arm's length like a Neolithic axe, as though to prove that the crudest of tools can clear a field if you're ruthless enough.

At Schpiegal's house, upstairs in Schipiegal's study amid the wild disarray of paper, she could hear the threat of that accent in the voice over the telephone, much as she'd felt the threat of some watcher downstairs with those cold, black panes of glass on all sides of her. Dutch was a urologist, she remembered that too. Speciality: resection of the prostate. She'd feared her father might call him in.

'I been doing some thinking,' Dutch said to her (the accent was faint but on view: the axe at rest, driven into the trunk of a nearby tree), 'and your daddy, he wants me to make with this prostate next week. But I'm not at all sure it's the right thing. You ought to call your daddy, know that?'

'Do you have doubts about operating?'

'Yeah, I got doubts.'

'Pop called you in?'

'Yeah.'

'What about Morgenstern?'

'What about him?'

'He doesn't seem to have any doubts. At least he hasn't mentioned any to me.'

'He ain't a surgeon.'

'But you've talked to him about it?'

'Nope.'

'He's the — what am I supposed to call him? primary physician?'

'Yeah, I know about that.'

'Shouldn't the two of you get together?'

'Me and Morgenstern?' He laughed. 'That'll be the day. It's

Christie I been talking to, and Christie has his mind all made up.'

Alice took in her breath. 'You know, uh, Dutch, this has nothing to do with my father. Not anymore.'

'Ah, come on. Don't be like that.'

'I don't want him around.'

'Yeah, yeah. I know about that, too. It'll pass.'

Christie had telephoned every day. He'd sent fruit and an oversized picture-postcard of Lake Michigan, where Peter had spent summers when he was a child. Alice pinned the postcard up on the wall so Peter could see it from his bed, but she wasn't ready to let Christie himself into the room. Felicity had come to visit on the second day – a bad hospital visitor (she said so herself), too breezy, too cheerful – and the talk had touched on very little of importance, certainly nothing as awkward as Alice's ban on her father.

Alice sighed. 'Anyhow, you don't agree with him?'

'Now don't make a mistake, Mrs Kessler. I love Christie. If he wants me to operate his little nephew, I'll operate him. And if what Christie wants is, I do it on a kitchen table with a kitchen knife, then I'll do it on a kitchen table with a kitchen knife.'

'Not without my permission, you won't,' she snapped.

'Well now, ma'am' – the hillbilly accent was abruptly fill-swing, mowing down brush on all sides – 'what I'm tryin' to say is I think we oughtta to take another gander at this whole shebang, beginnin' to end.'

But Peter had been a good teacher of tactics, and Alice had learned her lessons well; she let Dutch wait just a little too long for his comfort. 'Why would you want to do that?' she said then.

'Now you don't need no explainin' about such matters, do you, ma'am?'

'I'm afraid I do. What you suggest is just what Morgenstern's been doing. What else is there to do at this stage? He's run all kinds of tests.'

'What's the point in a whole bunch of tests you can't tell the meaning of?'

Alice glanced around at the heaps of paper that lined the room; again she let him wait. 'Don't you want to do this operation?' she said at last. 'Is that what you're telling me?'

'What I'm tellin' you is that there's just so much a man can take. The point is, is this the right thing for the man?'

iii

When Dutch arrived in the hospital the next morning, Alice didn't recognize him. The plumpness of years before was gone, just washed away. The face left behind was crude, shadowed, coarse-edged, lines scored deep into the cheeks. The clothes were sober. He was shorter than she'd remembered.

He shook Peter's hand. 'You look awful,' he said. 'What have you been doing to yourself?' There was only the faintest twang in his voice.

'I don't know. I really don't know,' Peter said. He was propped up on pillows, shaved, washed, brushed, fussed over. 'It's good to see you, Dutch.'

'Been a long time, hasn't it?'

'Too long.'

'What kind of a story you got to tell me today?'

'Will you do me the honour of believing it?'

'Probably not.'

Peter's smile was wan and slow, but at least it was a smile. 'How about The Indignities The Medical Profession Visits on Its Captives?'

'I know that one already,' Dutch said, patting his shoulder.

'No, you don't.'

'I wouldn't bet my life on that, if I was you.'

76

The examination that followed was like its predecessors in this hospital: binder, pencil, questions, proddings, palpatings. When it was over, Dutch sat down opposite his patient.

'You really are feeling pretty low, aren't you?'

Peter nodded.

'Look, I gotta ask you a question.'

'I'm listening.'

Dutch looked embarrassed. 'I'm sorry about this – uh – '

'What day is it?' Peter said. 'That your question?'

'It's supposed to be the infallible test of, uh' – Dutch shrugged – 'of whether you got your marbles or not.'

'In that case, I would be a good deal happier if I didn't know.'

'You do, though?'

'Let me see. I feel around me an uneasy equilibrium between good and evil,' Peter said, and Alice knew that dreamy delivery as well as she knew her own soul. 'And you're here – in part anyway – to have a look at my kidneys. That makes it October. As to the day, well, nobody could deny that I am in an excess of peril and that the threats against me have led – as threats in October tend to do – to incontinence. That should make it the eleventh.'

This short speech was the first real effort Peter had put into anything for months. Alice was touched, intrigued – and a little irked.

'You always did talk too much,' Dutch said. 'What is that guff anyhow? Numerology or something?'

'You have to take truth where you find it,' Peter said. Then he sank back against the pillows, his face suddenly pinched and pale.

Dutch turned to Alice. 'I don't know,' he said. 'I think we ought to get this man up out of the bed – get him walking – before we start messing him about with a knife.'

'He can't walk very well at the best of times,' Alice said.

'Yeah,' Dutch said. 'Yeah, I can see that.'

'He's had regular physiotherapy.'

'Done him any good?'

'It's better than nothing,' she said, but she wasn't as sure of that as she'd once been, and the twitch of Dutch's eyebrows didn't make her any surer. Peter hadn't wanted physiotherapy; he'd gone only because she'd insisted, and one day the physiotherapist had turned him over to a young assistant. There had been an accident. It hadn't seemed much at the time – an internal noise like sugar ground under a shoe and a momentary faint – but afterwards Peter had walked with bent knees. The pain was worse. Why hadn't she objected to the young assistant? She'd asked herself the question again and again.

'Well now, I'll tell you something.' Dutch leaned back in the plastic hospital chair. The once plump body was compact, efficient, irritatingly at ease with itself. 'There isn't much point in reaming out a prostate less of which a man can get to the can to urinate. See, when you do this to the man, he got a time period thereafter – couple of days, sometimes a couple of weeks – of what we call "urgency". What that means is, when he's got to urinate, he's got to urinate right now. Understand me?'

'Isn't that what a urinal is for?' she asked, pointing to the shiny aluminium pisspot on Peter's bedside table. But she herself had complained again and again about this most ill-designed piece of medical equipment – one of those simple items that should work, has to work, but doesn't work well at best and won't work at all for a man who's really ill.

Dutch's shrug was as dismissive as her own assessment, and thus it was that he put her in the wrong a second time in her own eyes – and in less than five minutes at that.

'So how do we get him to walk then?' she said, unable to keep the annoyance out of her voice.

'That's something we got to do some thinking about.'

78

'What about his back?'

'What about it?'

'Dr Morgenstern suggests a brace.'

Dutch laughed. The shadows in his face shifted and broke. 'They put one of those contraptions on me once. I'll never forget it. When I took it off, I thought to myself, "I ain't never gonna put that thing on again. I'll go to hell first." Worst half-hour I ever spent in my life. It's a waste of time.'

'I think it's a good idea,' Alice said.

'What do you know about it?'

'What he says sounds reasonable to me,' she said. 'Besides, what do *you* know about it?'

Dutch shrugged. 'Morgenstern's an old boy – so am I, come to think of it – but he's an internist, a gut man. He don't know anything about braces. He's just flailing around.'

'Why are you so hard on him?' Peter asked her later.

It was cold and dark when she got back to Macher-Daly House; there was to be a hard frost this night. She poured herself a drink and sat – a leather sofa, low-slung, expensive, no smell of dog – studying the fish in the fish-bowl, and out of the corner of her eye she caught an edge of movement somewhere deep in one of those retreating reflections. She swung around, her heart aflutter. There was nobody there. Nothing. She shook the ice in her drink to shake off the trembling in her hands and turned again towards the fish-bowl.

There it was again – no more than a quick dash, a flick of something – but she was certain this time.

She held herself rigid.

Over the far arm of the sofa appeared the tip of a ginger-coloured tail.

'Wiffles?' she said uncertainly, looking down.

The cat jumped back, its fur on end.

'Kitty? Here, kitty, kitty,' Alice said, reaching out.

The cat sniffed at her finger, drew back, sniffed again, and at that very moment she realized she knew how to make a hand for the Corn King.

CHAPTER 7

i

The day after Dutch first examined Peter – the tests Bob Morgenstern had ordered were still going on – Alice, who had fallen into Overton's hospital Wonderland by running after her father through dark corridors, found herself for the first time face to face with the Queen of Heart's logic, which ruled the place. She was shaving Peter when Dutch arrived the second time.

He threw himself down in the chair opposite Peter's bed, opened his binder with a sigh and said, 'They want this man out of here.'

'Want what?' Alice said. Peter hadn't been able to shave himself for over a year; she kept her eyes on his lathered face.

'Ever seen one of these?' Dutch held up a paper.

'What is it?' she said, not looking.

'I remember the first one *I* ever seen. I had a man in here – didn't know what was wrong with him – no idea at all. They wanted him out. Like Peter here.'

'I don't know what that means.'

'It means they wanted him out. Like I say.'

A man's beard is a place of traps. The razor skates over the cheeks but oh, beware of over-confidence: at the upper lip and just beneath the chin, it suddenly drags as though it's run into a gravel underlay. Who can control such anarchy? Alice had taken months to figure out that she had to press down all the harder to keep from grazing the skin.

'He'll get another in a day or two,' Dutch was saying. 'All depends on how the computer works.' He paused. 'You don't know what I'm talking about, do you?'

'Computers?' she said, eyes on Peter.

'No, ma'am. I'm talkin' about this here thing.' He held up the paper in his hand.

She twisted to glance at him over her shoulder and lathered her own nose in the process. The clothes this morning, she thought, aren't they just a shade jauntier? 'Are they moving us to Urology? They've sure as hell taken their time.'

'You got soap on your nose.'

She wiped her face with her sleeve and turned back to her work. 'I never did understand why they say they haven't got beds in this hospital when they do.'

'That ain't got nothin' to do with it.'

'Doesn't it? What is it then?'

'No, ma'am. Like I said before, when I say out, I mean out.'

Alice set the razor down beside the bowl of hot water and handed Peter a towel. 'Out of the hospital?' she said.

'Yeah.'

'That doesn't make any sense.'

'Nope.'

Dutch shifted his compact body in the chair, and despite her irritation with him – or perhaps because of it – she found herself wondering why the lines in his face were so very deep. Maybe it's just hereditary, she thought. Maybe his father – old Dr Hashman – looked just the same. Old Dr Hashman had been a urologist, too, and the son of a doctor: three generations.

82

'I was grandfathered in,' Dutch had said at that Overton cocktail party years ago. Why would she remember a thing like that?

'The first one of these I seen' – he held up the paper again – 'I didn't pay it no mind. This dumb nurse calls me up, and she says, "He's ready to leave." I says, "You a doctor?" She says, "No." I says, "Then don't tell me how to treat my patient." Well, she doesn't like that very much, and she gets huffy on me: she says, "I represent the Utilization Board of this hospital." '

It was a bright, crisp, blowy morning. The row of maple trees that lined one side of the helicopter landing-pad outside the hospital window glowed yellow and red.

'So I says to her, "Ma'am, this man is pissin' blood." She said, "I don't like your language." I tell her I don't like hers, either. Well, this particular man stayed in, but what I'm tellin' you about was eight years ago – maybe nine. It ain't anywhere near as easy as it was then.'

Alice took the towel back from Peter. 'They haven't even finished their tests,' she said. 'Nobody's decided anything.'

'Been here four days, ain't you?'

She nodded.

'You don't get as long as four days for a prostate job, leastways not for one without complications.'

'This one's sure as hell complicated.'

'Yeah. But I gotta fight for that. I can't rightly remember just how much you do get at this stage. The point is, you're already over the limit. Three days and three-fifths. Something like that; it changes all the time. What's three-fifths of a day, anyhow? Ten hours? Eleven? Who knows? They got it all down in a book of logarithms. I always hated logarithms.'

'More like fourteen,' Alice said.

'Fourteen what?'

'Hours,' she said. 'Three-fifths of a day. Is there really a book?' She eyed him suspiciously. 'Or are you just making that up?'

'Numbers have always seemed opaque to me,' Peter said wearily from his bed. It was the first time he'd spoken that morning, and there was a sheen of exhaustion to his skin.

'Fourteen, huh?' Dutch said to Alice. 'How did you work that out?'

'It's only arithmetic,' she said. 'What's a Utilization Board?'

'Bunch of dumb nurses.'

'What do they do?'

'Follow the rule book. Sure there's a rule book: I wouldn't tell you no tales, would I? They work the software. There's a couple of million bucks-worth of that.'

Alice turned to look at the maple trees again. The first leaves had fallen on the tarmac. As she watched, a gust of wind picked them up, swirled them around and whisked them away. Alice liked computers, although the first one she'd owned scolded her when she entered commands incorrectly. 'Silly,' it flashed up on the screen.

'Want a cup of coffee?' Dutch said to her.

'The coffee's terrible around here,' she said.

'It's near enough to passable in the private lounge for us important people. Come on, I'll treat you.'

'I don't think – ' she began.

'Hey, Peter, you mind if I take your wife out to a cup of coffee?'

Peter shook his head.

'Look, I'm not – ' she began again.

'Come on, woman,' he said, winking at Peter, walking out of the door, beckoning to her.

Alice knew where she was in the Oncology corridor and the elevator, but after that she lost track entirely. Hallway followed hallway, set of doors followed set of doors, back and forth, up some stairs, down some more. Dutch half-walked, half-ran; she

84

followed at a trot, irritated at him all over again. Hospitals are so depressing. Bare walls, dun colours, seamed linoleum like prison walls or subway trains.

Years ago I saw a picture of a soldier with no face. There was just a dish shape of skin where the eyes, nose and mouth should be: a triumph of medicine, the icon of what goes on in these blind, suffocating, featureless places, where the absence of screams is itself frightening, the means for screaming excised on entry by shame, inertia, opiates, and a fear of death so deep down, so bestial and so raw that the spirit shrivels into its shell like a poisoned snail at the merest whiff of it. Dutch and Alice manoeuvred past a traffic-jam of beds on trolleys, three of them, each with its own shoal of attendants in rustling white nylon, each sporting an inert body attached to jangling bottles and flashing meters.

'I'll never find my way out of here,' Alice said, afraid despite herself.

'That's what they all say, and yet here we are.'

The doctors' lounge was on the ground floor, which surprised her; she hadn't realized she'd gone down that far. Tall windows looked out into a small grove of maple trees, red and yellow like the ones visible from Peter's room, and across a landscaped greensward half-buried in fallen leaves. A hillock, strategically placed, cut out the cars that hurried back and forth on the road beyond. The room itself was large, airy, light, divided up by bookshelves and groupings of plants; except for the aura of plastic that clings like bloom on plums to all Midwestern public rooms, this could have been a gentler, older place, an elegant old hotel in New York perhaps. The chairs were leather, low and soft. A coffee-urn stood on a side-table.

'They treat you well, don't they?' she said, gazing around her.

'When it comes to furniture, they can't do enough to kiss the hem of our garment. You take milk? Sugar?' He filled two cups and set one down in front of her. 'You can't still be mad at your daddy,' he said then.

Alice's irritation flared anew. 'Do we have to talk about this now?' She herself was only half-aware that her cadence as she spoke was so much Peter's that Dutch recognized it even though he'd seen Peter only two or three times since they were children together.

'You got to talk about him sometime.'

'Why?'

'It ain't right. That's why.' She looked fixedly out at the trees, just as Peter would have. 'Whatever Christie done,' Dutch went on, 'he didn't mean no harm.'

'How would you know?'

'Try me.' She took a sip of the coffee, which was as good as the room promised, but kept her gaze averted. 'Come on, Alice. What'd he do?'

'He deserted us in the hospital,' she said then, her own impetuosity abruptly overruling Peter's tactics. 'He just dumped us there and wandered off.'

'It's been a couple of years since you seen him, isn't it?'

'Two – three maybe. Three, I guess.'

Dutch leaned back in his chair and stretched out his legs. 'He went to the airport on Monday looking for you, know that?'

'You mean Tuesday.'

'Nope. Monday.'

'It couldn't have been Monday.' Alice shook her head. 'It was only Monday that I called him. We couldn't possibly have got across the Atlantic that fast.'

'Yeah. That's what Felicity told him. He went anyways.'

'That doesn't make sense.'

A tremor – half amusement, half pity – shifted the harsh planes of his face. 'He ain't stepping around corners so good anymore, Alice. Got himself lost on the way home – always gets lost on the way home. By Tuesday he'd forgotten you were coming.'

'Oh,' she said.

'Yeah.'

'Poor Felicity.'

'Well, yeah, that too.'

'So what was he doing while I was trying so madly to get a bed for Peter?'

'Probably wandering around hoping he could figure out how come he was in Memorial when he don't have patients here anymore.'

She stared out at the greensward and its covering of bright fall leaves. 'He didn't seem very upset when he came to the room. He seemed sort of pleased with himself.'

Dutch laughed. 'Probably forgotten he'd forgotten. Figured if you'd got a room and everything, he must have done what he was supposed to while he wasn't noticing. You gonna forgive him?'

'I don't know.'

'Gimme a break, Alice.'

She studied his face. 'Okay, okay,' she said then.

'Good, 'cause he's waiting for us in reception.'

She took in a breath of protest – but let it out with a laugh. 'You don't lose much time, do you?'

'Not me.'

ii

Another half-walk, half-run through corridors that seemed, as before, never to end – only to turn, branch and recombine like some overgrown electrical diagram – and Dutch ushered Alice into the vast reception-hall where the plastic was pure plastic, not just aura of plastic as in the doctors' lounge, but raw material and essence, heart and soul of plastic: plastic chairs, plastic tables, everything plastic: plant-pots, the plants them-selves, lamps, window-shades, even window-frames.

She knew the entrance-hall well by this time. She came in through it each morning, left through it each evening. Several times she'd caught sight of Maybelle's frizz behind the glow of terminals at the central information desk. She'd bought a newspaper from the gift shop that stocked get-well cards, soft toys and chrysanthemums. One day she'd had lunch in the café that lurked behind its screen of plastic flowers: a three-decker sandwich and a milkshake, too expensive for regular eating but at least edible – not like the underground staff cafeteria, which specialized in solid-looking things apaddle in a viscous soup.

'Where is he?' she said to Dutch. 'Why didn't he meet us in the doctors' lounge?'

'He's scared of you.'

She wasn't sure how to take such a statement. 'My mother and I never got along very well,' she said.

'No kiddin'?'

Christie stood alone on the far side of the information desk, a shrunken, tentative figure, staring off in the wrong direction.

'Pop?' Alice said, touching his arm.

He turned, took a wobbly step into her arms and dropped his head on her shoulder. 'Forgive me, Allie?'

'Oh, Pop, I'm so sorry.'

'Did you talk to Dutch?' he whispered into her neck.

'He gave me a good scolding,' she whispered back.

'I don't mean that.' He shook his head impatiently. 'We must get a move on the prostate, Allie. We have to convince Dutch here.'

His concern was so naked that she hugged him tighter, and they walked arm in arm to chairs near the expanse of window fronting the reception-hall and looking out on the traffic of arrivals. Christie and Dutch sat. Alice remained standing, her back to the glass. The sun was low on the horizon; it glinted off the cars that drew up and released frightened-looking patients-to-be in the company of bluff and hearty bag-carriers, relatives, friends, social workers.

'Just how powerful is this book?' Alice said.

'What book?' Christie said.

'Dutch was telling me about it. It has logarithms in it.'

'It ain't really got logarithms in it, Alice.'

'So you were making it up after all.'

'You got kind of a literal streak, don't you?'

'Either there is a book or there isn't.'

Dutch shifted in his chair to keep the light out of his eyes as he looked up at her. 'Sure, there's a book.'

'So what's in it, if not logarithms?'

'I don't know what you're talking about,' said Christie, looking from one to the other of them.

'I been tryin' to explain to her about the relationship between principal diagnosis and Diagnosis Related Group.' Dutch gave a snort of laughter. 'Not too surprisingly, she's having trouble getting the hang of it.'

'Try again,' she said, her eyes on the glow of the computer screens at the information desk.

'Well, looking at those computers over there, you're looking in the right direction, I can tell you that much,' Dutch said. 'And yet, I don't know. People say they want science, technology, all that. Fact is, they don't mean it. They want magic. They want something that's going to work no matter what – incantations, eye of toad, ear of newt. Now here's this rule book, what's supposed to be pure, unadulterated science – '

'It's a rule book?'

'Ain't nothin' people love more than a rule book. This one lists all known diseases in order and calculates down to the last penny what it costs to cure them. Now ain't that a pip? Especially when we don't know *how* to cure most of 'em.'

'I don't understand,' Alice said. The plant beside her was a fern with fronds that arched out from a central stalk like the ferns in forests when dinosaurs still roamed. She reached out to touch it.

'Pages and pages of medical and surgical procedures, all pinned to fancy numbers – ' She snatched her hand back, and he interrupted himself. 'What's the matter?' he said. 'Did it bite?'

'It's – ' She frowned and leaned over to study the dun-coloured vegetation and its brown splotches. 'It's *alive!*'

Dutch laughed. 'They got F1 hybrids so ugly they take your breath away. Why don't you sit down?'

'I don't want to sit down. I want to know about this book.'

'Allie, honey,' Christie said. 'We've got to talk about Peter. We don't have much time.'

'But doesn't the book and the shortness of time – ?' she began, then left off, not knowing how to finish her thought.

On the other side of the vast hall a child started to sob.

'Dutch, tell me how I can convince you to do this operation,' Christie said urgently. 'Alice and I say Peter needs incentive first. You say he should walk first. It's the chicken and the egg.'

'Then it don't make no difference if we start with the walking.'

'You haven't seen much of him since you were little, have you?' Alice said then. 'He's changed a lot. People do.' The point wasn't very meaningful; she knew this. She also knew it was underhanded. So what? It wasn't arguable. Which is to say it was just the sort of point Peter might have used.

Dutch ran a hand over his face. 'Won't you please sit down? It's hurtin' my neck looking up at you. Not that you ain't worth it, of course. What'd your English urologist say? Come on, sit down.'

'Oh, he was just English,' she muttered. But she lowered herself onto the edge of a chair. 'You know how they are.'

'Tell me what the man said.'

90

'I can't see that it makes any difference.'

'Just tell me.'

She sighed irritably. 'He said Peter wouldn't make it past Christmas no matter what we did.'

'That all?'

Before Peter was ill, she'd worn her hair in a long, heavy braid that hung down her back and gave her a gentle, vulnerable look. When she realized his sickness was not temporary, she'd cropped her hair to emphasize her high cheekbones and the strength of her neck. She gave up jewellery and bright colours. She borrowed books from the library and learned which was the lower left quadrant and which vertebra was which, where the carotid artery ran and more or less how a kidney functions. She'd worried over the viscosity of blood and the classification of diuretics. She'd read case-histories, prepared lists of questions and spent hours on the telephone getting Christie to answer and comment. You can get a surprisingly good feel for the limitations of medicine this way.

'All I know for sure,' she said, 'is that no one of you knows for sure.'

'That Englishman was talking sense, Alice. You gotta see that.'

'Morgenstern isn't so gloomy.'

'Morgenstern's a jackass.'

'Is that the reason you're stalling? Morgenstern approves, so you don't?'

'Allie, honey,' Christie pleaded, 'this isn't going to help.'

'Isn't it? I know Dutch here doesn't get along with him.'

'You don't know anything about it,' Dutch said.

'He suggests a second opinion.'

'Nothing wrong with that.'

'We don't need a second opinion,' Christie said. 'What we need is the best urologist in town to do a prostate resection.'

Alice studied Dutch's shoes, which had thick soles and leather tooling. They were brown. 'What Morgenstern suggests,' she said, drawing again on her study of Peter's tactics, 'is that we consider looking for somebody else if you aren't willing to undertake the job.'

A flush spread across Dutch's face and neck. 'He said that, did he?'

'He indicated as much.'

'What's that jerk-off trying to do? Take away my patient?'

Christie looked from Dutch to Alice in dismay.

'I asked for his opinion,' she said, 'and he gave it.'

'All right! All right!' Dutch got up out of his chair. 'Tomorrow's Sunday. How about Monday? That soon enough for you?'

'What about your doubts?' she said.

'Lookee here, ma'am, I've said I'll do it. Who cares about my doubts? What more do you want? Blood?'

So the operation went ahead.

iii

The first hours after surgery are the riskiest; this is when patients suddenly up and die for no reason that anybody can figure out. For the first forty-eight hours after Peter's operation, while he slept his smiling morphine sleep, Alice dozed in the chair beside his bed.

There's an obstruction, so what does the surgeon do? He sticks in a knife and whittles away, much as Christie had whittled out the inside of a stick to make a flute for Alice when she was small. She'd kept this flute for years and years before she thought of showing it to Peter. It wasn't a childhood secret or anything; she'd just stored it away, just forgotten it. Peter was enchanted. He held it up to the light of the fire. It was evening, winter, dark and cold outside; they sat together in front of a log fire that roared and crackled in the ancient stone hearth of their ancient Devon house. He put the flute to his mouth and blew a few notes.

'I can do better than that,' Alice said. 'When I was little I could play an almost recognizable *Row, Row, Row Your Boat*.'

'On this? Could you?'

'I could.'

'Show me.'

She managed a round and a half, and he laughed that delighted laugh of his. She said (pleased with herself, happy in front of the fire), 'You can't beat me on that one.'

So with only a slight pause here and there (Peter prided himself on his speed at making up limericks), he said:

> 'There was a young man from Beirut
> Whose prick was shaped like a flute.
>   When he came it made sounds
>   Like old English rounds,
> And the ladies all thought it quite cute.'

He was cheating with Beirut, of course. Peter was never above cheating if it helped the rhyme. And my comparison isn't wholly accurate either – a toy flute and a prostatectomy – but it's close enough to elicit a sympathetic pang. The urologist uses a probe with a thin, egg-beater-like knife that he slips in through the urethra to whittle out the constricting collar of flesh from the inside. Recovery is much quicker than it used to be – the old operation called for an abdominal incision – pain is less severe, infection less likely. What's left where the whittling went on is as disagreeable as you'd expect, but a catheter provides protection for the first days. After that it's not too bad provided the patient drinks a lot of water.

On the morning of the second day after the operation, Alice heard Peter say out of nowhere, 'It's the time of year when leaves fall.'

She roused herself, half-thinking she'd imagined his voice;

his head was turned away from her. 'Peter?' she said quietly. 'Did you say something?'

He turned to face her. 'There's nobody else here.' His brows contracted in that fleeting bafflement so characteristic of him. 'Is there?'

'No, there's nobody.'

'Overton is at its prettiest under a layer of leaves with birds chirping and chattering all around, especially when you can see maples and elms and meadow-larks every – Why are you laughing?'

'I don't know,' she choked. 'I didn't think you could see the trees. It looks to me like they're all maples. Besides, I thought the elms in Overton were dead.'

He struggled to get himself upright in the bed. 'I hate these pillows,' he said petulantly. 'They refuse to stay up.'

'Tell me about the trees.'

'I can't see any.'

'Oh, Peter!'

'How can I see trees from this bed?'

'Why are you never logical?'

'Only because I am so eminently reasonable.'

'There's a rift somewhere today.'

'Don't you think it a little harsh to charge a sick man with lapses of logic and rifts of reason?' He frowned, mouthing the words, then said, 'With lisp of leaves and ripple of rain.'

'It isn't raining today. How do you feel?'

He smiled that quick smile of his. 'Hello, pretty Allie.'

iv

Back at Macher-Daly House for the night, Alice fixed a sandwich for herself – it was about nine-thirty – and was about to eat it when there was a knock on the door from the laundry-room.

94

'Peter's going to be all right!' she cried, flinging the door open, knowing it was Cordelia. 'He's not going to die!'

The black Labrador stood in the dark of the laundry-room alongside his mistress. They made an eerie couple, white-faced Cordelia, white-haired, dressed in white, aglow like Tinker Bell, her little wing folded across her chest – and the dog, visible only as a tense, black-on-black shape, fate incarnate with eyes that glittered.

'When did you hear this?' Cordelia said. 'The operation worked, did it? You and Christie were right all along. But it's kind of early days to be so sure, isn't it?'

'You should have seen him this morning. He was almost the Peter of old. Come drink a toast with me.'

Alice turned into the apartment and turned back almost at once, hearing the dog's claws clatter on the floor. 'Cordelia, the dog – he's followed you in.'

'Ahab?'

'Oh, God, you haven't called him Ahab, have you? Doesn't he ever obey?'

'He's with me for a purpose this evening. You and he have something to settle.'

'Ahab and I? Do we? What?' She poured out two shots of bourbon and handed one to Cordelia. 'Here's to Peter. Here's to recovery.' She held up her glass and clinked Cordelia's. 'Look, do we really have to have the dog here? I thought we'd agreed on that before I moved in.' Ahab made a low sound in his throat. 'He doesn't even like me.'

Cordelia cocked her head. 'He doesn't understand you any better than you understand him.' She swallowed back her drink in a single gulp, as she usually did. 'Isn't it too warm for you in here? You do know how to work the heat, don't you?' She set down her glass, went to the thermostat and turned it off. The apartment had been icy each night when Alice got back from the hospital. 'English people like cool rooms.'

'I'm not English.'

'You've got to make up with Ahab, you know. It's silly to have all this quarrelling going on. As a market analyst – '

'What quarrelling?' Alice said quickly, in hopes of staving off a lecture.

'You shouldn't have thrown a stone at him.'

'I didn't!' Alice cried, more surprised than indignant.

'He says you did.'

'Cordelia, this is a dog. He can't talk.'

'You must work it out between you. Is twenty minutes long enough?'

'Sit down, Cordelia,' Alice said firmly. 'Or take Ahab with you. I don't have anything to' – she struggled for the right word but could not find it – 'to say to him.'

But Cordelia swept out of the room and shut the door behind her.

Ahab stared at Alice. She stared back. He was big and sleek, running a little to fat, she thought, for the leader of a pack. There were a few grey hairs in his muzzle.

She picked up her glass and sat down on the sofa to face him. 'I didn't throw any stone at you, you stupid dog,' she said. Then she said (he pricked up his ears), 'In the place where dogs licked the blood of Naboth shall dogs lick thy blood, even thine.' She lifted her glass and toasted him as she'd toasted his mistress. 'That's what Elijah said about you. It's in Kings somewhere, I think.'

Ahab's front paws danced a little tattoo of impatience. She wondered what she would do if he attacked, but the worry wasn't real; there was an unexpected, liquid sadness in his eyes. (He must have been a beautiful dog once.) She could see herself telling Peter about him in the morning, and laughter suddenly bubbled up inside her.

'This is why we came to America, Ahab, old friend,' she cried. 'We were right. Don't you agree? How dare anybody say that man is dying? We did it. We fooled them. We gambled and we won. We won!'

She laughed again, while in front of her, eyes aglow, Ahab watched her every move.

Part Two

CHAPTER 8

i

Kesslers had been doctors in Overton since the middle of the nineteenth century – an ancient dynasty by American standards. Peter's great-grandfather had practically founded Overton; his grandfather was one of the first children born there. They were a moneyed, smart, handsome people, although the men of the family were feckless, as Aunt Squeak often said.

True to family tradition, Peter's father won and lost three fortunes on the stock market before he died at the age of fifty. The first one went in the great crash of 1929, when Peter was just a year old. Aunt Squeak (who was a doctor herself and an investor of serious talent) helped for several years afterwards, a cheque here and a cheque there, always discreet, so as not to offend her brother's male pride. The second fortune, Edison Life, I think – some ambitious life-insurance flotation, at any rate – bought a big house on the outskirts of town; Dr Kessler sent Peter to Choate, the Eton of America, where Peter was even happier than he'd been in Overton.

It's true that he was bad at Latin and worse at French – truly dreadful at French – but he was good at English. 'Masterly for a boy his age' is what his report card said. This was right and proper. After all, Peter was eleven, and eleven is perfect. His mother planned his birthday party for the Easter holidays.

'I want to stay eleven,' he said to her when he got home. It was a business-like request in a business-like voice (only his mother could have detected the hint of a tremor in it). She was on her knees, gardening; the roses were in full bloom.

'I'm afraid there's very little I can do about that,' she said.

'You can if you try.'

'Come help me weed. There's a – '

'I hate weeding.'

'Oh, dear,' she said. She put down her trowel and gathered him into her arms. 'What's on your mind? Tell mommy.'

He buried his face in her neck. 'I hate twelve.'

'Oh, dear,' she said again. 'I'm getting ready to plant columbine. I'd be – '

'I hate this party.' His voice was muffled.

'We'll go to Waskeegee Rock for a picnic. We'll have potato salad and hot dogs and a fire to roast them on. Marshmallows too. There'll be lots of presents.' He hid his face deeper in her neck; his tears trickled down under her collar. 'Don't cry like this. It'll be better tomorrow.'

'It won't.'

'There, there, Peter. You always love parties. You know you do.'

'I'm not crying because of the party. I'm crying because I don't want to be grown up.' He pulled away from her, abruptly angry. 'Besides, I'm not crying.'

'When you're grown up you can do anything you want.'

The tears fell faster. 'You're grown up,' he wept, 'and you can't do what you want. You always have to ask daddy.'

'When you grow up, you'll be the daddy.'

This thought had not crossed his mind before. He stared at her aghast.

Working on his own in the years that followed (with the aid

of magic incantations), he managed to stay a child until he was almost sixteen. He held on to smooth skin and a hairless body longer than any of his friends; he remained graceful in the way only children can be graceful. He used to catch his eye in mirrors and laugh delightedly at the perfection he saw there – and at the trick he'd played on fate.

But during the spring he was to be sixteen, his hands grew too large for his pockets. Because he didn't get his height until three years later, the proportions went awry: nose too big, neck too wide, shoulders too broad. There was a smell of musk. At Choate the cooks put saltpetre in his peaches to keep his attention off girls; he could see it floating there in little fatty pools. But he spent his Junior Year at Overton High because Edison Life went bust; there was no saltpetre at Overton High. So it was that in June, in a cornfield that squeaked as it grew, the sacred Penny Gosling comforted him by losing her virginity and taking his at the same time, and so revealing – oh, sacred Penny Gosling – that there just might be compensations in the business of growing up after all.

Peter went back to Choate for his Senior Year and his father's final fortune; he wrote Penny twice a week and pretended to himself that her letters didn't disappoint him. But he knew too much about words already; he could rhyme them and pace them. He could conjure up whatever he liked with them (cornfields are easy); sometimes, on a good day, he could not tell where he left off and the words began. He edited Choate's Poetry Magazine, its newspaper and its yearbook – all three. He wrote most of the poems and the articles himself, putting other boys' names on the ones he thought less good.

Meantime, he applied to the University of Wisconsin, even though Harvard and Princeton were both ready to accept him.

'I think you're nuts,' said Dr Kessler. 'But, what the hell, one pre-med school isn't all that different from another.'

'I don't care about that,' Peter said.

103

His father snorted. It was a Sunday morning during the Christmas vacation. Dr Kessler didn't look up from his paper. 'With Choate behind you, it'll be a breeze,' he said.

'I don't want to be a doctor.'

The newspaper still had Dr Kessler's attention. 'Vascular surgery is the place to go. The research is getting a little specialized for Christie and me.'

'I'm not going to be a doctor,' Peter said.

His father looked up briefly. 'Don't talk nonsense.'

'I want to be a writer.'

Dr Kessler shook his newspaper and opened it to another page.

'I am *not* going to be a doctor,' Peter said again.

There was no response. An hour went by. Then a day, a week, a month. Like all Kessler men, Peter's father ruled by silence, and Peter was not able to be ruled at all. The situation was not unfamiliar. They both shrugged it off. 'This too will pass,' they said, each in his own way.

ii

Peter only narrowly missed the draft, although you could just as well say that Word War II came to a stop rather than threaten him with combat. Not that he'd have been afraid. Of course not. He couldn't remember being afraid of anything except the grey mist that hung midstairs in his mother's house, swinging a little forward and a little back, when he dreamed. He knew – as what eighteen-year-old doesn't? – that he was the culmination of the universe, the end towards which, from the beginning of time and throughout the ages, all its turbulence had been directed: he was its pinnacle, its ultimate flowering. How could it harm him? In fact, how absurd of it to arrange itself in any other way than to his convenience – and quite simply, he did not consider a European battlefield convenient.

But he was interested in the machinations that led to the battlefield. In his daydreams he saw himself as The Chronicler of Events, and the reason he wanted to go to the University of Wisconsin was because Colin Murphy O'Dwyer taught there. O'Dwyer was as fine a wordsmith as any in America, a political commentator and one-time leader-writer for the *New York Times*, Wisconsin born and bred, come home to teach a new generation what he'd learned in the big city of the East. Peter loved Wisconsin University from his very first day. He loved the Deke house, of which he was a member. He loved the freedom. He loved getting drunk. He followed O'Dwyer around like a puppy; he wrote home to explain the way of the world to his mother, who kept all his letters in the original envelopes. As she said to her neighbours, 'This is history.'

Because he was very intelligent – as well as exuberant and very young – and because he was in Wisconsin and looking for a political figure to lampoon, he paid attention before most people did to Senator Joseph McCarthy, the great Red-baiter, who destroyed so many lives.

'He's a liar!' Peter cried, almost dancing with glee along a path through campus grounds with O'Dwyer himself. The grass was coarse but very green even though there had been no rain for weeks. Peter had just come from a week of research in the *Milwaukee Journal* morgue. 'He lied about his schooling. He lied about his war record. He lied about his judgeship. He lied about sugar. He lied about housing. You know his limp? Do you know how he got it?'

'I read about it somewhere,' said O'Dwyer, who was a small, nervous man with long upper lip and a tiny, button-like nose. 'He was a Marine. Wasn't it a shrapnel wound?'

'That's what he says. Ten pounds, he said. Did you know he said that? Ten pounds of shrapnel in one leg. How can you get ten pounds of shrapnel in one leg? Think of the bulk. Where would you fit it?' Peter wasn't a doctor's son for nothing.

'Around the kneecap? In the groin?' Peter's excitement made him fall into half-sentences (of which he disapproved, although O'Dwyer did not). O'Dwyer, watching him, laughed and felt an edge of excitement himself. 'It's so gloriously absurd,' Peter went on. 'No, no, no. He caught his foot in a bucket on the good ship *Chandeleur*. He broke a bone in his foot. A bucket! It's right here. I found this report by one of his shipmates. *I* found it. What do you think of that?'

His enthusiasm was so infectious that the *Milwaukee Journal* itself ran excerpts of the article he wrote for the University of Wisconsin's newspaper.

Peter's father died a week after the issue came out. And so it was that the silence between father and son never came to the negotiated settlement both of them simply assumed.

It was a minor operation, nothing that should kill a man, but Dr Kessler was in a coma when Christie called the University. Peter didn't believe his father would die despite what Christie said. How could he? He was Peter's father. Besides, they hadn't yet made up that quarrel. Peter took the train home through a night lit only occasionally by bleak, distant towns; he stayed awake for the whole trip, writing about it in his notebook. Once in Overton, he made notes on the raw, bright neon of the hospital hallways. While he sat in the waiting-room outside intensive care, he worked on the contrast between train and hallway, movement and quiet, dark and light. He fell asleep on the floor with his diary open in his hand.

They waked him to tell him his father was dead.

Two days later his grandfather, Old Dr Kessler, died too.

But it was Christie who wept, who was inconsolable, who drank too much and too often, who bolted from the room when people appeared. Peter felt only a tingling in his cheeks and from time to time a sudden breathlessness. Which was odd because he'd never had asthma. He helped Aunt Squeak sort out the two wills and the scrambled finances. There were many debts. In the months afterwards, he ran a bowling alley to pay the tuition that had been eaten up in two probates. It was then that he grew, the way some do, to well over six feet in as many months.

The proportions of his body were again perfect, but this time around, mirrors gave him no real pleasure. It was all so alien, so blatant, so external. His arms and legs seemed to wander off on their own; he kept them in order only by holding them tense, and the tension in him made him as innocently awkward as a fawn. He didn't think about his father much, but almost every night for that first year after Dr Kessler's death he dreamed about the grey mist that hung midstairs in his mother's house, swinging a little forward and a little back, whenever he approached it. It was then that the people began to say there was something fey about Peter Kessler. Everybody noticed it.

At twenty-one he graduated from the University of Wisconsin, packed O'Dwyer's letters of recommendation in the Paris luggage that was his father's only legacy to him, and went to New York to make his fortune.

CHAPTER 9

i

I understand it's different now, but in those days, New York was the only place to go if you wanted to write, paint, sing – do anything related, centrally or peripherally, to the arts. People went in droves. Angela Leslie, Alice's mother, was among them. She arrived with her first husband, Jude Leslie, who used to tell her she glowed yellow, a pure, startling yellow, like a field of mustard in June. She had the almond eyes and blonde hair that Alice was to inherit from her – curly hair, oval face, short upper lip, retroussé nose, a crisp, fresh look – very pretty. Jude was her high-school sweetheart from Salteen, Kansas. He wanted to be an actor; she wanted to write.

They were luckier there than most, I suppose; every year New York eats up millions of young hopefuls from the Middle West. After a couple of years waiting on tables in a Polish café, Angela managed to get a job as a dogsbody on a theatrical rag called *Backstage*, but Jude's endless auditions resulted only in a bit part here and there; for money he played the professional bridge circuit. Six years later he was drinking his winnings as well as most of Angela's meagre salary.

They were both ready to go back to Salteen when he just

happened to see an advertisement in *On the Spot*, the Today Corporation's flagship magazine. It read:

* * * * * * * * * *
WRITERS WANTED
* * * * * * * * * *

She laughed when he showed it to her; like most Middle Westerners in New York, she'd quickly developed a bitter side. 'Ridiculous,' she said. 'Nobody wants writers.'

'It's a new political journal,' he said, pointing to the small print. His hands trembled as they always did in the morning, but he loved her despite his failures. What's more, he believed in her. 'What have you got to lose? They're going to call it *Postscript.*'

'I think *Postscript*'s a stupid name for a magazine.' Then she sighed. 'I don't know anything about politics. What would they want with me? I haven't got a hope in hell.'

He urged. Reluctantly she sent in her CV. She could hardly believe it when she got an appointment with the editor: three o'clock on a Wednesday afternoon. In fact, in her heart, she didn't really believe it, and so she wasn't all that surprised when, on the unseasonably hot Wednesday in May, the bus she'd taken broke down. She didn't get to the Today Corporation's huge building until three-thirty. The elevator was out of service; the *Postscript* offices were on the tenth floor. She had to run up the stairs, and she arrived panting, asweat, thoroughly out of sorts. The tenth floor had not yet been divided into rooms. Building materials, desks, chairs, typewriters, filing-cabinets stood in disorder against the walls. No sign of the editor – nobody but a boy, office-boy most probably, lounging against a packing crate beside a window on the far side of the empty space. He was reading a book.

She waited for a few minutes, and when nobody else showed up she called across to him, 'Hey, you!'

The boy looked up. 'Me?' he said.

'I'm supposed to be meeting Peter Kessler here.'

'Oh?' He returned to his book.

'He's the editor. Or that's what they tell me, anyway.'

The boy looked up again. 'Yes.'

'Has he already gone? Not that I can blame him. I certainly wouldn't hang around this God-forsaken place if I had any choice in the matter. It's too god-damned hot. Has he?'

'Has he what?'

'Has he gone?' she said irritably. 'There's nobody here but the two of us, is there?'

'You're right about that.'

The trouble is, he was too arrogant, too sure of himself for an office-boy; but she'd have sworn he wasn't more than sixteen years old, and besides he was an astonishingly beautiful boy – and the way he leaned against the desk, that tension in him, oh dear. 'Well, you can't be – ' she began and then faltered.

'I'm afraid I can.'

'Oh, God.'

'A little late, aren't you, Miss Leslie?'

'For Christ's sake, why didn't you say something?'

'I thought I just did.'

'Why let me flounder like that?' she said, angry now. 'It's Mrs Leslie, by the way.'

'My apologies, Mrs Leslie,' Peter said, bowing his head in her direction. 'What else would you like me to tell you before you jump to another and equally mistaken conclusion?'

'That's not fair.'

'You know, one of the things that's always amazed me is why people think what's fair or not fair has any bearing on the matter – this or any other matter.'

'Why don't you tell me a little about the job?' she said, angrier still.

Despite Peter's elegant demeanour, his heart was askip inside

110

his well-cut suit. He'd arrived in New York from Wisconsin just a few months before, and his interview with Angela was, in fact, the very first interview he'd conducted since his University days, when he'd interviewed only students. Above all, he wanted to hide this from Angela. He was careful to keep his face averted (the habit wasn't yet wholly ingrained), and he fiddled – the bored, nonchalant professional – with a piece of loose strapping on the crate he lounged against.

'*Postscript* is a new venture,' he said, trying on a frown of preoccupation, eyes glued to the crate. 'I'm going to need people with real commitment.'

'You don't think I'm up to real commitment?'

'That's what I'm trying to find out.'

'I thought you wanted writers.'

'I do.'

'So what kind of writers do you want?'

'Are you speaking practically?'

'We could start with an ideal.'

'Ideally, I'd have half a dozen just like me.'

The conjunction of mischief and complacency was so unexpected that Angela, angry as she was, had to fight back a giggle. 'You write well, do you?' she said, as sourly as she could manage.

'Very.'

'How are you as an editor?'

'I can't think of anyone better.'

The laughter broke out despite her. 'Are you always this conceited?'

'I consider it my most charming trait.'

She walked over to the packing-box. Pretty though she was, she was a poor dresser. Her slip was showing and her seams were crooked. The dress she wore neither suited her nor fitted her. She'd pulled her hair back into an untidy bun; wisps escaped here and there. Hairpins stuck out.

'What are you reading?' she asked. She'd lost the job: she knew it. In her mind she was packing to go back to Kansas. Her father would send her fare; he owned a garage on an empty corner in Salteen – not much of a living – but he loved her almost as much as Jude did. Besides, she was no fool; she could see this brat was getting a kick out of the situation.

He handed her the book.

She took it and looked at its cover. '*Madame Bovary*,' she said.

Peter glanced at the book in her hand, glanced at her, then nodded. To him *Madame Bovary* was the book of all books. He never wavered in his love of it, not throughout the rest of his life. Besides, the great O'Dwyer had inscribed this copy: 'Here's to the promise of Peter Kessler, from Colin Murphy O'Dwyer.' Peter saw that Angela hadn't noticed the inscription; he itched to point it out to her. What a handsome young man this is, he figured she was thinking, and just imagine being so sophisticated as to read *Madame Bovary* – *Madame Bovary*! – while waiting to interview writers for a political journal.

But Angela was never predictable. 'I always thought Emma was a silly bitch,' she said.

The most important letter Peter had carried with him to New York was to J. J. Hingham, publisher of *On the Spot*, America's foremost news magazine in those days. O'Dwyer asked J. J. to give Peter a job doing bits and pieces on the political scene. J. J. obliged, then noticed that the kid was good – more than good. J. J. was impressed and amused. Smitten too, and in those days nobody admitted to feelings like that. When the idea for *Postscript* came up, J. J. backed it – very discreetly – just for the pleasure of watching the kid play at being editor. He was ready to kill the magazine altogether as soon as the first issue was out.

Until that time, though, Peter was the youngest editor in publishing; and as Angela Leslie walked out of the *Postscript* offices, he decided her reaction to *Madame Bovary* was really very funny. But in that same moment, perhaps because she was his first interview and he'd been so nervous, he forgot her. He tended to forget people anyway when they were out of sight.

She came to mind again only after he'd interviewed a dozen other candidates. He'd been calmer with the others and so had managed to frighten them a little, which was right and proper – after all, he was editor, wasn't he? – but he couldn't help feeling contempt for them because of it. They were so suited and so staid. They were so boring. There were so old – thirty years old at least, and three were over forty, practically as old as his father had been, and his father was already dead. Not like Mrs Leslie in her ill-fitting clothes. Besides, there was the retroussé nose and the almond-shaped eyes, which were blue.

So at two o'clock in the morning, a week after his interview with her – the surface of his desk buried under paste, scissors, cut-up photographs, blocks of type (he was playing with a cover design) – he got out her résumé and picked up the telephone.

'Mrs Leslie?' he said.

'Who the hell is this?' He recognized her voice immediately, although he'd forgotten it just as he'd forgotten her. She had one of those deep voices, throaty, resonant, unusual in a woman.

'It's Peter Kessler.'

'Do you know what time it is?'

'Does it matter? Is it late?'

She took in her breath. 'Tomorrow at seven in the morning I go back home to Salteen, Kansas.' She was holding a battered kettle in her hand, half full, making coffee. Jude had just passed out on top of the suitcases, and she had to rouse him before she could go on. 'I've been packing since yesterday.'

Peter was disconcerted. 'Are you sure Salteen – is there really a place called Salteen? – is the best of all possible places for you?'

'My husband's drunk up all the money. And, yeah, I guess I'm tired of looking for what isn't there. What can I do for you?'

Peter never worried about money himself; he assumed he could get it if he needed it – just as he assumed that if he were to go looking for something he would find it. But he was always on the side of anybody in need, so he was very gentle when he said, 'If you still want that job, it's yours.'

The kettle clattered to the floor.

'Mrs Leslie?'

Angela clutched the receiver to her.

'Are you all right?' he said.

'Yes, I – ' She'd scalded her foot, but she hardly noticed the pain. 'I don't know anything about politics,' she whispered.

'Good for you.'

'You're sure?'

'Of course I'm sure,' Peter said, a little stiffly.

'Then of course I want the job. I've never wanted anything so much in my life.'

'That's what I like to hear. I'll see you tomorrow at eight. *Postscript* offices.'

ii

There was nothing Peter loved so much as a pile of manuscripts on his desk. Cutting, adding, rearranging – the joy of it! Again and again he went over every line of every story of that first issue of *Postscript*. He rewrote it all. He designed the pages. He pasted them up. He rented a car so he could deliver them with his own hands to the print plant in New Jersey.

Alice never saw a real live printing-press herself, but – years later – she could hear in Peter's voice how beautiful a machine it was: how it smelled of ink, how it clack-clacked as the hot type got locked into frames, how the presses thundered –

presses big enough to tower above your head and shake the ground beneath your feet — how the finished pages chuck-chuck-chucked onto the floor in neat piles. In the beginning was the Word, the greatest power God had to give. And to whom did He give it? He gave it to Adam — and to Peter.

Putting that first issue to bed took three days and two nights. Peter's staff struggled to keep up with him, napping wherever they could on the floor while he worked on, changing this page, then that, then this phrase, then that. Some of them couldn't stand the pace; he forgave them because, after all, they were past thirty years old and couldn't help it. Besides, they tried. Everybody tried — everybody except Angela, that is. Angela said a New Jersey printer could manage to put out a magazine without the help of some college passman from Wisconsin. She didn't even show up at the party that ran through yet another night of celebration and champagne; she went home to bed. Peter didn't care. Foolish woman. Sleeping is so dull.

When J. J. Hingham saw this first issue on the stands, he grabbed at the pain in his chest (he had angina anyway). The lead article was called 'His Majesty's Witch-Finder General'. The analogy between witch-hunting and Red-baiting is famous now — a cliché of the period — but Peter was the very first person to use it. Senator Joseph McCarthy was just edging into the fullness of his power, and one of the many unsolved mysteries of that period is why he did not wipe out Peter Kessler there and then.

It would have been easy.

iii

Witches exalt what is evil and spit upon what is sacred. They want only to destroy whatever we hold dear. They are crafty and devious too; you can't identify one just by looking — the

115

signs are deep and subtle – and sometimes witches themselves don't know the extent of their guilt. What a terrifying time it was three hundred and fifty years ago when England was infested. What a public service Matthew Hopkins provided when he came up with his method for identifying them: strip, threaten, bind, whip, thumbscrew and rack. For intractable cases: strappado, squassation, tearing and dismemberment. The remarkable thing is that the method works. It is, in fact, infallible. Apply it, and witches confess. Names get named. Is it any wonder that a grateful sovereign dubbed Hopkins 'His Majesty's Witch-Finder General'?

Such was Peter's little history lesson, and the public response to it gave J. J. a second shock. *The New York Times* asked, 'Has the hunt for Communists gone too far?' The *Herald Tribune* asked, 'Is there somebody out there saying the king has no clothes?' J. J., who had more courage and foresight that he is usually credited with, signalled to his intermediaries that Peter was to be offered the editor's job on a six-months' trial.

Peter was a little irked; it had never occurred to him that the job wasn't permanent.

The second issue came out. The third. The fourth. Peter bubbled. He fizzed: ideas, research, interviews, consultation, writing, editorial, paste-up, whole nights at the printers and, of course, drunken parties to follow. Some days he worked so hard and partied so long that he didn't know what day it was or what week or what month. By Tuesday afternoon he'd often forgotten whether Monday was last Friday or next Saturday. On one morning-after following one wild party-of-the-night-before (*Postscript* had been up and running for a month beyond its six months; there was no question of killing it now), he woke, sat naked on the edge of his bed – a canopied affair like Tinker Bell's bed in Neverland – and was reaching unsteadily for a cigarette when he heard noises from the living-room beyond.

116

They weren't the noises of some bumbler who'd passed out on the floor and just wakened to find himself in a strange place. They were too efficient, too, well, what? – it was hard to put a finger on it – too proprietary.

He crept back between the sheets, puzzled and intrigued. Anybody with any sense (to say nothing of a reputation as budding crusader on very dangerous ground) would have been frightened. Not Peter. He pulled the covers over his head and awaited developments. Footsteps approached the door. He smiled in anticipation inside his bed-tent. The door opened.

'Good morning.'

He jolted upright. The voice was unmistakable. 'Mrs Leslie?' he said in wonder. He peeped out from his canopy and there she stood, Alice's mother, in the doorway, as naked as he was himself – nakeder, considering that he had the sheets to cover him.

He wasn't at all sure what to do. It wasn't just that she shunned his enthusiasm for printers and didn't show up at parties. Almost every aspect of their relationship at the office had been as prickly as its start. He thought she might quit any day. This worried him because, although he hadn't told her so, she was the best writer he had; he'd come to assign her the best stories – the ones that without her he would have trusted only to himself. He never saw her outside the office. That, of course, was as it should be. She was five years older than he. Besides, every day her stocking seams were as crooked as they had been at that first meeting. Her slip usually showed too, and wherever she went she dropped a trail of hairpins from that ill-conceived and ill-executed bun.

'Good morning,' he said politely, holding the sheets up to his chin. There was no bun in her hair now; blonde curls fluffed about her bare shoulders.

She smiled at him but didn't reply.

117

He had no idea how to proceed (which was unlike him). 'Can I – um – get you something?'

'Like what?'

'A martini?' he said, and felt foolish at once.

She laughed. 'Maybe later.'

There was a pause.

He said, 'Your stockings aren't crooked this morning.'

'Are they usually?'

'No slip showing either.'

'No.'

She didn't move. He watched her, sheets still up under his chin. 'Not a stray' – his voice cracked – 'stray hairpin in sight.'

'Am I always such a mess as that?'

There was another pause.

'Mrs Leslie? Angela?'

'Yes?'

'Would you – um – like to lie down?'

'That might be nice,' she said.

Ever afterwards, Angela maintained that she'd spent the night in his bed with him. Peter pointed out that she'd never been to his apartment before. How could she possibly have slept in his bed? Either way, as lovers often do, they enjoyed the loverly pit-a-pat over just what had gone on. Besides, Peter loved mystery almost as he loved manuscripts. Not knowing how they'd got together added to the enchantment of the affair.

CHAPTER 10

i

Peter used to tell Angela dazzling tales. There's the one about how he defied J. J. Hingham with pheasant *sous cloche* and a Venetian blind. Very funny but, as Angela said (and Alice, too, when her time came), when he told stories like this you could never be sure they were real. There's the one about how he threw dice with Albert Einstein and won the ornate pewter hookah that stood on his mantelpiece; that had to be at least partially true because Angela met Einstein once, and he said it was entirely true. Of course when Peter rescued Angela from Old Iron Pants, she was there herself, so she knew all of that was true.

What was so fascinating about Peter, though, is that some of his adventures were real adventures — serious adventures — that showed a breathtaking (if reckless) courage and out-of-the-way skills not even his mother knew he had. The most impressive of these stories — to me anyway — is how he saved his uncle Christie from the toils of his old enemy Senator Joe McCarthy.

Peter's uncle Christie, Alice's father, wasn't a Kessler, not really. But if I'm to explain who he was, I've got to go back again – I do apologize for this – and pick up a final thread. One day old Dr Kessler, Peter's grandfather, just plain found Christie. This was during the flu epidemic of 1918, which was quite an epidemic; it spread through half the world and took more than twenty million lives. In Overton, people wore gauze masks in the street. The small Victorian hospital was crammed (1918 was long before Aunt Squeak set up her foundation and built Memorial Hospital). Doctors tended victims all day. Doctors' telephones rang all night.

One of the Kesslers' telephone calls was from Christie's mother, who was new to Overton, the wife of a World War One pilot by the dashing name of Hawk Kittyhawk. Captain Kittyhawk had gone missing in action, shot down somewhere over Europe, nobody knew precisely where. By the time Old Dr Kessler got to Mrs Kittyhawk, he could do no more than close her eyes for her. It was then that the child emerged from behind the mahogany bureau where he'd been hiding. His face was red with fury.

'What's your name?' Dr Kessler said.

'Christian Nation Kittyhawk. I'm six years old. My mother is dead, isn't she?'

Dr Kessler nodded.

'Why didn't you save her, you silly old man?'

Dr Kessler had the devil's arched eyebrows that Peter was to inherit from him; usually he was impatient – imperious even – but this night he was just tired. More than tired. He'd been up most of the night every night for at least a month. He shook his head wearily and spoke the truth. 'We're next to helpless at the best of times, and this isn't the best of times.'

120

'When I be a doctor, I'm gonna do more. I'm gonna save them all.'

'What did you call me? A silly old man?' Dr Kessler's impatience spurted in a mechanical sort of way. 'Well, don't you bet on playing saviour, you silly little boy.' The spurt collapsed abruptly, and he sat down on the bed beside the dead woman. 'Where are your other relatives?'

'Don't need any.'

'Aunts? Uncles?'

'Don't have any.'

'Grandmother? Grandfather? There must be somebody.'

'What do you care?'

'How boring children are,' Dr Kessler said under his breath. 'Well, what's to become of you then?' he said out loud.

Christie's lower lip trembled. 'You keep away from me.' Then he burst into tears.

Dr Kessler made a quick search for letters or an address book – some sign of relatives, any sign – but found nothing. So he took the screaming Christie home. What else was he to do? Besides, his own son – Peter's father – was away in medical school. (Old Dr Kessler wasn't all that old yet.) Perhaps relatives would come forth at the funeral. The child sobbed all night. Old Dr Kessler's wife rocked him; she sang to him. He sobbed on and was still sobbing when Dr Kessler and Aunt Squeak reappeared the next morning, red-eyed and pasty-faced from yet another night of house calls. Aunt Squeak was the only woman in practice in Overton in those days. Her patients called her Miss Doctor Kessler, which annoyed her.

'We've got a second case of pneumonia on Washington Avenue,' Dr Kessler said to her as his wife put a cup of coffee down in front of him.

'Who is it?'

'What's numia?' Christie said, choking back his tears.

'What's what?' Dr Kessler said irritably.

'It's a special kind of sickness.' Aunt Squeak responded to the child's voice before she'd taken in the child himself. She frowned. Then she thrust her head forward to peer at him. 'Who are you? I've never seen you before. Where did you come from?' She didn't wait for answers; she never did. 'It gets hard for the patient to breathe because the lungs fill up with water.'

'What is lungs?'

'Not now, boy,' Old Dr Kessler said. Christie screwed up his face and began to bawl again. 'Be still!' Christie bawled harder. 'Oh, all right,' the doctor said in exasperation, 'all right. Tell him, Squeak. Do hush boy. *I'll* tell you. Just what is it you want to know?'

At his mother's funeral, Christie sat between Aunt Squeak and Old Dr Kessler; first the one whispered into his ear, then the other. By this time they'd gone over pneumonia in great detail, so it was appendectomies and gastrectomies that kept him quiet through sermon and prayers. His eyes filled with tears only when the voices stopped. But no relatives came forth. Dr Kessler and Aunt Squeak took him home again.

Days passed. Then weeks. Christie was not the easiest child to have around. He held the Kesslers responsible for what had happened to his mother; he was given to tantrums. Yet his enthusiasm for anything medical was so fetching in such a medically-minded family that they grew fond of him. He loved riding with the doctors on their rounds, in the front seat of Dr Kessler's yellow Packard Twin Six or Miss Doctor Kessler's massive Crane-Simplex, which was guaranteed for life (what powerful arms Aunt Squeak had before arthritis took her over). He loved answering the door during surgery hours between one and two. He loved Aunt Squeak's black bag with its smell of Lysol and ether; he loved the ampoules of morphine in Dr Kessler's brown leather case. Years went by.

Dr Kessler and his wife filed adoption papers. Christie went

122

to Choate when he was eleven as all Kessler men did. He was a better student than any of the others; he graduated top of his class with a scholarship to Harvard in his pocket.

But early that summer – the one before his Freshman year at Harvard – he disappeared. He left no note. The Kesslers were frantic; they were afraid he was dead or sick or lost. There'd been no argument, no disagreement. They were afraid he'd been abducted (such an eminent family, so well known for its ancient lineage and its lavish dinner-table). They called in the police; a state-wide search turned up nothing. They awaited a ransom notice. No notice came.

Two months later, tired and deeply tanned, Christie reappeared. He walked into the house as though nothing had happened and called out, 'Anybody home?'

Just like that.

He'd grown some, but he was never to grow as tall as Kesslers grew. He never mastered their imperious control of themselves, either, and he didn't have their slender, elegant build or their long, thin hands and feet. His charms were very much his own: a ragged sensuality clung to him despite years of dancing, deportment, Choate and military camp. He had curly dark hair and a dimple in his chin.

The Kesslers were on the patio: a hot evening, a pitcher of martinis and a pitcher of lemonade sweating on the glass out-door table, potato salad and a cold ham in the ice-box. The atmosphere Christie walked into froze at once, as icy as the pitchers of drink.

'Would you care to tell us where you have been?' Old Dr Kessler said. Nobody else spoke.

Christie said simply, 'I had things to do.'

'Things?' Old Dr Kessler raised his Mephistophelean eyebrows, now white and bushy. 'Did you indeed? What things?'

'Personal things.'

Old Dr Kessler took a measured sip of his drink. 'Have you no idea how much pain you've caused?'

Christie smiled and said, 'A little pain is good for the soul.'

He would say no more. The Kesslers, who usually had an answer for everything, were flummoxed. That fall Christie went to Harvard as scheduled and got the A's the Kesslers expected of him. But when the next summer came, he disappeared again. He did give warning this second time; he said he'd be somewhere along the eastern coast of the country. That's all, though. He would not tell them how long he intended to be gone. He would not agree even to send a postcard. As before he returned tanned, tired, uncommunicative.

The next summer it was the same, and the next.

As he moved on into medical school and the habit continued, the Kesslers stopped questioning him. Sometimes he was gone for a month, sometimes a few weeks. He was always tanned, always tired, when he returned. The Kesslers forgave him everything because he won ribbons and prizes from Harvard. He knew this, and he loved them for it. He was twenty-seven when World War Two broke out, deep in a research fellowship at Columbia. By the time the draft started up, he was too old and too valuable medically to be caught by it. He had a trick knee anyway. Johns Hopkins tried to recruit him. So did Mayo. He turned them down: he wanted only to practise medicine with the Kesslers in Overton. That's all he'd ever wanted to do, and when the war was over, that's precisely what he set about doing. He had a real knack for family practice too; he wasn't hard-edged the way so many doctors are, especially the ones who haven't been ill themselves.

'He's deep,' the people of Overton said. 'Oh, he's a deep one.' They said the death of his mother explained it. People love an easy explanation. They said she accounted for his summer disappearances too. They even said she was the reason why he didn't marry, despite the dimple in his chin and a cotillion of eager Overton belles.

It's true that when Peter's father and grandfather died in the same week, Christie was profoundly upset in ways no one had seen him upset before; it's true that he got drunk and stayed drunk for several weeks. But this was the only evidence anybody saw that he had feeling for anybody or anything outside his work – which made his compassion for his patients all the more endearing. Then came the Korean War.

With this war, Christie's luck ran out. With this war came the Doctor Draft Law, and Christie was one of the first to be called up: unmarried, no longer involved in important research, never served before. He hadn't even read about the legislation. The letter of induction arrived out of nowhere; the mailman just handed it to him one morning as he was setting out on his rounds.

When I was little we used to try to make ourselves faint out in the playhouse in the back yard. God knows why. We squatted down, head between the knees, eyes shut, and breathed in and out a dozen times as deeply as we could. Then we jumped up and waited to faint. It never really worked – at least on me – although I managed to cause a buzzing in my ears as well as a queer, distant look to the horizon. That's how Christie felt, I think, standing there on the front lawn of the Kessler house with the induction letter in his hand: bees buzzing inside his head, dogs barking in the distance, his life finished, over, done with.

That night he threw a tantrum like the tantrums he'd had when he first came to the Kesslers. He shouted. He sulked. He wept. He broke things. He called the Mayor who patiently explained that the Doctor Draft Law was the law of the land; nothing could be done. He called the governor, his representatives to Congress, both state and federal, the AMA. Nothing could be done. He called lawyers. Nothing could be done.

125

The Army clerk who swore him in asked if he was a member of the Communist Party.

'The Constitution doesn't guarantee me the right to practise medicine in the way I'm trained to practise,' Christie said, quivering with rage (Old Dr Kessler would have recognized the furious little boy emerging from behind a mahogany bureau). 'But I always thought it guaranteed me from freedom of association. Am I mistaken?'

The clerk looked down at the paper in his hand and back up at Christie; the directive had just come in – a voluntary measure, not as yet a requirement. 'You know, I think you're right. Sure it does. Freedom of Association. Civics, right? Eighth Grade. I always kinda liked Civics.' He shook his head and put the unsigned paper down on his desk. 'What'll the fuckers think up next?'

Christie was still serving his time – he was one of many medical consultants to the Defense Department in Washington – when the Army McCarthy Hearings burst onto American television sets. The country trembled with excitement coast to coast. What counts when you hunt witches is the mark of Cain that is hidden deep beneath hair and clothing. One such mark – all but invisible in the scheme of things – was that loyalty oath Christie had not signed. McCarthy's investigators turned it up in some discarded filing-cabinet. They added it to the document that became known (for reasons that have no bearing on my story) as the Hoover Memorandum. A subpoena went out at once to Christian Kessler, MD, citizen of Overton.

iii

'Suppose I sold you – uh, told you,' Christie said over the telephone to Peter a week later, his voice shaking this time with whisky as well as rage and indignation – 'that you were talking to another of those Fifth-Amendment Communists?'

126

Peter was working on a story of Angela's; she'd come to his apartment for the purpose, and he'd made a pitcher of martinis (martinis had become a delicious private joke between them) to help them on their way. They sat, glasses in hand, in his living-room, which had as much of a Neverland feel to it as his bedroom. On the intricately carved mantelpiece, above the fireplace, between the two windows draperied in gold, a pert little bull from Peru faced a bright-eyed Chinese monkey (each astonished to find the other there). The striped carpet was too bold for any room in any other house, but here its force enriched the already rich textures.

'Christie, you are the noblest of the Kesslers,' Peter said, plans already half-formed and half-discarded in his head, new ones taking shape, strategies, tactics. Would this work? How about that? 'Have you talked to a lawyer?'

'Yeah, yeah. Sure I have. A couple. I say to them, "I'm in the Hoover Memorandum." They say, "Ooooh, dear me – egad – so sorry. Would you mind leaving by the back door?" Ah, Jesus, Peter, you get mixed up in this, they tear you limb from limb.'

'Not me,' Peter said. 'I'm invulnerable.'

Angela laughed, shaking her head, only half amused by his half-amused vanities.

'There's a serious – ' Christie began 'Who's that with you?'

'Angela.'

'The writer you told me about? I thought you couldn't stand her.'

'She has managed to persuade me of the error of my ways,' Peter said softly.

'You tell Angela for me that she has a lovely laugh.'

This was true. It was a knowing laugh, deep-pitched to begin with, down the scale even farther, then bubbling up all fresh like some New Zealand geyser. Peter turned away from the telephone and patted her on the head. 'Angela, you have a lovely laugh.'

'You didn't tell me she was pretty. She's got to be pretty to sound like that. Is she as — ?'

'I know how to handle this,' Peter interrupted. There was a sudden thrill in his voice. 'You're in Overton. Am I right? Go back to Washington. I'll join you there tomorrow. They haven't got a chance against us, Christie — not against us Kesslers.'

Angela laughed again, and Christie, ruin just around the corner, suddenly yearned for a back yard of his own with perhaps a potato patch and a clump of daisies. His whole body, kept so carefully in check for so many years, ached for a lawn that needed mowing every Saturday, a toddler in the sandbox, and certainly — oh, most certainly — that lovely, deep laugh coming from the kitchen.

As for Peter, he hung up the telephone with a smile of pure enchantment on his face. 'This is going to be fun,' he said, and Angela felt, as she had so often before, that it was his cleverness alone that intrigued him, not Christie's predicament at all.

Peter did so irritate her. Sudden fascinations engrossed him completely and were completely forgotten with such speed that she'd given up keeping track of them. But dammit all, this time a real issue was at stake. This time it was serious. Deadly serious. How dare he treat a Senate investigation like just another of his games? He laughed when she said as much to him (his laugh was, in fact, quite as wonderful as her own, innocent where hers was knowing, but abubble in much the same way), and he said to her:

'What's the matter with you, Angela? Don't you believe? Come on, clap your hands to show you do. Otherwise, Tinker Bell will die, and it will be all your fault.'

In Washington the next day he began with the telephone. During the rest of the week he took time out only to visit an optometrist and a theatrical hairdresser. Just what more he

128

did remains a secret. Myself, I suspect O'Dwyer helped him. O'Dwyer was not a man of courage despite his exalted reputation as a political commentator; he would have been terrified at the thought of personal exposure. So would J. J. Hingham, and yet I'm sure he helped too. Between them, these two men knew everybody who was anybody in Washington. Equally important, neither one would have denied Peter anything he asked.

If I'm right, this is why Peter only joked when Angela pressed him later for the whole story. He'd given his word, and when he gave his word, he stuck to it. He was loyal that way.

iv

But speak of volcanoes ready to erupt! The Senate Caucus Room is a caldera of a room, and there were so many people crowded into it for the hearing that they had to move in slow whorls like lava; the temperature in Washington was fearfully hot – only May, but heavy, sticky, suffocating. Everybody smoked in the 1950s, so this lava of people even seethed as lava should. Wisps and corkscrews of cigarette smoke floated up towards the vault of the ceiling, around the tops of the marble columns – Corinthian and vulgar but huge and impressive – and the tops of the red brocade curtains, drawn to either side of a wall of windows where the television crew's parade-ground bleachers stood. The needs of television took up that entire expanse; for years the Army McCarthy Hearings held the record as the biggest television spectacular of all time.

On the bleachers, above the crowd, producers and directors flailed and gesticulated. In front of them, cameramen manoeuvred cameras on twenty-foot-high trolleys; sound men arranged and rearranged microphones; electricians threaded miles of wire and tended banks of flood lamps, which threw a great shaft of light – smoke-laden like everything else – straight down the centre of the Caucus Room, slicing it in two halves: attorneys, aides, witnesses, relatives, reporters, photographers on one side and – on the other – the members of the Permanent Subcommittee on Investigations, who sat at a table so long that you had to turn your head to see it end to end. At the far right of this table, flanked by bodyguards, sat the brooding presence who had brought the hearings about: Senator Joseph McCarthy. A few years back you'd have seen a good-looking man with heavy-lashed eyes and a softness to the five o'clock shadow, a crude face but appealing in an incongruous sort of way, rather like velveteen stretched over some farm tool, a spade or a shovel perhaps. Those days were past. He'd done his best to disguise his complexion with pancake of a startling cream-coloured shade, but he still looked like the splotchy drunkard he'd become.

Opposite him, on the other side of that shaft of light, the Chief Army Counsel Joseph Welch was as upright as a high-church vicar; the uniformed Army officers ranged around him were as fresh-faced as choirboys. The contrast wasn't intended. Television was so new then that nobody realized how changed people are in front of a screen that sees everything, misses nothing – how pitiless we become when we're slouched at home watching it all, knowing perfectly well that we can't be seen and judged ourselves.

Peter had told Angela what would happen if his plan worked – the very plan that had come to him wholly formed during his conversation with Christie. He'd given her the outline of it not ten minutes after hanging up the telephone.

'You can't be serious,' she'd said.

Peter was so pleased with himself that he couldn't sit still. He jumped up and paced across the bold stripes on the rug.

'You'll never get away with it,' she said. 'You'll never even get started. It's out of the question.'

'Yes I will. Or rather, *I* won't but Welch will.'

'Peter, the idea's ridiculous.'

'If I can find a way to get to Welch, I can explain it to him. If I can explain it to him, he'll do it.'

'McCarthy won't fall for anything so simple.'

'The greatest ideas are always the greatest simplifications.'

'Oh, do sit down or something. At least stand still. You're driving me nuts.'

'He'll have no choice – not in front of all those cameras. He'll do whatever he's asked to do, however he's asked to do it.' Peter stopped, but only to peer at the bright-eyed Chinese monkey on the mantelpiece; he moved it a fraction of an inch farther away from the pert little bull and began to pace again. 'That's what's so smart of me. He'll see the trap, and he'll have to walk into it just the same.'

'You're practically crowing,' she cried. 'You must know you haven't got a cat's chance in hell. How can you be so pleased with yourself?'

Peter only laughed and paced faster; she watched, her eyes following him back and forth, back and forth, like a fan at a tennis match.

He said he'd telephone when the plan was ready to go into operation. The call came through on Wednesday afternoon; he'd been in Washington almost a week.

'Tomorrow,' he said. 'Watch tomorrow and Friday, and all will be revealed.'

'You've talked to Welch?'

'Just watch.'

She had no television. Neither did Peter. She went around the corner to Maurice Denning's store; Maurice had a set in his back room. Angela was not much given to self-examination, but this day she knew what she was about. From the very first interview with Peter in the *Postscript* offices, her feelings about him had been decidedly mixed. She loved the look of him; she'd lusted after him from the moment she laid eyes on

131

him, but the conceit of the boy! That, combined with such an uncanny gift for words. How could she bear it? What she'd wanted from the beginning was to watch him fall on his face – only once, but really fall – and here at last he was about to do just that, and right out in public too. He'd never be able to explain this one away. As she sat down on the chaise-longue in Maurice's back room she could already feel the warm glow of the satisfaction to come.

Television was black and white in those days; resolution was poor. Partly for this reason – but mostly because she'd been so certain – it took her almost an hour before she realized that she was in fact seeing Peter among the grey figures on the screen. He stood behind the Army Counsel's table – precisely where he'd said he would be standing – half lost in a haze of assistants who ferried messages, bought cigarettes, cleaned ashtrays. He wore the heavy-rimmed spectacles he'd told her about, hair slicked back, eyebrows shaved into simple crescents. She felt a flicker of annoyance. She couldn't deny he'd got this far. But what the hell. So he was there. So what. Nobody was paying any attention to him.

Chief Army Counsel Joseph Welch stood to speak.

'I'd like to call Senator McCarthy to the stand,' he said.

Angela's warm glow disappeared at once. 'God-damn you,' she said under her breath, meaning Peter, not McCarthy (who sat staring down at the papers in front of him, as shocked as she was herself), and not Maurice either (who had the misfortune to be on hand); she turned on him fiercely. 'I wish you'd keep that god-damned dog of yours out of here.'

Maurice held a Pekinese in his arms 'I thought you liked dogs,' he said, a little petulant.

Angela had discovered this television set when she was looking for a brass trivet for Peter's birthday; Maurice had one with a cockerel in full crow on it. She'd admired the Pekinese then; she didn't like dogs much, but Maurice and his dog looked so much alike – the same squashed profile, overfed, ill-defined and ill-tempered – that it amused her to flatter the man by flattering his dog.

On the screen McCarthy shrugged and slowly manoeuvred his body upright 'God *damn* you,' Angela said.

McCarthy waded through the mass of people in the Senate Caucus Room. She jumped up from the chaise-longue and began to pace as Peter had paced before her. McCarthy had sworn – he'd said it again and again – that he would never take the oath that he himself had administered so many times to so many of his victims; but in front of all those cameras, he sat in the witness chair and spoke out the oath despite himself, just as Peter had said he would.

What a queer voice the man had – a simulated kind of sound, monotonic and resonant at the same time – broken occasionally by a chuckle that upset the flow like washboard ruts on a road. With the oath finished, he leaned forward over the witness table, peered out through slits in the swollen flesh around his eyes and spoke in an urgent conspiratorial whisper.

Angela paced faster. Maurice's Pekinese bounded and yapped in his arms.

'Can't you keep that god-damned thing quiet?' she shouted at him.

'You're the one who's upsetting him. If you sat down, he'd stop barking.'

She couldn't. She just couldn't. She paced faster still. The dog shot out of Maurice's arms in a frenzy and snapped at her heels while McCarthy paused for breath and Welch held up the famous letter – the Hoover Memorandum that would ruin Christie if it ever got read out loud.

Welch said: 'Senator McCarthy, when you took the stand you knew of course that you were going to be asked about this letter, did you not?'

There was irritation in the famous monotone. 'I assumed that would be the subject.'

'And you, of course, knew you were going to be asked the source from which you got it.'

'I won't answer any such question.'

For one moment Angela forgot her outrage at Peter. She stood stock still. The Pekinese stood stock still with her. With this very sentence – these very same words – McCarthy had ruined thousands of people. This is how you catch a witch. This is how you catch a Fifth-Amendment Communist. What's a Great Inquisitor doing in such a trap?

Welch said: 'Senator McCarthy, the oath you took included a promise, a solemn promise by you to tell the truth and nothing but the truth. Did you have some mental reservation when you took the oath, some Fifth-Amendment notion that you could measure out what you would tell?'

'I don't take the Fifth Amendment,' McCarthy said.

'Then tell us who delivered the document to you.'

The quiet was so deep that Angela could hear the Senator's breathing; she could see the sweat ooze through his pancake.

'You can go on until doomsday,' McCarthy said. 'You will not get the names of my informants, who rely upon me to protect them.'

'Will you tell us where you were when you got the document?'

'No.'

'Were you in Washington?'

'I will not tell you.'

'How soon after you got it did you show it to anyone?'

'I don't remember.'

'To whom did you first show it?'

'I don't recall.'

Oh, dear God, how glorious is the smell of fresh blood, especially when it's the blood of a Great Inquisitor. The Peki-

134

nese growled, and by this time most of the human audience – numbering some twenty million, all of them safely ensconced in front of their televisions – growled with him.

Welch – tall, old, thin, dapper – paused, then said, 'You are of course aware, Senator McCarthy, that if you do not answer my questions and are not taking the Fifth, you are in contempt of Congress.'

In a just world, McCarthy would have gone up in flames there and then like Overton's annual Corn King. But who says the world is just? Certainly not Peter. People were mortally afraid of what a cornered McCarthy might do. When this day of hearings closed, there were hurried consultations. A compromise was reached. The next morning a letter arrived from the Attorney-General himself. Welch read it into the record.

Why is brilliance such an outrage? Why do we always try to crush it? Angela stood in front of Maurice's television possessed of devils. She felt her heart was going to burst. She really did. How dare Peter know such things? How dare he penetrate with that child's mind of his into depths she could not reach? There was that dry old stick reading out just precisely what that brat had said he'd be reading out.

Henceforward the Hoover Memorandum was a classified document. Senator McCarthy was safe: you can't be in contempt of Congress for refusing to answer questions about a classified document. But – and oh, this was the clever part – nobody can publish a classified document. If nobody can publish it, no part of it is going to appear in the newspapers.

Which is to say Christie's name, reputation and professional standing would remain intact.

Peter flew back to New York that very evening. He collapsed into Angela's arms and Angela's bed.

'Did you see what I did?' he said, an hour later.

She lifted herself up on one elbow. 'You look like Cupid with those eyebrows.'

'But I did do it, didn't I?'

'Yes,' she said. 'Yes, you did.'

'Oh, I was wonderful! Wasn't I wonderful, Angela?'

She laughed. 'You were.'

'Tell me about it.'

'You were absolutely wonderful.'

He'd never liked Angela's apartment. The chairs were ugly. The cheap Danish bedstead oppressed him. He hated the picture on the wall, a photograph of an old woman bent over a bowl of dough. That fleeting bafflement crossed his face, and Angela (a little baffled herself) pulled him to her.

'Angela?'

'Um?'

'Say it once more.'

'You were absolutely wonderful.'

He drew in a ragged breath. Then he turned in her arms and slept.

But he cried out in his sleep that night. He often had nightmares, and from time to time he cried out like this. Angela asked him once or twice what he dreamed about, but he would never say; he told her that the moment he awoke, he forgot. Myself, I'd guess he dreamed of the grey mist that used to hang midstairs in his mother's house, swinging a little forward and a little back and pinning him there with the perfection of eleven years old forever behind him and a lifetime yet to go. Angela wouldn't have understood. Not really. But that night she rocked

136

him in her arms as she had before, as she would again — as her daughter Alice was to rock him in years to come.

Part Three

CHAPTER 11

i

Peter's mother died in Overton's Memorial Hospital, where he himself lay right now. There'd been a reception after the funeral, an elegant Overton affair, as befitted the Kesslers' station: roast beef, several salads and a sparkling wine of truly dreadful quality. Alice had talked to an old man there who said, 'Maude was the most beautiful woman I ever knew' – Maude was Peter's mother – 'and she remained beautiful to the day she died.'

Alice had met her Aunt Maude only the one time, over Peter's baby pictures; she'd seen no signs of beauty in that irritable old person with the rheumy eyes and the spittle at the corners of her mouth. So she'd smiled at the old man over her glass and nodded sympathy, thinking to herself, poor creature, is he functionally blind? And what about the half-puzzled, half-pleading expression on his face? Is all this some form of self-deception? Is it a flaw of age? a survival mechanism of some sort?

But now, helping the young nurse give Peter his bath – a pretty young nurse, dark-haired, doe-eyed, nervous but controlling it well, new at the job but gentle and efficient – Alice suddenly understood. 'Peter's not just another middle-aged man,' she wanted to cry. 'Look at him: here's the child of the pictures in Aunt Maude's suitcase; here's the line of his cheek where the mischief shows. Can't you see? Here's the boy dancing alongside O'Dwyer at the University of Wisconsin. Right here, dammit, right in the eye that used to twinkle. Here's the man who found a join of river and tributary on Dartmoor, where we had a picnic and the wayfaring tree was in bloom. They're all here, all these Peter Kesslers, a whole series of them, one superimposed on another – an image as multilayered as the CAT scan of his cerebellum. This sickness, this age: it's nothing but a patina. Nothing but verdigris on bronze.'

Alice glanced up at the nurse with these thoughts on her face, and the nurse smiled, nodding sympathy, just as Alice had nodded sympathy to the old man at her Aunt Maude's funeral.

Early that morning, the morning of the third day after Peter's operation, Dutch Hashman had removed the catheter. A man has to drink after a prostatectomy if he's going to get well. Peter said he wasn't thirsty. The bed-bath came not long after lunch, and still he refused to drink. Alice was lathering his arm when the fine-grained Bob Morgenstern came by on his rounds.

The young nurse hesitated, startled when she saw him, then took courage. 'Good afternoon, Dr Hashman,' she said. She had a soft, sweet voice.

Bob froze.

'This is Dr Morgenstern,' Alice said hurriedly.

The little nurse was covered in confusion. 'But I thought – I'm so sorry. You see – '

'It's not as though I haven't been around a while,' Bob said through his teeth.

'But *she* hasn't,' Alice said, taken aback.

Bob didn't look up. 'I suppose I've been called worse things' – there was no hint of apology – 'but not often. Can you dry him off for me? I'm in something of a hurry today.'

142

The examination was brief. Peter said nothing. Bob said little. When he was finished, he leaned against the wall to scribble something in his binder, stared out of the window a moment, then, without a further word, turned and headed out of the room.

'Hey,' Alice called after him. He did not stop. She rushed after him as she had before. His pace quickened. So did hers. He made a dash for the stairwell. She dashed too and cornered him there on the landing.

'Peter won't drink,' she said. She was a little breathless after her sprint. 'Why won't he drink? Please tell me. I want to know.'

'Yes, yes,' Bob said, edging away from her, a little breathless himself, 'he must drink. Hydration is absolutely – '

'But he won't.'

' – absolutely essential. You must force the liquids.'

It was hard for her to keep from plucking at his coat. 'I haven't been able to get a drop down him all morning,' she said. 'Not a sip. Nothing.'

'You must try. He must try. Now I must – '

He slipped past her and hurried away down the stairs.

Alice did not know what to make of it. It meant something. But what? What *could* it mean? She fretted throughout the evening, while she worked with pliers and wire cutters on the skeleton for the Corn King's hand. She'd found chicken-wire in Rowan's garage; she finished two fingers by midnight – a short plank would support the wrist and palm – but she could not get her mind off Bob Morgenstern.

ii

The next morning she was at the hospital not long after seven, waiting for Dutch to come by on his rounds. He was usually there by eight-fifteen. She checked her watch – Peter's really

143

– again and again. When he did appear, the dapper suit was gone; he was wearing a heavy knitted cap, as brightly coloured as Christmas wrapping paper, and a leather flight jacket with 'I love Arabella' printed on it in large pink letters. Ivy and rose buds entwined themselves around the A.

By this time Peter had taken no fluid for twenty-four hours.

Dutch leaned forward, his hands on his knees. 'You ain't gonna urinate less often if you drink less, Peter. It's just gonna hurt more. If there's no water going in, what's coming out has got to be pretty acidic. You can see that.'

'Is that why he won't drink?' Alice said, struck by how obvious the reasoning was. 'He won't speak to me about it. Morgenstern doesn't seem to know what's going on, either.'

'Morgenstern never did know anything. What's the urine look like, Peter?'

As soon as the catheter was gone, Alice had seen that Peter was too weak to get to the bathroom on his own; he couldn't use even the shiny aluminium urinal by himself. A paper coffee-cup worked better, but not much better – too light, too unsteady, too easily knocked over. He gave up. Alice did what she could, but she had to be alert and quick, and sometimes she wasn't.

'You see the urine, Alice?' She nodded. 'What's it look like?'

'Bloody,' she said. 'Thick.'

'Got any?'

She handed him the cup with perhaps an ounce in it, perhaps two.

Dutch frowned. 'Peter, if you drink, it'll get easier. I give you my word on that. There'll be more of it, but it'll hurt an awful lot less – starting right away.'

Peter kept his head turned away towards the window.

'Peter?' Dutch said.

There was no response.

'Peter, we gotta talk about this.'

144

Beyond the glass, the first snow flurry of the season swirled and eddied, big flakes, soft and wet as first flakes so often are; it was way too early in the year for snow. The grey was impenetrable. Nothing could be seen, not even the outline of those autumn-coloured maples at one side of the heliport.

Dutch sighed, got up and stood by the bed a moment, irresolute. Then he patted Peter's hand and gestured for Alice to come with him.

'What does it mean?' she said as soon as they reached the safety of the corridor.

He shook his head. 'I never did understand Peter. It ain't all that uncommon – not drinking – but you don't expect a man that bright to act that stupid. Let's sit down a bit, huh?'

'Is it fear?'

'Oh, it's that all right.'

They walked the fifty yards to the Day Room in silence. All the wards in Memorial Hospital have a Day Room for patients and relatives. They're all the same, these rooms; blue plastic sofa that can serve as a bed (a woman was stretched out asleep on this one), linoleum floor, white plastic tables with cigarette burns, coffee-machine and candy-machine shoulder to shoulder against the wall, windows overlooking the snowstorm outside. In these surroundings, Dutch's flight jacket with its ivy-entwined message had a charm Alice would probably not have noticed in it otherwise.

She said, 'You look snappy this morning.'

'Day off.'

'Who's Arabella?'

'Go-go joint out at the edge of town. Best-looking women this side of the Mississippi.'

'You don't say. And you're a regular?'

'I gotta pay my respects, don't I?'

He ushered her to a chair. The room was empty except for the sleeping woman on the sofa.

'Sit down,' Dutch said. 'I'll get you a cup of coffee.' He turned away and turned back almost at once. 'They got topless dancing out at Arabella's.' He looked down at her with an exaggerated grin.

'At eight in the morning?'

'You got some old-fashioned ideas, don't you? Besides, it's nearly nine.' She shrugged, and he turned to punch buttons on the coffee-machine. 'You want milk? Sugar?' The coffee Dutch handed her was too hot to drink; she set it down on the table. He threw himself into a chair opposite her. 'I tell a lie,' he said. 'Really I'm going out to take a look at my oil well.'

'In a snowstorm?'

'Why not? You can see an oil well in a snowstorm just as good as on a sunny day. It ain't nothing but a hole in the ground with a donkey working over it. Aren't you impressed that I got an oil well all my own?'

'I'm not sure I believe anything you say.'

'Who else can you believe around this place?'

She considered Bob Morgenstern for a moment and realized she'd already granted Dutch more than she ever thought she would. She said, 'Has this, um, oil well made you rich?'

'Depends on how you look at it. I just got my cheque for the year's receipts this morning. That's why I'm going out to pay my respects. To my oil well, that is. Want to see?' He rummaged in his jacket pocket. 'Here. Now what do you think of that?'

The cheque was made out to Dr Septimus Hashman III in the amount of $70. Alice laughed despite herself. 'These are very modest riches,' she said. 'I didn't know your name was Septimus.'

He took the cheque from her and studied it fondly. 'The first year I got only one dollar. Way I look at it is, in ten years my profits have increased seventy times over. Can't say that about many investments, can you?' The sleeping woman on

146

the sofa began to snore. He folded the cheque and put it back in his pocket, took a drink of his coffee, grimaced, set the cup down. 'Now, how come I want to talk to you is, I'm gonna be getting another of those Notices any day now. Tomorrow. Next day maybe. I can hold them off for a bit, but you're gonna need to find some place for Peter to go. I want you to be ready when I can't hold them off any more. Understand me?'

Alice looked at him aghast. 'You can't mean it.'

'Yeah. But he's going to have to go.'

'I don't believe you. I just plain don't believe you.'

'You're a hard one to convert, aren't you?' He took off his knitted cap, stretched it out into a muff of bright colours over his hands, stared out of the window, then down at his shoes; but when he spoke, he looked at her. 'I'll tell you something. I've had fun being a doctor. I admit that. If I could start back where I was and go through it all again, there isn't anything I'd do different. But suppose you ask me, would I go into medicine now? I'd say to you, "Hell no. I'll go to work in the fields first." I wouldn't have anybody I cared about go into it either.'

He glanced down at his shoes again, then back up at her. 'Now if you ask me why I feel this way, I'll say because in the years I've been practising, I've watched an honourable profession get pushed into mediocrity. I've watched medicine subverted by attempts to supervise where there is no expertise in the supervisor and to regulate where there is no expertise in the regulator. I have no qualm with doctors who make a million dollars a year doing heart operations at five thousand dollars a pop. I hate to see it happen, but there are always going to be doctors on the make. This other business is different. Here what you're doing is jingle-jangling the knobs around so that *all* hospitals and *all* doctors can clean up. You've suddenly developed this relationship where the whole point is cash-flow,

147

where the hospital is out to take care of itself and screw the doctors and the doctor is out to take care of himself and screw the hospital. And the patient is caught in between and screwed by everybody. It's a rip-off. It's got nothing to do with quality of care. Nothing at all.'

He stretched out the cap and released it. 'I don't know what can be done about the situation. I'm not saying you have to change human nature. I don't want to reinvent the wheel. But I feel sad for the people, who deserve better. I feel sad for my old friend Peter, who's one of the people. As I say, sense doesn't have anything to do with what's happening to him. Nor does humanity or decency or mercy or any other fine virtue. This has to do with cost – and cost alone.'

It was the first speech she'd ever heard him make without a single trace of the hillbilly accent, and this alarmed her more than the words themselves. Her mind lurched sideways as it sometimes did when she was upset, and she said, 'Have you really done twenty thousand prostate operations – you and your father between you?'

'Listen, you gotta – ' He stopped short. 'Who told you that?'

'You did. Years ago – at Pop's house.'

He put his knitted cap on again and pulled it down over his ears. 'Only reason I told you that is, you're from a medical family. Only reason I'm telling you what I'm telling you now is, you're from a medical family. Listen to me: this is important.'

Alice reached for her coffee but drew back her hand without touching the cup. 'A man as sick as this needs full-time nurses,' she said. 'What am I going to do about this – this Notice of – what is it?'

'Non-coverage. Means the government won't pay for him anymore.'

'They won't pay what?'

'Hospital bill. No money, no bed. That's the way Medicare works, and Peter's on Medicare.'

'Oh, is that all it is?' The relief made her almost giddy. 'My God, you had me scared. Peter's an idiot about things like that – you understand him better than you say – but I'm not. I got him a million dollars worth of private insurance. I insisted. He was furious. But he's got it. He doesn't need Medicare. He's all right.'

Dutch shoved his knitted cap back on his head. 'Well, uh, look, I – '

'Couldn't we maybe put the catheter back?' she interrupted. 'Just for a day or two? Just until the healing's a little further along? I'll take him home to England as soon as I can.'

'You ain't gettin' this man home to England.'

'I got him here: I can get him back.'

Throughout the rest of the morning, Alice put a glass of water again and again to Peter's lips, which were parched. He would not drink. She pleaded. She scolded. She forced. The water ran down his chin onto his hospital gown. Sometime during the middle of the afternoon Dutch ordered an intravenous drip over the telephone.

iii

That evening a physiotherapist appeared with the brace for Peter's back, a long, bony brace, made of stiff linen and cotton-covered struts. She held it up. 'Will you try it on for me, Mr Kessler?' she said. She was a small, cheery woman with neat hands and shoulder-length hair.

He turned to Alice. 'What shall I do?'

'Perhaps another day,' Alice began uncertainly.

'President Kennedy wore one much like this,' the physiotherapist said with an encouraging smile. 'Why don't we at least give it a try?'

'That was more than thirty years ago,' Alice said, horrified. 'Hasn't there been any change in the design since then?'

'These really work very well – sometimes anyway. You never know until you try, do you?'

Alice expected Peter to resist, but he did not. He let the physiotherapist and a nurse manoeuvre him upright and strap him in.

'Try to take a step, Mr Kessler,' the physiotherapist said.

He swivelled his head around to face her and swayed.

'Try, Mr Kessler.'

He shut his eyes.

'I'll just get you started,' the physiotherapist said. She pushed at the heel of one of his feet with the toe of her sturdy white shoe. This time the sway brought him down, flat across the bed.

'Do you think – ' Alice began.

'Let's give it another try,' said the nurse.

They got him up. Alice supported his right side; the physiotherapist supported his left, which was tied by tubes to the shoulder-high scaffolding of his intravenous drip. Together they half-dragged, half-paced a little way up the hallway outside and back down again, bottle of liquid ajangle, tubes swaying.

Late that evening, Alice ran into Dutch in the corridor.

'You still around?' he said to her. 'Don't you never get out of here?'

'You're still around yourself, I see.'

He had a patient's binder in his hands, loose-leafed. He was again the dapper doctor in muted tones of grey. 'I been home. I changed my clothes. Besides, in case you ain't noticed: I work here.'

'At this time of night?'

The dark shadows of his face shifted a little. 'Well, maybe not exactly. Tonight's my night at the Lambert Ladies' Annual Quilting Bee. I'm gonna explain to them about sperm counts.'

'The Lambert Ladies. Really.'

'They asked me special.'

150

'I'll bet they did.'

He made a note on the page in front of him and shut the binder. 'You're not staying here again tonight, are you, Alice?'

'No, no,' she said. 'I'm just leaving now.'

'Don't tell me: you're gonna spend the evening by yourself in that fish-bowl joint of Cordelia's. That ain't the happiest place in Overton, you know.'

She smiled. 'I rather like it. The reflections in those windows – they remind me of something. I don't know what. I keep trying to guess. Besides, Cordelia's usually there at night. I don't think I've ever been completely alone. Schpiegal as well.'

He tossed the binder on the desk of the nurses' station and walked along with her.

'Why don't you do something different for a change? Go see somebody. You got friends in Overton, don't you? Go see your daddy. He misses you. Go see Felicity. Catch a movie.'

Alice shrugged.

'Well, then, why don't you play bingo? Go dancing?'

She turned a wry smile on him. 'Arabella's Go-Go Joint?'

To her surprise, he said, 'Why not? I'll drive you out.'

'What about the Lambert Ladies?'

'We'll manage something.'

The idea was so absurd – so unexpected – that she said, 'What'll I dance there? I'm not much of a dancer.'

'The Go-Go, of course. What else do you do at a Go-Go joint?'

'Is there really such a dance as a Go-Go?'

'I'll teach ya,' he said. 'Watch me.' Hands on hips, eyes on his feet, he executed a few jazzy steps as they made their way down the corridor. 'It's a cinch.'

Alice watched him smiling. 'I don't trust you,' she said. 'You tell me fairy-tales.' He turned a small circle, his arms extended, and she shook her head. 'I do not for one minute believe that's a Go-Go.'

'Ah, come on, what else could it be? Where's your faith, woman? If there's a Go-Go Joint, there's got to be a Go-Go to go with it.'

But the magic of the fancy disappeared as abruptly as it had come, and she turned again towards the elevator. After all, what were the hours ahead for? Their single purpose was to be slipped past: absorbed and excreted as quickly and quietly as possible, much as her gut would absorb and excrete the bourbon that, in her mind, was already poured, iced, sipped, finished, in the hopes that it would aid the elusive sleep that, in her mind, had already been slept – or not slept. In her mind, she was already back here, in this hospital corridor, tomorrow morning. Actually getting back and forth was no more than a technicality. Besides, it never occurred to her that he could be serious.

'Well, if I can't bring myself up to the joys of Arabella in person,' she said, 'tell her I'll drink her health.'

'You got a supply?'

'I certainly do.'

'Ice? Soda? A glass?'

'I'm not going to drink it out of the bottle.'

They walked the rest of the way to the elevator in silence and waited there in silence. When the elevator arrived, he ushered her in – the old-fashioned gentleman in his gentlemanly flannels – and as she went past him, he touched her arm.

'What you're doing is wrong, Alice,' he said. He shifted from one foot to the other, looked down, looked up again. 'You can't live this man's life for him.'

CHAPTER 12

i

So what the hell does a comment like that mean? I don't know. I've thought about it for years and I still don't know. Back at Cordelia's apartment, Alice sipped a drink and worked on a strut, made from an old wooden spoon, to support the Corn King's thumb. What a stupid waste: a chicken-wire skeleton for the hand of an effigy to be burned in a month's time according to a ritual that had long since lost its meaning.

Prostatectomy: a failure. Brace for the back: a failure. Homely percale doctor: a failure. Government money: a failure. At least she'd managed to force supplementary insurance down Peter. Live his life for him? Is that what this struggle was called? What are you supposed to do? step aside? There's loyalty and there's betrayal. Where does living a man's life for him come into it? Besides, what do you say of someone who knew that the most important moment in her relationship with a man was the moment she realized he wasn't perfect after all? And the triviality of the incident! My God, it would have served nobody who wasn't lying in wait for it. How do you atone for something like that?

It began one evening years ago; they were sitting in front of their log fire in Devon. Peter was telling her about the Countess of Salisbury's garter, the medieval ball and the dancing.

'Way back in those days, girls wore brightly coloured ribbons around their legs,' he was saying. He stared fixedly away from her while they talked – this trick he'd learned from his father, who knew how to use boredom as a weapon. 'Dropping a ribbon meant exactly what it sounds as though it means, and when the Countess's blue garter fell to the floor, the dancing and music stopped at once. There was a scandalized hush, and in the midst of it' – he smiled, eyes on the fire – 'Edward the Third bent down, picked up the garter, tied it around his own leg and said that famous sentence, *Honi soit qui mal y pense.*'

How absurd we are when the hormones are in full flow. The flickering light on his cheek, the tension in his fingers around the glass: Alice had to fight to bring her mind to bear on a garter. Had he really said a garter? What did a garter have to do with anything? '*Honi* what?' she said, not caring, just wanting to hear his voice start up again. 'What does it mean?' She had some Spanish and some German – no French. 'You never told me you were good in French.'

Her gaze was so intent (he glanced at her quickly) that he resisted lying to her only because the lie was too far-fetched to maintain. 'I can still hear old Mr Fowler at Choate: "A little louder and a little faster, if you please, Mr Kessler." '

'You *weren't* good at it?'

'I was awful.'

'I don't believe you.'

She didn't. She just plain didn't. She thought he was teasing her; he often teased her. Besides, her mind was no more on French than on that ancient garter. Felicity once said to her, 'You aren't in love with Peter. You're obsessed by him.' It was true. Alice knew it. In rare moments of clarity she said to herself: I hate this. I can't bear it. How can my head be empty of everything but this one man? Why does every thought have

154

to end in him? Who was it that wrestled the angel? Is that what I'm doing?

Such clarity never stayed with her long; one touch, one glance was enough, and there she was, drowning in him as before. So, as had become her habit, she set out the very next morning to learn French – do as he did, be as he was. She found a local teacher and set up lessons.

And Peter? He knew she hadn't believed his denial, although he could hardly have been plainer. He also knew, in the months that followed – he whose accent had been a school joke and his mother's despair – that she didn't practise with him because she feared his disdain. It made him smile whenever he thought about it; he loved incongruities. But the fact is, he didn't think about it very much. Besides, if faith in his French gave her such pleasure, who was he to disabuse her?

They decided to take the last two weeks of June in Brittany; they bundled up Tad, who was three years old – a happy little boy, never still, always chattering, afraid of nothing (much to their despair) – and crossed on the car ferry from Plymouth to Roscoff. They stopped for lunch in a small Breton town.

She was just inside the door of the restaurant, Tad astraddle on her hip, twisting this way and that to take in everything at once, when the headwaiter addressed her. '*Madame?*' he said.

'Funny talk!' Tad cried and lurched out towards the man, grabbing her long braid for support.

She glanced to her side for Peter; the eyes of headwaiters usually sought him out, sliding off her like boiled eggs off a plate. No Peter. She looked behind her. No Peter. He was nowhere to be seen.

Alice took in her breath. '*Une table pour trois,*' she said, and to her delight the headwaiter nodded as though she'd said something sensible. He turned to lead her to a table. She was so relieved, so pleased with herself that she would have followed him anywhere, Peter for once wholly out of mind.

And, wholly out of mind, he reappeared, trotting beside her as though he'd been there all along. They sat down at a pretty table with a red tablecloth, a small vase of pinks and a high chair for Tad; a huge waitress with tusk-like teeth appeared, a walrus of a waitress. Peter was reaching out to take the menu from her when the headwaiter rushed over and – with a flourish and a smile – redirected it to Alice, saying in a contemptuous aside, '*Monsieur ne parle pas un mot.*'

There are revelations and revelations. You see what I mean by triviality, though. Who could make anything of this? But Alice did. She was shocked. Her Peter? who was perfect? couldn't speak French? and had let her think he could? for months? She cocked her head and studied him with wonder on her face. His cheeks became as pink as the flowers; they began to compete with the red tablecloth itself.

She burst out laughing: if a man blushes, you forgive him everything.

Well, almost everything. The fact is, she'd never before been in a position to forgive Peter. What is there to forgive in perfection? There was serious triumph here. She was suddenly abubble with it. Her heart swelled in her chest, and in that moment she claimed back a goodly portion of the territory that he had ruled for so long inside her mind. Even now she could tell you with certainty that the walrus of a waitress had on a green uniform with a yellow collar and cuffs – and that there was a spot of gravy on the apron, which was embroidered with forget-me-nots.

No wonder then that when the social worker walked into Peter's hospital room in Overton, Alice could almost see those Breton pinks again and the red of that tablecloth.

'Mrs Kessler?' the social worker said. She was as big as the waitress, huge, blubbery and as wide as a door. The teeth had been unusual in a Frenchwoman; they were outrageous in an American, stuck – stuffed – into her mouth like parsnips into an old meat-grinder. 'Dr Hashman thought it might be a good idea if I had a word with you.'

'Oh, dear, I don't think he understands,' Alice said.

'Mr Kessler?'

'Dr Hashman.'

'I know this is all very difficult for you – ' The social worker stopped short. 'I'm Mrs Carpenter,' she said.

Alice nodded, unsmiling, although it did seem to her an error in judgement – aesthetically speaking – to join up the Walrus and the Carpenter, especially in this Wonderland of a place. 'It's about hospital insurance, isn't it?'

'Aren't you smart. Dr Hashman said you were. It's the law, you know. There's nothing we can – '

'Is it really? Nobody's said that before. What law?'

'What law?' Mrs Carpenter blinked her round, black eyes. 'Well, um, *the* law. Let's talk about it in my office, shall we? We won't disturb Mr Kessler there.'

Mrs Carpenter's office nestled behind the nurses' station, behind the desk and the massive, slowly turning carousels that held the patients' binders. It was a tiny place, not at all right – Alice was sure of it – for a walrus to live in, or a carpenter either, for that matter. Alice slid into a straight chair beside the door. Mrs Carpenter squeezed what she could of herself between desk and bookcase.

'Let me try to explain,' she said. 'If you're sixty-five or over and on Medicare, your disease process becomes a government matter as – '

'Peter's prostate?' Alice laughed. 'An affair of state? What do you know: it even rhymes.'

'Please, Mrs Kessler. I'm just trying to explain the situation to you.'

'Of course, of course. I'm sorry. Go on.'

'Your disease process becomes a government matter as soon as you walk into the hospital.' Mrs Carpenter gave a little

157

jiggle; the rest of her bulk slid down into place. 'Diagnosis is a government matter. Admission is a government matter. Treatment is a government matter. Recovery is a government matter. It's very, very carefully – '

'What's this got to do with *private* insurance?'

'The point is that private insurance is a government matter too. It's regulated by the government, and if the government says a patient is well, then his insurance can't keep him in the hospital. It's a way of protecting the patient, do you see? If an insurance company kept him in the hospital when he didn't need to be there, that would be exploiting him, wouldn't it?'

'Have I got the wrong kind of insurance? or not enough?' Alice said, suddenly afraid. 'Is that what it is? I haven't got enough coverage?'

'No, no, no. You're fine. Don't worry. You've got everything you need.'

'Well – then – ' Alice stammered. 'It will pay for everything.'

'It'll pay for as much as any other insurance, Mrs Kessler. But there are limits. There have to be. If the doctors say Mr Kessler is well – and the government always agrees when the doctors say a patient is well – you can't expect an insurance company to keep on paying for him. They'd go broke in no time, and then where would we be?'

'But he isn't well. Nobody thinks so.'

Mrs Carpenter took in her breath and tried again. 'The question comes down to what the hospital can do to help Mr Kessler. A hospital has limits on it, just like an insurance company. When the hospital has done everything it can, we must turn somewhere else.' Pinned up on the wall above Mrs Carpenter's desk was a photograph of three children wearing Mickey Mouse ears. Alice thought of the oysters, whose coats were brushed and whose shoes were clean and neat. The walrus had eaten more oysters than the carpenter. Or was it the other way around?

158

'We process all the details,' Mrs Carpenter went on, 'every single one, down to the last aspirin. We've got the finest software in the country. We don't leave anything to chance. All a Notice of Non-coverage means is that the hospital has done everything it can, and it's time to move on to the next stage.'

'What about Dr Hashman? He knows there's more the hospital can do.' Alice's hands trembled a little. 'What about Dr Morgenstern? Have you talked to him?'

'If you have lots of people looking after your rights, there's bound to be some disagreement among them. That's just human nature.'

'I see,' said Alice. 'So it's Morgenstern, is it? He says Peter's recovered, doesn't he?' Mrs Carpenter opened her mouth to speak but Alice rushed on. 'At least that explains why he keeps trying to avoid me. Let me see if I've got this straight. As a result of what he's said, my million-dollars-worth of insurance is useless, and the hospital is going to throw Peter out, sick or well. That's it, isn't it?'

'Of course not, Mrs Kessler. Nobody would do such a thing. I'm saying exactly the opposite. The decision is not Dr Morgenstern's or any other individual's.' Mrs Carpenter's cheeks jiggled with distress and good intentions. 'The hospital has processed all the information and decided it has done all it can for him, and now – '

'This is what Hashman was talking about?'

'I would imagine so.'

'When?'

'What do you mean?'

'How long before Peter has to go?'

'Oh, dear, you are confusing the – '

'Let me put it another way. How much longer is Memorial prepared to keep him?'

Mrs Carpenter looked down at her desk. 'Two days,' she said.

So while Alice watched Peter's agony and waited for him to need her and her paper cup, she combed the half-truths of her layman's knowledge in search of some weapon to extend this deadline long enough to get him in shape for the trip back to Devon. She sorted and classified what had been done for him already, and noted that all the investigations so far had been physical.

Her heart beat a little faster. Did it matter? Could it?

He was plainly depressed. Suppose the depression could be lifted, might he drink? If he drank, maybe he'd feel like trying to walk. If he tried to walk – Why not call in a psychiatrist? Some of the antidepressants were very effective. She'd read about them in the newspapers. It was possible, wasn't it? Isn't anything possible? at least in theory?

ii

She was so enchanted with this idea that when she caught a glimpse of Bob Morgenstern hurrying away down the hall outside, she hurried after him, caught him by the arm and held firm; this time he couldn't escape her without shaking himself loose.

'I think Peter's depressed,' she said, full of excitement.

'What?'

'Depressed. He's depressed. Don't you agree?'

'I don't know what that means. Now I'm in a – '

She held his arm tighter. 'I know you don't think you can do anything more for his body, but surely somebody can look into his state of mind.'

'I'm not a psychiatrist. I don't know anything about depression. I don't believe in it.'

'How can you not believe in depression?' she said indignantly.

'Why should I believe in it? I've never dealt with it. I don't

160

know what you're talking about. Now I really must get back to my office. I have patients waiting.'

Alice noticed that the fine-spun cotton of his soul had taken on that fragile look that sheets get before they develop holes in the wash. 'He won't eat,' she said. 'It seems almost as if he can't eat. Isn't this a sign of depression?'

'Look, Mrs Kessler, I don't know anything about – '

'If it isn't depression, why can't he eat?'

He sighed irritably. 'I don't know.'

Alice frowned. 'He doesn't even seem hungry.'

'Maybe he isn't.'

'But why isn't he?'

'I don't know.'

'Is it age? He's not old enough for that, is he?'

'I don't know.'

'Is it disease?'

'I don't know.'

'Is he dying?'

'I don't know.'

'You must know that at least. Is he? Tell me.'

'No, I don't know that. I can't answer any of these questions, Mrs Kessler. All I know is you have to get him out of here within the next two days.'

'That's *all* you know?' The rage she felt was so abrupt and so strong that the words were out before she thought to stop them. 'You've got to know something more. Are you a doctor, or aren't you?'

Bob flipped his stethoscope back and forth between the fingers of his free hand. 'There are times when I wonder about that.' He sighed and stared off down the hallway as he spoke. 'But yes, I am allowed to know certain things. Not the things I learned in medical school. Not those. Those are all outdated. Ask the computers. It's computers that tell me what I know these days; what do do, how and when to do it and – oh, most important of all – when to stop doing it. They tell me Peter now produces a stream of urine that exceeds thirteen cubic centimetres in thirty seconds. And what *that* means is, we made him all better.'

'He pees tiny little bits,' Alice cried. 'I catch them in a coffee cup.'

'Oh, well, what's a computer know of such details? A computer can't urinate at the best of times. Or drink a cup of coffee, for that matter. That leaves us only with the question, what would Peter's stream measure if it weren't for you and your coffee cup.'

'It's exactly the same whether I catch it or not,' Alice said.

'That's not the question, though, is it? The question is, what is its precise volume? Computers are nothing if not precise. So how do we measure it? What's the procedure? You won't find it in the handbook. Let's see: a shot-glass and a stop-watch maybe? "Here, sir, just let fly when I say 'Go!' " No, I really don't have any idea. But having ideas is not my job. Urology isn't my job either. You've got Hashman for that. Remember? But then maybe volume of stream isn't this week's criterion. Medicine isn't static, you know. Maybe this week the deciding factor is – let me see – ah, yes, how about this? I understand your husband no longer has to get up at night to urinate.'

'He can't walk.' She let go of his arm and took a step away from him. 'How can you say – ? You know he can't walk.'

'Well, if he can't walk, he doesn't get up at night to urinate, does he? That's logical, isn't it? And if he doesn't get up at night to urinate, he can't stay in the hospital anymore. This may not sound like medicine, but I assure you it is. Medicine at its most modern. Government seal of approval. The best.'

Beyond him the corridor window looked out over the hospital parking-lot and its attendant buildings and from there to the tangle of highways on Overton's distant fringe; all the hallway windows at Memorial ended in this view.

He sighed. 'You're going to have to find a nursing-home to put him in. It's as simple as that. That's what they want, every single one of them – computers, utilization boards, armies of bureaucrats, acres and acres of US-government-certified criteria. Maybe it all springs from nothing but witchcraft, but it's the law of the land and it's what the system's geared for. That's where the conveyor-belt ends. And that's what you're going to have to do.' He walked over to the window. She followed warily. 'There's one over there. See it? Across the parking lot?' A cement-screeded building squatted there, purpose-built, grey windows. 'And there, catty-corner, there's another one.'

'You don't mean this.'

'Yes, I do.'

'I don't like the sound of a nursing-home.'

'Not many people do. You're not going to have any choice, you know.'

'I'm taking him back to England. Somehow or other I have to get him well enough for that, and if this hospital evicts him, I'll take care of him myself.'

Bob stared out of the window a minute, then shrugged. 'Okay. I did my best.'

'I don't know that your best is good enough,' she said.

The bas-relief billiard ball on his forehead gleamed in the light from the window; the parking-lot outside was unexpectedly empty at this afternoon hour, an acre of ill-defined macadam connecting the ill-assorted buildings around it. Between the nursing-homes on the far side of the parking-lot and the highways in the distance lay the desolate reaches of Overton's poor sections. 'If it's any comfort to you, I don't feel so good about nursing-homes myself,' he said then. 'Nothing personal. Well, maybe a little personal. But whatever happens, keep in mind that what I tell you is not truth. It is only law.'

'That's what Mrs Carpenter said.'

'Who?'

'Social worker.'

'Quite right too. Quite right. How nice and clean the law is. How sweet-smelling. Don't you think?'

'Not like a nursing-home?'

'No,' he said. 'Not like that.'

iii

It's amazing how canny you become when you finally realize that the need is imperative. An American nursing-home is not a good place to end up, and just the look of those squat grey buildings gave Alice the shivers. She called Christie first, and so it was that she had a little room for manoeuvre in her telephone call to Dutch, who said (as she'd expected him to), 'Aw, come on, Alice. There ain't no psychiatric case here. You know that.'

'Pop agrees with me,' she said at once. 'I just talked to him about it.'

'A man in Peter's condition: if he *ain't* depressed, then you know he's away with the fairies.'

'Pop and I want to consult a psychiatrist.'

'What for? There isn't anything wrong with Peter's mind.'

'You're just like Morgenstern,' she said, pulling in the battering-ram a little reluctantly – not because it was a low trick, only because she'd used it before and feared (as she'd told her father) that Dutch might have strengthened his defences against it. She held her breath – and was gratified to hear the anger rise in him.

'There ain't no similarity whatever between me and Morgenstern. No way. Understand me?'

'Oh, yes, there is. This time you are as one. He says he doesn't believe in depression.'

'That's a dumb thing to say. I don't agree with nothin' he says.'

164

'Except about depression.'

'Not about depression neither.'

'It sounds to me like you do.'

'Alice, what are you trying to do to me?'

'I want a psychiatric assessment.'

'I'm tellin' you it's a waste of time.'

'Peter needs to stay in the hospital, and you know it.' She made a stab in the dark. 'All I need to do is get him well enough for the trip to England. Maybe he could spend a few days in the psychiatric ward. I think it sounds like a good idea.'

'Alice – '

'If Pop and I can't get help from you, we'll go back to Morgenstern. Maybe if he knows that you – '

'Lookee here, ma'am' – the hillbilly accent was in full swing – 'you cain't keep beatin' this old horse with the same old stick.'

Peter used to say: if you can't fight dirty, fight clean. 'I don't know why not,' she said. 'You always respond so promisingly.'

He laughed then. 'All right. All right. Lemme think. I dunno. It's just remotely possible that you might have a – ' His voiced lightened. 'They got different rules down in Psychiatry. I don't know just what, but they're different. It's just possible that – Why not? In fact, they owe me one.'

So it was that early the following morning a shoal of nurses and porters manoeuvred Peter out of his room, still in his bed (bottles and bags adangle and ajangle, monitoring machines bleeping and flashing), pushed him into the elevator and rode him down to the fifth floor and sanctuary in the psychiatric ward.

Psychiatric wards are different from other wards. Disorder and inertia hang over them like boiled-cabbage smells from the kitchen. In Overton's Open Ward, the nurses wear jeans and shirts – no uniforms – but jeans and shirts manage to evoke only the disorder of home, not homeliness.

There are pictures on the walls, too, but the pictures are so inept, so meagre, so plainly the work of sick people with no more talent in art than they have in life, that they fool nobody, least of all the sick themselves. Other wards don't have pictures. Other wards are too busy for such things, so the pictures serve only to underline the fact that nothing happens here. There's no bustle of staff and equipment, no rush of emergency, no visitors, no sense of something to be accomplished today – a test, an operation, a preparation for home-going – nothing to be accomplished tomorrow or the next day or the day after that.

The psychiatrist in charge was Dr Novali, a youngish man, thirty-five maybe – about Alice's age – very tall, six foot six, maybe six foot eight, thin and angular like a locust. His consulting-room was at the end of the hallway near the elevators. Patients in various states of disarray waited for him on benches – women in bathrobes or ill-fitting dresses, men in slippers, eyes blank, posture stooped, heads hanging. The psychiatric consultation is the one meaningful activity of the day, and Dr Novali wasn't due for several hours yet. Or perhaps he'd already come and gone. It didn't matter. They might as well wait here for tomorrow as anywhere else.

Peter's room was long and narrow. The windows looked out over the same view that Memorial's corridors overlooked: tarmac ringed by nursing-homes, then ramshackle housing and beyond that to the distant cloverleaf. Orderlies pushed Peter's bed into one end of the room; at the opposite end, another man lay on a bed already in place. Alice's heart sank at the sight of him. He had a wasteland of a face, tired through and through, like the dust-bowl soil of the Thirties, when her father was young. He lay on his back, fully dressed on the made-up bed, to watch the ceremony of Peter's hook-up to new sources of electricity. She wondered vaguely why he wasn't waiting outside Dr Novali's office like the others. Was he less crazy than they? Crazier maybe? The space around Peter's bed was tight. Either she took herself over to the tired man and introduced herself in a decent, civilized manner, or she escaped into the corridor. She chose the corridor.

There was a small electric organ at the other end, away from Dr Novali's office; she wandered towards it. It was an old instrument, battered, scarred, varnish bubbling. Christie used to play one like it. A Hammond organ: Alice had always hated the sound; a sentimental tawdry, down-graded thing, suited to this place, she thought, hating the place, too – sanctuary or no – fearing it and ashamed of her fear. Opposite the organ, the hallway opened out into an area with plastic chairs, tables, a television, but no windows; the only light was from fluorescent fixtures in the ceiling. Nobody was about.

She picked up a magazine from one of the tables, flipped its pages, then swung around at a noise behind her to see Peter's room-mate standing there. He was quite short, an inch or two shorter than she. Standing up, he looked even older. His head was huge, heavy, badly balanced on his neck. The skin on his face sagged into syrupy folds that gathered themselves into a ridge above his eyes and a crop beneath his neck.

'What's the matter with him?' he said to her, jerking that mammoth head in the direction of the room where Peter lay.

'Practically everything,' she said.

He leaned backwards, scanned the corridor behind him, then said, 'I thought *I* was sick. But, Jesus, that's a different league. He shouldn't be here, not even to get more days. I mean, what about us?'

Alice didn't quite know how to answer, so she said, 'How many days have you got?'

His face collapsed in front of her. She thought of mud-flats being washed out to sea on the spring tide. 'I got only twenty-three. That's why I'm so upset. See?'

'*Only* twenty-three? Isn't that a very long time?' With that long, she could probably get Peter in shape for the journey.

'I already been in here a hundred and sixty-seven. I been sick for years: years, years, years. After I had eighty-nine days – that was earlier this year – they told me I better get out so's I'd have some left for later, see? I got out and tried to strangle my wife.' Alice nodded, not shocked (she wasn't sure why) – not frightened either – but, by this time, delightedly aware that she'd made a brilliant move in bringing Peter here. 'Don't get me wrong, I don't hear voices or anything. That's why they say I'm not schizophrenic. She had red hair when we got married. Red, red, red. In curls down her back. Prettiest thing I ever laid eyes on. See what I mean?'

Alice nodded again.

'I got a collection of hunting-knives so I was in the Closed Ward for eighty-three days after. Time was getting so tight that they moved me down here five days ago. They got no choice: I got to get well in twenty-three days.'

The numbers are all prime, she thought. How very odd. That must be accident; what they added up to was formidable. 'Do you really get a hundred and ninety days here?' she said, hardly able to take it in. 'Does it matter what's wrong?'

'Don't you know anything?' he said, suddenly exasperated; he stamped his feet and turned in a circle around himself. 'I'm not getting better quick enough, see? Even without this. And with him in the room. I still feel – ' He stopped short, stuck his face close to hers and studied her intently. 'You can add,' he said.

'I'm good with numbers.'

'I am too. Most people can't add. It's how they get 'em. Is he going to die here?'

'I don't know,' said Alice.

'Where's he going to die then?'

Alice looked at him, her mind a blank. 'I don't know.'

'Maybe you *can* add, but you sure don't know anything, do you? Ignorance of the law is no excuse. Unless you're lying to me. That could be. Everybody around here lies.'

He probably hid the sedatives they gave him, Alice thought, or flushed them down the john – not easy in a psychiatric ward. She was impressed. That would explain why he didn't spend the day slouched on the benches outside Dr Novali's office. 'I'm afraid I don't understand much about the way this hospital functions' – her earnestness was absolute – 'but I assure you I'm not lying to you.' He narrowed his eyes. 'Why would I bother?' she said. 'I don't know you well enough.' The little man stamped his feet as he had before. She went on in a rush, 'I am sorry, really I am. I do appreciate that it isn't good for you to have somebody as sick as he is in the same room with you.'

He turned abruptly, scuttled down the corridor and back into the room where Peter lay.

Alice waited until she saw the people from Oncology leave; then she went back to the room, too. Peter's room-mate was on his bed again. One of the psychiatric nurses, a large, wiry black woman, sat on Peter's bed, holding his hand. She turned to Alice at once. 'He says he's in pain.'

'I know,' Alice said. 'I don't know what to do about it.'

'Talk to your doctor, Mrs Kessler.'

'Morgenstern insists he *isn't* in pain.'

'It's no wonder he can't sleep. You can't sleep when you're in pain.'

Alice leaned against the end of the bed. 'Morgenstern says he doesn't believe in panic attacks, either.'

'Mr Kessler has panic attacks?'

'I'm not just imagining panic attacks, am I? They are real, aren't they? People do have them?'

'Of course they do,' the nurse said. 'I can get something for those. But you'll have to get Dr Morgenstern to prescribe for the pain.'

'I don't think he will.' Alice couldn't keep the despair she felt out of her voice; the pain had seemed to her to increase by the hour.

'Corner him. Talk to him.' The nurse reached out her free hand to Alice. 'I'm Sharon,' she said.

Alice shook the hand.

From the other end of the room, Peter's room-mate watched. As soon as Sharon left, he rose up on his elbow. 'Psst! Hey! You!'

'Me?' Alice said.

'Yeah, you. You *really* don't know much, do you?'

'No.'

'Come here.' Alice hesitated. 'Come, come, come. We haven't got all day.' Alice walked over to him. 'Closer.' She hesitated again. 'Closer.' As soon as she stood by his bed, he reached out, grabbed her – his hand around the back of her neck – and pulled her down to him. 'I'm the White Knight,' he whispered into her ear.

'I'm Alice Kessler,' she whispered back.

She tried to pull herself upright. He yanked her back. 'Listen here, Alice Kessler,' he said. 'You can fire a doctor.'

'Can you? How?'

'Sssh! Don't struggle like that. They don't like it. All you've got to do is say, "You're fired." You get more days.'

170

'Are you sure about this?'

'You think I'm lying?'

'No.'

'Then I must be telling the truth.'

'If I fire Morgenstern,' Alice said, 'then what?'

'Hire another doctor.'

'Shouldn't I find him first? the other doctor?'

'Probably.'

'How do I do that?'

'I've already said too much,' he said. 'If they find out, they'll cut my days. They can. They'll blame the computer, but by then it'll be too late. They can do anything.'

It never crossed Alice's mind that the White Knight might not know what he was talking about.

'Thank you,' she whispered. 'It's very kind of you.'

He let go of her, and as she pulled herself upright, he winked. A wink looks odd in so wrinkled a face. The skin closed over like syrup; Alice was almost afraid the eye wouldn't emerge again. When it did, he said, 'It's because of the numbers.'

She began her search for Bob Morgenstern's replacement at once. Her father had suggested Morgenstern in the first place, so she couldn't call him. She called Dutch Hashman's office. This was his day off; he couldn't be reached until tomorrow. She tried Dr Novali; Dr Novali was in Chicago for two days. 'He's getting married soon,' his secretary said. 'There's so much to do.'

Who was left? Alice was determined, absolutely determined, to get another doctor before nightfall. She's an atheist – Alice is – but she burns for her sins even so, and she burns more for the ones that aren't her fault than for the ones that are. Now that she knew how to avoid it, Peter was not going to suffer another night of pain. Not a single one. Never again. The switch had to be made at once.

She decided to talk to Cordelia Macher-Daly.

v

The dogs weren't lying in the laundry-room at Macher-Daly House when Alice got back there; she could hear them, though, and the sound was wrong, low and insistent, somewhere between a growl and a moan – not right at all. Alice tapped on the door that connected the laundry-room to the kitchen of the main house; it opened at once. 'Thank God you've come,' Cordelia said. Her white hair was in tufts; there were scratches on her face. 'I've been waiting for you.'

'What's the matter? Is Schpiegal all right? The dogs sound funny. That is the dogs, isn't it?'

'Come,' Cordelia said, leading her through the kitchen, where towers of dirty dishes – on counters, draining-board, stove – rattled and teetered with every footfall. Spoons jiggled in open cans of dog food. Why does everything to do with dogs smell bad? The dining-room beyond was darker than before; the smell was worse here, wet dog this time, Alice figured, and something else too. Blood? Could it be blood? There'd been rain for most of the morning.

Ahab lay on the floor in the corner.

'My God, Cordelia, what's the matter with him?' Alice peered into the gloom; she could make out only the dog's silhouette and the whites of his eyes, but she could see that he quivered as he lay there. She'd never seen anything like it. Living things don't quiver that way, all of them apiece – aspic on an intercity train maybe, a can of paint in a paint-mixer, but not something alive, not a dog.

'It's his paw.' Cordelia said. 'I don't know what to do.'

'His paw?'

'Back paw. Wait a minute. I'll turn on the light.'

172

She turned on the floor lamp. Alice sat down heavily in one of the rickety chairs. 'How'd that happen?' she said.

Bone protruded from a red, clotted stump, which was all that remained of Ahab's leg. The four other dogs lay facing him, making that keening sound, eerie, sad and yet threatening somehow. Was it hunger? Not quite. Besides, the dogs were fat, overfed. Greed? Why not? thought Alice. One slip of the foot and the pack is at your throat. Christie used to say that. What happens when you lose the foot itself? Does everything end up in betrayal? Is that what life is? Endless betrayal? The white shapeless dog lay a little closer to Ahab than the others.

'I heard them,' Cordelia said, 'and when I got to them –' She broke off.

'I don't know anything about animals,' Alice said softly.

'Who does?'

'Shouldn't we get him to a vet or something?'

Cordelia shook her head. 'He won't let me near him. He snaps at me. He bit me. My Ahab. He actually – I called the vet an hour ago and they said they'd send somebody out after lunch. Do you want a sandwich?' Cordelia paced back and forth beside the table and in front of the dogs. 'How about a glass of wine? I'm having one. I'm going to drink a whole bottle. Maybe two.' She poured out two glasses of wine and handed one to Alice. 'We can't talk here – not in front of him.' She jerked her head towards the living-room. Alice followed, then glanced back. As she did, the shapeless white dog crawled forward and licked the carpet where it was soaked with Ahab's blood.

In the living-room Alice put her glass down on a heap of papers and took a second heap out of one of the chairs; she stood irresolute a minute, papers in hand, and, finding no surface free, sat down with them on her lap.

'These seem to be old bills,' she said, glancing at them idly.

'Why don't you let me have some of them? I'm ready to start fleshing out the Corn King's hand.'

Cordelia looked at her in alarm. 'I'm not sure you wholly appreciate the pre-eminent importance of a full and accurate record of events. Of course you're not a market analyst . . .'

Alice made little sense of the stream of words that followed until she caught the phrase 'an essential written history'. She said, 'But, Cordelia, this is only an old grocery bill from – my God, it goes all the way back to 1978. And this one – '

'Are you sure you don't want a sandwich?'

'I ate at the hospital,' Alice said, although she hadn't.

'How can you ask me to sort through old records now? I can't think of anything but Ahab. I have to make a decision.' Cordelia cradled her little wing in her good arm and rocked her body back and forth. 'What good is a three-legged dog? As a market analyst, I must pursue . . .'

Alice studied this three-legged Cordelia, talking on and on, and thought, as she put the pile of old bills on the floor beside her, that it might be wiser for three-legged creatures to forget the questions and make common cause with one another.

'. . . and all I come up with,' Cordelia was saying, 'is, do I patch him up and let the others tear him limb from limb behind my back? or do I snuff him myself? What do you do with old kings? The king is dead. Long live the king. Schpiegal used to say – '

'Where is Schpiegal anyway?' Alice interrupted. 'Is he taking his nap?'

'Charlie found him a bed. He hated to go, and God knows, I feel guilty. Charlie had to convince us both that the time had come. Emotional ties always present difficulties in terminal situations, but with my analytical – '

'A bed? What do you mean, a bed? A hospital bed? Did you say terminal? Is he dying?' Alice found herself speaking as fast as she could, fearful that Cordelia would veer off again. 'I had no idea he was so sick.'

'When you gotta go, you gotta go,' Cordelia said, but her heart wasn't in it.

'I haven't seen you at the hospital. We must have been just missing each other. Why didn't you tell me about this?'

A pale gleam of sunshine – the first of the day – filtered through the room, lighting up swirls of dust in the air. 'He isn't at Memorial.' Cordelia sighed. 'At least he wasn't *here* when all this happened.'

'You haven't put him in a nursing-home, have you? Who is this Charlie, anyway?'

'Doctor.'

'Your doctor?'

'And Schpiegal's. It's more like a small hospital. Charlie's on the board, and it's got a wonderful reputation in town. In medical matters, a market analyst has certain . . .'

How could anybody talk so relentlessly? Alice squirmed in her chair, resisting as best she could the desire to check her watch. A small hospital probably had different rules from a big place like Memorial – a pity the idea hadn't occurred to her before. She couldn't remember any small hospitals in Overton, but she'd never paid much attention before. She waited for a slackening in Cordelia's monologue.

'Is he any good? This Charlie?' she interrupted. 'Do you like him? Have you had him long?'

'Charlie? You mean my doctor? He's young and he doesn't live in Overton. Sure I like him. Schpiegal likes him. But to get back – '

'He's managed to get Schpiegal a hospital bed? one that nobody can throw him out of?'

'Of course nobody's going to throw him out. What gives you such weird ideas?'

'You're sure?'

175

'Charlie wouldn't let anything like that happen. He doesn't have a lot of personal problems either – nice in a doctor, don't you think?' Cordelia said, that sudden shrewdness of hers appearing oasis-like, as it sometimes did, in the desert of her talk. 'A lot of these guys are so wrapped up in playing doctor that they hardly notice whether there's a patient in front of them or not. Why do you want to know?'

'I'm going to fire Morgenstern.'

Cordelia let out a screech of laughter. 'Good for you. I fired him once myself. Did I tell you that? That's why I got Charlie in the first place. He's good with Schpiegal – with me too, and I'm not all that easy. And what a relief to have somebody who knows his way around the red tape the rest of them get tied up in. He arranged everything. All I did was sign the papers.' She shut her eyes and held her wing snug against her chest. 'What am I going to do about Ahab?'

'I don't know,' Alice said. 'I wish I did. What am I going to do about Morgenstern?'

Cordelia opened her eyes. 'That's easy. Why don't you call Charlie right now?'

So Alice called him. He listened; he was reassuring. 'They get a bit out of touch, these old guys,' he said. 'After all, they went to medical school almost half a century ago. The bureaucracy is a little beyond them, and they don't seem to realize just how much we can do to help people like your husband. The psychiatric ward, you say? Fine. I'll look in on him this evening.'

Alice put down the phone, steeled herself, called Morgenstern and fired him. His teeth chattered a little as he spoke – with sheer relief, Alice thought.

Charlie was as smooth all over as a mannequin in a men's department-store window. He wasn't tall. He wasn't short. He wasn't plump, or thin, or blond or brown-haired. Alice figured he was youngish – though she couldn't put an age on him – worked over by a good orthodontist, probably a bit of liposuction and a nose job. Mannequins aren't at their best close-up; no feature seems quite complete: nose runs into cheek, cheek slides into ear. The fact is, Charlie gave her the creeps. But she'd liked Morgenstern, so who was she to judge? Besides, Charlie examined Peter with the care that Morgenstern and the English doctors before him had once lavished, and that Morgenstern – like the English doctors – had come to lavish no more.

'I suggest we take out the drip,' he said. His voice had the resonance and pedantry of a speaking clock. 'Perhaps he will eat then. I will get a neurologist in here as soon as I can. Some of this rigidity could be Parkinson's. If it is, we can help.' He prescribed a pain-killer.

That night Peter slept for the first time in weeks.

CHAPTER 13

i

Of course, once the headwaiter in that Breton restaurant of
years before showed Alice that Peter was not perfect in mind
– and once illness got it through her head that he was not
perfect in body – she began to realize she'd seen evidence of
flaws in him elsewhere, flaws she'd missed or simply put aside.
You get used to perfection just as you get used to anything
else.

He was impatient and impulsive. Plainly he was. He was
easily bored. He was feckless like his father, always trying to
save a penny here or there and frittering away important sums
on a whim. Take the garage doors in Devon. They were ancient
when she and Peter bought the house. They needed replacing.
He insisted on trying to repair them instead, fifteen pounds
here, a hundred there, replacing this board, then that, then
hinges and locks. When the doors literally collapsed under this
approach, he insisted on designing the replacement himself; he
hired a handyman to help him build them out of quarter-inch
plywood – quarter-inch plywood, I ask you! – that, once nailed
into place, sagged on its overhead pulley, twisted in its frame,

juddered in the slightest breeze and stuck out into the street at eye level, endangering passers-by.

One morning while the handyman was still at work on the doors – Peter had just got the idea of reinforcing them with second-hand struts – Alice brought home an old record of a Bach Prelude in C Major that she'd found in the local market. Peter was asleep, bored by his project, although he would not admit it. He often slept at odd times during the day and stayed awake much of the night. She put the record on the turntable, and he awoke at once, smiling in delight.

'What is that?' he said, the smile deepening. 'What a glorious piece of music.'

'My father used to play it.'

'Did he? I never heard him. Put it on again.' He shut his eyes while she played the record a second time. 'You know,' he said then, 'that hasn't got any chords in it. I could play it myself if I had a piano to play it on.'

So they went out that very morning and brought a piano, an upright to be sure, but pretty and not all that small either, made out of oak with keys of real ivory. The shop couldn't deliver it until the following week, so Peter hired a firm to move it that afternoon. He sat down to play the moment it arrived. He couldn't read music, nor could Alice; so he played the record and began to pick out the notes on the keyboard. He practised for hours, way into the night, and in two days he'd mastered the prelude. It wasn't perfect – a little syncopated – but a remarkable feat for somebody who'd never had a lesson. He played the one piece every day for a month. Then he stopped. Never played it again. Never learned to play anything else. The piano became a room divider with books atop it.

You have to be very, very careful with the past. You have to gag it and chain it inside you – watch it like the growling beast it is – because if it gets loose and goes on the rampage it will tear your heart out. That's what it did to Alice when she heard

179

the Bach Prelude in the psychiatric ward as she got out of the elevator. The battered Hammond organ at the end of the corridor did not do justice to the charm of the piece, and she knew perfectly well that Peter could not be playing it. Dutch Hashman was at the keybord. She walked towards him, knowing at once that he knew she was there, although he kept on playing. She stood beside the organ and waited.

'I tried to reach you yesterday,' she said when he finished.

'Yeah,' he said. He kept his eyes and his fingers on the keys.

'My father used to play that.'

'Yeah?'

'I fired Morgenstern last night.'

'Yeah.'

'You know about this?'

'Yeah.'

'Do you know Charlie? Charlie Pederson?'

He took in his breath and looked up at her. 'Who doesn't know Charlie Pederson? He's a jackass. Of course, he's young enough to be my son – which just might account for my view of it.'

'He seemed quite good last night. I though you'd be relieved to have Morgenstern out of the way.'

Dutch shrugged.

'Aren't you?' she pressed.

'Sure. Yeah, you're probably right. Who knows?' He got up from the organ, then reached down and dusted his fingers along the keys. 'I haven't played one of these in forty-five years.'

'Tell me,' she said.

'Tell you what?'

'What's wrong with Charlie Pederson.'

'What for?'

'Tell me.'

'Got his fingers into too many pies. Let's have a cup of coffee. They got a machine down the hall in the kitchen.'

180

'You hate coffee,' she said. She wasn't sure why she knew this was true, but she did. They turned together, walked past the row of somnolent figures waiting outside Dr Novali's office and on to the inmates' kitchen, a bleak room like a practice kitchen in an underfunded cooking-school: ill-fitting plastic doors, cracked basin, crude, hand-lettered signs giving directions:

Do NOT put
Soup in the
kettle

Attach a label with
YOUR NAME ON IT
to food in the refrigerator

Alice sat in a folding chair at a plastic-topped, cigarette-scarred table. 'Charlie's going to call in a neurologist,' she said as Dutch poured out coffee into two plastic cups.

'What for?'

'He thinks some of the rigidity might be Parkinson's.'

Dutch gave a short laugh. 'You are the limit. Parkinson's!'

She nodded. 'I know it's bad.'

'It's worse than *bad*. I wouldn't wish it on my worst enemy, and here you are praying Peter's got it.'

'At least it's something Charlie can deal with.'

'No it ain't.'

'If it's Parkinson's, he says they can do something.'

'Alice, there isn't anything anybody can do.'

She put down her cup, got up abruptly and turned away. Then she turned back and sat down again. 'I am not going to give up.'

'Why not? You gotta give up sometime. Just make sure they don't ship him out of here. Understand me?'

'In fact, I do understand you. But they don't want him here. His nurse took me aside and told me she wasn't trained to deal with people in his condition. And his room-mate – ' She shrugged.

'Don't pay 'em no mind. A nurse is a nurse. As long as he's here, everything's gonna be all right. And if I was you – ' He broke off.

'What?'

'Ain't none of my business, is it?'

'If you were me, what?'

'If I was you, I'd get that boy of yours over here.'

The window of this dreary kitchen looked out, as the window of Peter's room did, over the poorer sections of town to the knotted highway interchanges. If all the people rushing north exchanged jobs with all the people rushing south, she thought, wouldn't life be simpler? 'You think I should send for Tad,' she said. 'I see. How long has Peter got?' she said.

'Nobody can tell you that.'

'Ask Morgenstern anything, he says, "I don't know." '

Dutch laughed. 'He's protecting his backside.'

'So are you.'

'Alice, I can't tell you how long a man is going to live. Nobody can do that. I can see he's dying but I don't know when he's going to die. I ain't God. I can only guess.'

'Then guess.'

He sighed. 'Christmas maybe.'

'That's what the English said.'

'They got good doctors in England.'

'It's barely November.'

'That isn't the point. The point is, you want this boy – Tad – to be able to talk to his father again or not? I don't know: I don't know what difference it makes. Maybe none.'

Alice frowned. 'He's only eleven.'

'He's gotta know sometime.'

'Peter always said all of eleven was perfect.'

'Everybody's got his quirks.'

182

'It's such a fragile age.'

'What other kind of age is there?'

She telephoned Switzerland that evening; the headmaster put Tad on the first plane out of Berne. Alice went to meet him at the local airport where she and Peter had arrived only a month before. She watched him skip down the stairs of the plane, eyes asparkle, tugging – puppy on a leash – at the stewardess's hand, just like Peter in the photographs at his mother's house years ago – the same fine features, the same electric tingle in the air around him, that extraordinary exhilaration, clouded – look quick! did you see it? – by the fleeting bafflement she had struggled so long (and so fruitlessly) to track down in Peter.

She ran across the tarmac and caught him up in her arms; he hugged her happily, already wriggling to free himself so he could see everything around him at once. He danced alongside her through the airport lounge and into the car. She sat with him there for a few minutes, doing what she could to prepare him. It wasn't much, and he was too excited to pay attention. Even so, at the hospital, upstairs in the psychiatric ward, he paused only a little. He checked with Alice over his shoulder. She nodded and smiled.

'Hello,' he said to Peter, and kissed him.

Peter traced the curve of the boy's cheek and agreed to eat a bite of ice-cream in celebration of his arrival. Tad held the spoon to his father's lips. Peter ate, watching Tad's every move, staring into his face with a hungry, unblinking gaze, as though the secret of the universe could be found there. Alice was proud of her child.

On the way out, Tad said casually, 'Where's daddy?'

'What do you mean?' Alice said.

'You said we were going to see daddy.'

'You've just seen him.'

183

'Where?' Tad swung around. 'Is he here? Is he at home? Where's home?'

'Tad, that was daddy in the hospital.'

'Don't be silly, mummy,' Tad giggled. 'That's only an old man.'

They drove to Cordelia's apartment in silence. While Alice fixed supper, she asked Tad about school, friends, Switzerland. He answered distractedly, in fragments and half sentences. When she put a pork chop and a baked potato down in front of him, he said, 'Is that old man really daddy? He doesn't look like daddy.'

'He's very sick, Tad.'

'I am never going to grow up.'

'Young people get sick too.'

'Not children.'

'Besides, there are good things about growing up.'

Tad shook his head angrily. 'I won't. I won't. You can't make me.'

'Okay,' she said.

ii

Tad had come, well, as a surprise to Peter: Tad's getting born, that is. Or rather, Tad's getting conceived. Alice said to Peter one day – they'd been married several years by this time and she was twenty-three – she said, 'I don't know whether you're going to like this or not, but I'm pregnant.'

He said nothing, not a word.

She knew he was angry. When Christie got angry, he went red. He shouted. Peter went white and still. She'd seen him this way too often in the eighteen months since *Faith Like a Jackal* had come out. *Faith Like a Jackal* was the third novel in his quartet – and the first to fail. How could such a thing happen? A book of Peter's fail? He'd sold five thousand copies.

No more. Alice knew *Jackal* by heart; she'd typed it through all of its various drafts, and she'd watched every inch of its creation. It was probably *Jackal* that had turned her passion for him into awe. With her own eyes she'd seen Peter make ordinary words into lines almost too beautiful to bear, lines that rose, dazzled and subsided – lines that left her with a fresh, salty taste in her mouth and a purely physical exhilaration, as though she'd dived through a wave on some stormy shore.

And yet the book failed.

Well, what the hell. These things happen. Sometimes the luck runs out. Sometimes the devil himself takes an interest. After all, he has to amuse himself too, doesn't he? Reviews a month too late, some inexplicable failure in distributing copies – and already the buzz is gone. That's the phrase they use in the trade: if the buzz is gone, you're dead.

Nothing like this had ever happened to Peter before. He brooded. He got angry over trifles. He woke at night and sat by himself in the dark. He drank too much. He wrote reviews and the occasional article, as he always had, but he could work up no interest in fiction – certainly none in the final volume of his quartet. Which is to say, he wasn't himself at all.

Alice had hoped the idea of a baby might cheer him up, distract him, spur him on. She was carrying orange-juice to the breakfast-table when she made her announcement and saw his anger. She stood, glasses in hand, and waited for him to speak. When he did not, she bent down towards him.

'Peter?' she said. 'Can I have offended you?'

He pulled back from her.

She set the glasses on the table. 'You don't want a baby?'

'Oh, for Christ's sake, Allie.'

'What's that supposed to mean?'

'I hate this.'

'My being pregnant?'

He kept his face turned aggressively away from her. 'If you've decided to leave me, why don't you just do it? Forget the bear-baiting.'

Alice took a drink of orange-juice and studied his angry profile. 'I can't follow your logic,' she said.

'So now you're going to tell me who the father is,' he said. 'Well, I don't want to know. It's your business, and I'd very much appreciate it if you kept it that way.'

'Do you seriously think you aren't the father?'

'I'm not going to be drawn into this.'

'You're already in it.'

Frost crystallized in the air around him. 'Just how much of a fool do you think I am?'

'I don't think you're any part of a fool.'

'Then cut the crap.'

'What crap?'

He glanced at her, then away. The cold he gave off was so extreme that she half expected the balmy spring morning to freeze over with him.

'We're not going to get anywhere unless we talk about it,' she said.

'You embarrass me.' Open windows looked out into River-side Park, over a huge tree and to the Palisades beyond. The walls of the room were oak-panelled; it was one of those old buildings, once grand, now cut up into airy, three-room apartments. 'No pill. No condom. No withdrawal. And no babies. Fair enough. But how many years has this being going on now? Five? Six? Isn't that enough to convince you? What do you expect me to think has been going on all these years? Divine intervention?'

'You embarrass me too,' she said.

'I'm glad to hear it.'

'I've never been to bed with anybody but you. You know that. Some couples just take longer than others.'

He shrugged.

'Why should I bother to lie?' she went on. 'I don't care enough about going to bed to lie about it.'

He was so angry that he faced her. 'You really pile it on, don't you?'

The Park was abloom just as Alice was herself, sun on the leaves – the dapple, the light, the delicate richness of the colour. The apartment faced east; sunlight fell across the table and caught red glints in her hair.

'Have you ever had a sperm count?' she said.

'I will not talk about this.'

'Because you think the baby isn't yours?'

He picked up the newspaper and stared into it.

'Okay,' she said. 'I'll arrange an abortion.'

He put the newspaper down then. He folded it, set it aside. He shifted his untouched orange-juice an inch farther away from him. 'I thought you wanted the baby.'

'If you don't want it, I don't want it.'

He frowned. 'Do you – ?' he began, but his voice cracked and he had to cough to start it again. 'Do you really mean that?'

'Of course I mean it.'

'You aren't – um – in love with this other guy? or something?'

'This other guy? What other guy?'

'You're sure?'

'I've never been surer of anything.'

He smiled that sudden smile of his. The frost around him cleared in a wash as bright as the sunlight from the window. 'In that case,' he said, 'anything you do is all right by me. If you want this baby, I want this baby. We'll have it together. I don't care whose it is.'

'It's going to be a boy,' she said, 'and you just wait and see. He's going to look exactly like you.'

She'd certainly been right about that. Even as a tiny baby,

Tad looked as though he'd been cloned, as though Alice had made no contribution to his genetic make-up. Perhaps Peter should have guessed the implications of this. Perhaps he did. But what good would it have done if he had?

CHAPTER 14

i

You start seeing flaws in a person – as Alice started seeing flaws in Peter – and you know there are others. It's just the way of things. But if you decide to track a few of them down, you have to know what questions to ask, where to begin your search. You say there. I say here. Nobody really knows, and if the flaw is well hidden it's only by the most outrageous of chances that you hit near the mark. Which is why Alice knows nothing of what follows; her investigations were too haphazard to get her even in range. How did I find out about it? I shut my eyes, spun around three times and pinned the tail on the donkey – and so discovered Angela's first husband, Jude Leslie, failed actor and bridge pro, on a winter night in 1953. That's when the skeleton in the Kessler cupboard started to rattle.

On this night Angela got back to her apartment from the *Postscript* offices to find Jude splayed out in a chair in her living-room. They'd separated after a bitter, all-night fight, and she'd rented this small apartment in the Village, not far from Peter. Her choice of neighbourhood was fortuitous; she had no designs on him – not yet. She lusted after him; she knew he was a first-rate editor, but he still irritated the hell out of her.

Besides, to live alone after years of marriage: the joy of it! A laundry-basket without a man's socks, shirts and stench of musk; a bathroom without a man's stubble scumming up the basin; whole mornings without a man to feed and clean up after — all this, to say nothing of that unparalleled luxury: sleep without a hairy torso weighing down the middle of the mattress or a couple of meaty legs wandering around where they don't belong. A daily maid did her wash and had dinner ready in the oven when she got home from work. She could smell tonight's casserole over the sour liquor breath that clung to Jude.

'How did you get in here?' she said. She half removed her winter coat, then — she had a sore throat and it was a very cold night — slipped it back on again.

'Magic,' he said.

'You're drunk.'

'Very.'

'Did you bribe the super?'

He grinned a lopsided grin at her. 'What's as magical as twenty-five bucks? Want a drink?'

She eyed him in disgust. 'Certainly not.'

The grin disappeared. 'You're right. I am —' His chin trembled. 'I saw your picture in *Postscript* yesterday — no, this morning. So long ago. What am I going to do, Angela? Tell me what to do. I feel like I'm dying.'

Jude wasn't a particularly beautiful man, but when he was sober he was ebullient, funny, warm-hearted and imaginative in bed. Angela told Peter that her education in sex had come from her biology teacher, who addressed his class saying, 'The position's ridiculous and the pleasure is vastly overrated. Are there any questions?' This wasn't entirely true. Before she was twelve, Ronny Malone's hands were groping around under her school clothes while the porch swing creaked.

She was sixteen when she first sat on that porch swing with Jude, who kissed her and then broke into song right there and

190

then, holding her in his arms. A couple of months later, they managed a furtive coupling on the steps of the local Baptist Church. Angela told Peter about it; she said it happened on her wedding night. This was not entirely true, either, since she didn't marry until she was seventeen. But there was no mistaking her enchantment. Ever afterwards she maintained — earnestly rather than humorously (humour was not her forte) — that there was something special about stone steps.

On that winter's night in 1953, drunken Jude said, 'I can't go on — Can't see you, hear you, my angel, my Angela — Can't bear it.'

She sighed irritably. 'It's too late for this kind of conversation.'

'The damn town's beaten us.'

'Speak for yourself, Jude. I like New York, except that I haven't eaten all day, and I'm hungry.'

'God, I'm sorry. You muss — must be starving.'

The concern in his voice was immediate, and it annoyed her because she knew that, drunk as he was, it was real; it bespoke that tiresome commitment of little towns like Salteen, where porch swings creak and Brownie troops bake cookies. The very thought of it made her feel queasy. She'd made her vows to the big city independence that Peter embodied by never seeming to notice how she felt. She turned her back on Jude and walked into the kitchen. He followed her. While she removed the casserole from the oven he leaned against the kitchen cabinets to watch. She opened the refrigerator to retrieve bread and butter — and sneezed.

'You okay, Angela?' He squinted to get her into focus.

'It was only a sneeze, for Christ's sake.'

'Why you got your coat on?'

'Because I'm cold.'

'I wanna go home.'

'Then go.'

'You don't understand. I want *us* to go home.'

191

'There is no *us* anymore.' She took out silverware and laid the table.

'S'only an argument. All married people have arguments.'

'We aren't married.'

'Course we're married. What are you talking about?'

'Have it your own way,' she said, exasperated. 'But the answer is no. You bore the bejesus out of me.'

Fights like these are as ritualized as recipes in a cook book. It hardly matters who's involved or what the provocation is. 'The answer is no,' Jude repeated after her and half under his breath, as though he could hardly make out her meaning. And yet she'd said precisely the same thing before – more than once, most notably on the night she left him. She began to slice the bread.

'You been screwing some other guy, haven't you?' he said. You see? Absolutely standard. Daily fare: vegetable soup, bacon and eggs.

'Don't be ridiculous.'

'Who is he?'

'Who is who?'

'Guy you're screwing.'

She shrugged. 'He's a lot better looking than you. Younger. More money.'

She said this as lightly as she'd said it on the night she left him; the difference is that now her commitment to Peter was far deeper than she knew; Jude sensed it, and the argument headed abruptly into the area of spicy foods, where you have to measure your ingredients carefully or one of your guests might choke. No drunk is very good at this sort of thing. Angela wasn't good at it by nature.

Jude yanked her to him, and for the first time she was alarmed. 'You whore,' he said. He didn't really mean it; he was more than a little shocked to hear the word himself, and he cast around in some confusion. But when she said nothing

– had she accepted the charge? had it meant nothing to her? – he was abruptly angry. Even so, neither of them expected the blow, a full-fisted blow that threw her to the floor and sent the casserole flying against the wall – that didn't break her jaw only because he was too drunk to deliver it properly.

Why did God make men bigger than women? For the purposes of rape. Angela had never realized this profound truth before, but she'd always known she was smarter than Jude was. She let him force her into the bedroom – token resistance, just enough to keep his suspicions at bay. She let him push her down on the bed. She let him throw himself down on top of her.

Then she said, as though the thought had just struck her, 'Wait a minute. I think I do have to take off this coat.'

Taken by surprise – the point was so reasonable (underneath his drunkenness and his disappointments, Jude was as reasonable a man as any) – he moved aside. She jumped up and ran – ran out of the apartment, down the stairs in the dark, hearing him fumble along behind her, too drunk to catch her, hearing him shout the threats that she prayed (a few minutes later, trembling, crouched in a doorway, her breath whistling in and out through her teeth) she'd never have to put to the test. It was only because Peter was so close by that she ran to him (or at least this is what she told herself); and it was only because she was afraid – and he was so insistent – that she moved in with him. She gave up the maid and the cooked dinner. She gave up the clean bathroom basin.

ii

Peter loved his apartment. He loved its Neverland feel. He loved arranging and rearranging things, furniture, knick-knacks, pictures. To celebrate Angela's arrival he added Einstein's pewter hookah to the mantelpiece where the pert little

bull from Peru and the bright-eyed Chinese monkey, now in
a brief alliance, gazed out into the room (startled at the goings-
on they saw there). He bought two straight-backed chairs –
carved, ornate, uncomfortable – so he and Angela could eat
and work together at his five-legged dining-table.

With Angela newly installed, he couldn't resist rearranging
her, too. She was five years older than he, but she was a garage
mechanic's daughter from a tiny town in Kansas. Peter bought
her clothes. He teased her into keeping her stockings straight.
He took her home to his mother, who cut her hair so that it
ringed her face with curls and showed off her gamine charm.
He told her which books to read and which dress to wear for
which occasion; how to talk to a head waiter, how to order
from a menu, how to talk over somebody else to get her way.
The standards of the American class system are so low and the
secrets so near the surface that with a willing guide and a little
determination, a humbly-born mechanic's daughter can stake
out a place in the upper classes easily enough to shock an
Englishman. Day by day Angela watched herself inch up the
social ladder to become somebody that no girl from Salteen
ever dreamed of becoming.

But the price was heavy. In the days of the McCarthy hearings she'd delighted in mocking Peter behind his back; she'd
amused herself with plans to dent that undented conceit of his.
No more. One day she awoke and saw to her horror that she
had fallen so deeply in love with him that she would never
own her own soul again. As soon as he walked out of a room,
all she thought about was gathering to herself joy, peace, love,
comfort so she could deliver them to him; but as soon as the
door shut behind him, nothing anywhere seemed worth
the gathering up. She used to sit on the boldly striped carpet
alone and weep like some poor demented creature.

This she did not like at all.

Besides, he slept with other women. He was quite open

about it. She sometimes thought that the only reason he wanted her to live with him – and he did seem to want her there – was that she had come to fit in so well with the furniture. It wasn't dignified. It wasn't right. She thought about leaving him, but she couldn't do it. Life without him terrified her. She toyed with the idea of killing him instead, and then herself, as drunken Jude (stumbling down the stairs after her) had threatened to kill her and then himself. Then she decided, still thinking of Jude, what the hell, there are easier ways to get at him.

She set out at once to find Maurice Denning. She seduced him – his resistance was minor – on the Empire chaise-longue in his back room where she'd watched Peter's triumph on television. Then she rushed home to the apartment, caught Peter's attention, dredged up a façade of reluctance and said, struggling for a suggestive but inconclusive word, that she'd become much *interested* in this man.

'Maurice Denning?' he said. 'Have you really? The antiques store around the corner from us? The guy with the fat dog? Hey, why don't you fix a martini? I remembered to freeze the glasses this time. Wasn't I clever?'

Angela wasn't sure what she'd expected, but certainly not this. 'The dog's not fat,' she said. 'It's Pekinese.'

'That's a noble piece of furniture he has in the window. I've never seen a table quite like it before, although people must have been putting lions' feet on tables for thousands of years. Where do you suppose the idea came from? He's had this one there for a very long time. How much does he want for it?'

'How the hell should I know?'

'I thought you were interested in him. Isn't that what you said?'

'I'm interested in the man, not his furniture.'

'Denning? Are you sure?'

'Of course I'm sure.'

'Isn't he a little decrepit for your taste?'

Angela ruffled her shoulders. 'He's only twenty-eight. Just my age.'

'If I got that table with the lions' feet, we could get rid of this one. You've never liked it. You know, I find it difficult to understand why you don't. It has such delicate legs.'

Evening sun shone in pale streaks through the drapery. 'God-damn you, Peter Kessler, I couldn't care less about the table. Or its legs. Or the one in Maurice's window, either.'

Peter looked down at his hands. 'There's more to tell, is there?' Angela nodded. When the gravity of her manner did not lift, he said, 'Is this serious?'

'I'm going to bed with him.'

'You already said *that*,' he said irritably, although in fact she had been careful not to say anything of the kind, 'but is it *serious*?'

She took in a shuddering breath. 'You don't care.'

'I care about everything that happens to you.'

He got up, went to the fireplace and moved the pert bull on the mantel an inch farther away from the Chinese monkey. 'What do you want from me, Angela?' he said then.

'Some response. Something to comfort me. Something – ' She stopped and stared at his implacable back. 'Have you no heart?'

Peter did not turn his face to her, and when he spoke, it was in the dreamy sort of way that he indulged in when he was least to be trusted. 'You must keep in mind that the days are growing longer,' he said, 'which is the way you like them to grow. This winter of discontent won't last. Things are not so bleak or so distant as you fear, although much of the trouble (as you suggest) comes from my limitations, which are many, rather than yours, which are surprisingly few. At any rate, the shaping of spring is going on, secretly, silently (all the best

196

things are secret), and one day sooner than you think we can sit again together in the spread of its warmth.'

She burst into tears.

He turned, eyes atwinkle much like the Chinese monkey's. 'That is, unless you really want to join forces with Maurice Denning and his fat dog. Now what about that martini?'

The next morning, Peter went out and bought the dining-table with lions' feet. He bargained for it, got a discount, was delighted with himself.

'We'll have to do some work on the surface,' he said happily to her, as though her distress of the night before had never happened. 'We need some wine glasses to go with it, don't you think? A couple of weeks ago I saw some beautiful stem glasses on the East side – the kind that make that special sound when you flick them with your fingernail. After all, I got your friend Denning to take off nearly forty dollars. We might as well spend my hard-earned profits. Wasn't it remarkable of me to get him down so far? Aren't you impressed?'

'I think I had something to do with that,' Angela said.

'Maybe a little.' A smile played at the edges of his mouth.

'More than a little' she said.

'What shall we have for our first feast on the table with the lions' feet? Since your mother was English, why don't we celebrate your English blood and the new table with roast beef and Yorkshire pudding?'

To her amazement she forgave him everything. She ditched Maurice, which was no hardship; she tried to steady her feelings. But within a month, she took a second lover, and this time she chose more carefully. Then she took another. Then another. Peter hardly seemed to notice.

'You make me so tired,' she said to him late one evening; Angela was one of those women who love a good fight.

They'd been working all day on one of her articles for the current issue of *Postscript*; they'd worked through dinner at a

197

small fish restaurant, and now – late at night – they were still at work, sitting at Maurice Denning's table with pages spread out in front of them. Drapes cut out any hint of the city beyond the windows; light from hanging lamps fell on the striped carpet in yellow pools much as light had fallen on the boulevard of Washington Avenue when Peter was eleven years old. One of these pools came from the lamp over the table; Angela worked sideways to keep out of the way of her own shadow, which floated half on the table and half on the floor.

'There's just this one paragraph left that I do not feel entirely happy about,' he said, not looking up. 'It has a tentative feel I think we ought to eradicate. Right here where you say – '

'I want to know about – what's her name? your latest?'

' – that you think – '

'I want to hear about this girl of yours.'

'No you don't,' he said. He drew a line through a sentence of the manuscript. 'Maybe if we cut this phrase and – '

'She's only a secretary. She doesn't *do* anything.'

' – and go straight to the – '

'How can you be interested in such a person?'

'Come on, Angela. It's late. Let's get this done first.'

'What's her name? Tell me. Come on.'

At dinner that evening he'd ordered Finnan Haddie, which didn't appear on the menu often; it's a dull, flabby fish. He'd ordered it only because the charm of its name so beguiled him; he'd ordered it a month before for the same reason, unable then as now to remember that so charming a sound could be associated with so undistinguished a taste.

'Ariadne,' he said to Angela, and to her despair she could hear that the sound of this name pleased him in just the same way. '*Ariadne auf Naxos*. That's what her father calls her. Her real name is even – '

'I don't want to hear about it.'

198

Peter looked quickly at her and as always, her heart – the whole of her body – constricted at his glance. 'I thought you did,' he said.

Angela swung out of her chair and walked over to the fireplace; she reached out, stroked a finger down the back of the pert bull, then clutched him in her hand. 'Why do you torture me this way?'

'Do we really have to go through one of these scenes tonight? Whatever is the matter this time, it can't be that little bull's fault.'

'You can't play the innocent bystander all your life, Peter.'

Peter reached up and tapped the lamp that hung over the table. It swayed back and forth, and the yellow pools on the floor shifted and changed.

'Say something, damn you,' Angela cried.

He bent over the pages again. 'What do you want me to say?'

'Tell me why you chase after these girls.'

'I never chase after girls.'

'Tell me.'

Peter studied the wall beyond the table. 'I think I'm – what's the right word? – perhaps curious,' he said.

He probably thought this habit of looking away from anybody he talked to gave him a Byronic air – that it hinted at thoughts too deep for ordinary mortals. Whatever he thought, he knew it maddened Angela. Which is to say, it was a good trick, and there were few things Peter loved more than a trick that worked.

'Curious!' she cried. 'My God, whatever can that mean?'

'I'd like to know – ' He frowned, picked up his pencil and deleted a phrase from the manuscript.

'Go on! Go on! What do you want to know?'

'Perhaps if I spend time with somebody else, I just might

199

come to see why you are so important to me. Maybe I can isolate the critical element and make some sense of it.'

What was poor Angela to do? What he gave with one hand he took away with the other. 'You're a little boy pulling wings off flies – and I'm one of the flies.'

'That's not fair,' he said, nettled at last. 'I don't want to hurt anybody, least of all you. I'd do anything I could to prevent your getting hurt. I'm not bloodless like that – and you know it – or bloodthirsty.'

'You're just selfish.'

'Look, Angela, don't you think this is getting a little out of hand? I don't know what you have in mind, but if there's something you want to say, why not just say it?'

'I want a child.'

He glanced at her quickly, then turned his face back to the wall.

'Peter?'

He turned farther away from her.

'Answer me, damn you,' she said. 'Say something.'

'What do you want to talk about this now for?'

'I want *your* baby. I want your child – and your family. I want the experience of childbirth. I want to know what it's like.'

'I'm only twenty-five,' he said, and that look of bafflement crossed his forehead.

'I'm thirty. I can't wait much longer.'

He shivered. 'The idea of being somebody's father. It sounds so' – for once he seemed entirely at a loss – 'so *old*. I hate that.' He bent over the table once more and inserted a word into the page in front of him. His dark hair fell over his forehead, and when he spoke again, his voice had that dreamy tone she feared above all.

'You do have, let us say, a capacity for entangling yourself, your thoughts and your audience. These things go by seasons

200

in you, and this particular season is one I've come to know too well.' He glanced at her again: 'Every time you find yourself a new guy to go to bed with, you seem to find yourself doing battle with what you describe, variously and ingenuously, as my shortcomings. This is as intriguing as it is cruel, but it's way too late at night for either intrigue or cruelty. We still have work to do.'

Pity poor Angela. Her emotions, never well controlled, slid from explosion to implosion and back again. She gripped the back of the chair. 'I bet you can't have children anyway,' she cried.

Pity poor Angela. It was outrage speaking, and outrage makes everybody stupid. When she thought about it later, she was painfully – agonizingly – aware of the illogic of her position, and of the trap she'd fallen into. Even at the time she could have torn out her own tongue, because she could hear the fresh sea breeze of relief sweep across him.

'You are doubtless right,' he said. 'Which more or less puts an end to this conversation, doesn't it?'

'You don't love me.'

'Oh, Angela, haven't you had enough for one night?'

'You want to know who this new guy is?'

'Not particularly.'

'It's Christie. Your uncle Christie. He loves me. He wants to marry me, and he wants children as much as I do. One baby isn't enough. I want three or four. So does he. I love kids. I'm going to take him up on his offer – start to finish.'

Peter had not cried since the shock of his twelfth birthday. If you hold your breath, say the magic words and never – never, never – let on what you're thinking, you can ward off the evils at the bottom of the garden. But the evils had not come so close since the fateful birthday. I happen to know for a fact (although I won't admit it in public, no matter how many times you ask me) that a tear rolled down his cheek even though he said the magic words, not once but over and over; and he held his breath as tight as he could. Fortunately for him, he kept his face turned away from Angela, and so it was that the most important criterion — secrecy — prevailed. But the cost for her was terrible. The moment passed, and she never knew how much he loved her.

'Lucky Angela,' he said, turning to face her at last. 'Mrs Christian Nation Kittyhawk Kessler. What a glorious name you're going to carry around with you.'

iii

As for Christie, he was not wholly innocent in all this. He'd wanted Angela ever since he'd heard her laugh over the telephone at the height of the McCarthy threat. But he knew how to wait for what he wanted, a rare quality. He knew how to avoid detours too. Look at the temptations he'd resisted to become a family doctor in Overton: he could have gone anywhere in medicine — done anything — but he didn't. He wanted a family practice, and a family practice is precisely what he'd secured for himself. Then he wanted Angela. The only complication was his nephew Peter, whom he loved and to whom he owed so much. Because of Peter, he held back. Because of Peter, he waited.

And yet the irony of it is that the affair gelled only because Peter sent Angela to him.

Christie had come out of the army within weeks of the Senate hearings — a quick, quiet discharge — and returned to the Kessler family practice in Overton. A year or so passed. He became consultant to Overton's Board of Public Health; Boards of Public Health have far more power over the welfare of a town's citizenry than any one doctor or, for that matter, all doctors put together. Christie knew this (all doctors do). It was only natural that he give some of his time to such a body: just

202

as it was only natural for Peter to call him in as a consultant for *Postscript*'s fluoride story, which was basically a public-health story: just as it was only natural for Peter to assign the story – a headliner in its day and very controversial – to *Postscript*'s best reporter, Angela Leslie.

Christie agreed to meet her in the Kessler Medical Group offices, across the street from the newly opened Memorial Hospital. An apple tree bloomed outside the building, petals dropping down, blowing everywhere, an inch deep on the pavement. All his life Christie remembered that first view of her outside the building – he knew her at once even though he'd never seen so much as a photograph of her – a Primavera of a woman walking in the sunshine with apple blossoms aswirl around her ankles.

He played at reluctance. It didn't come readily either; he had that tomcat's ease with his body – that way of moving some men have, as though their skin feels good to them. But he played his part well. There wasn't a hint of flirtation during the three hours he spent with her in his office. And yet Angela saw the passion in him; she just assumed – with some justice too – that it was passion for medicine alone: these were the great days of the profession.

These were the days of discovery, of enlightenment, of hope. Dutch Hashman once said, waxing lyrical as he sometimes did, 'These were the days when the blue of the night met the gold of the dawn.' Sentimental perhaps (inaccurately quoted too), but deeply felt – and not only by such as Christie and him. Practically every day some new horizon opened up in surgery, technology, public health, pharmacology. It looked as though the secrets were just standing up and volunteering to confess, one by one. The wolves – the bureaucrats and the money-makers – were still weak, still only shadows. It was exhilarating to breathe the air, and Christie had good, big lungs.

But a month after Angela got back to New York, Peter's

mother called with the news that Christie was dead. He'd gone off on that strange yearly disappearance of his, telling the Kesslers somewhat more than he usually did – a river in Canada, he'd said – and two weeks later, an empty, battered canoe had fetched up on a Canadian riverbank; a credit card, wedged beneath the seat, bore the name of Christian N. K. Kessler. No body. The authorities held out little hope: the rapids were fierce; the mountain lions hungry. Peter flew to Canada to find out what he could; from there he'd fly to the Middle West.

Less than two hours after Angela returned from taking Peter to the airport, she got a telephone call. 'This is Christie Kessler,' the voice said. 'I'd like to take you out to dinner tonight. Is that possible?'

'You're supposed to be dead,' she cried, shocked – titillated really – by the oddness of it and surprised, too, at how delighted she was to find him still alive.

'I have a melodramatic streak,' he said.

'You sure as hell have. Where have you been all this time?'

'I had things to do,' he said, just as he'd said years before to the old Kesslers.

'Things to do?' She laughed, shocked again. 'What things?'

'I love to hear you laugh. You will have dinner with me tonight, won't you?'

'Shouldn't you be in Overton?'

'Not yet.'

'What do you mean, "not yet"?' He didn't reply at once and she said uncertainly, 'They do know you're all right, don't they?'

'Not yet.'

'Christie – '

'It's not easy to explain,' he interrupted. 'I'd rather take you out to dinner first.'

New York was hot the way it often is in the summer, a bread-oven that's fired during the day and smoulders during the night; in the 1950s, in summer, you woke with swollen feet and a hangover whether you'd gone to bed drunk or not. Christie took Angela to a bistro in the Village: prosciutto, cannelloni and a bottle of wine. They sat in a hot breeze that blew between open doors to the east and west, both of them asweat. Candles guttered on the table. Christie ordered a second bottle.

'How beautiful red wine is,' he said, looking not at the wine but at her. 'No wonder Christ chose it for his blood.' He touched her glass with his. Their fingers brushed. No more.

He had bruises on his face and a bandaged hand, but he evaded questions about them. He evaded questions about the Kesslers too. She was puzzled. She was profoundly flattered. She liked the dimple in his chin. She took him back to Peter's apartment, but to her consternation, she got no more response out of him this time than she had during their first meeting in Overton, when his reticence so pleased her.

'How did the Kesslers take it?' she said as he shook her hand at the door, formally, like a Swiss diplomat.

'Take what?'

'News of your miraculous resurrection,' she said with a touch of Kessler-like impatience.

'I haven't called them.'

She gasped. 'That's hardly fair.'

'What has fair got to do with it?'

'I thought doctors swore not to cause unnecessary pain.'

He shook his head and was crestfallen.

'I'm sorry,' she said (and she was). 'Why don't you come to lunch tomorrow?'

He accepted at once.

He arrived with two dozen red roses; she put them in water and stuck them on Peter's mantelpiece, amusing herself with the thought of how Peter would hate them there. She cooked for Christie herself, and they talked easily throughout the afternoon, separated by a slate coffee-table — a long oval shape and a cold surface — while the sky darkened and rumbles of thunder began. Towards evening, in the middle of a discussion of something else, she said, 'Won't you tell me what happened?'

He kept his eyes on her, which can be somewhat disconcerting when you're used to a man like Peter who stares away from you all the time. 'I'm afraid to,' he said.

'Are you? Really? Of telling me?'

'You most of all.'

'I have a lower-middle-class soul and a prosaic nature to go with it,' she said smiling. 'I crave the melodrama you promise. Also I want to know why you keep this secret to yourself.'

He looked away, looked up again. 'My father — ' he began, then stopped short.

'He must be frantic, poor bastard.'

'I don't mean the Kesslers.'

'Your real father's dead, isn't he?'

'Yes,' he whispered. 'Yes, you're right about that.' Pain appeared so suddenly on his face — and was so raw in this Neverland world of Peter's — that she reached out to cover it just for decency's sake, but drew back across the slate coffee-table without touching him. He seemed not to notice. 'Yes,' he said again. 'I buried him three days ago.'

A statuette of African children stood on this table and gawped at the pert little bull, whose present job was to keep them at bay. Peter liked setting new tasks for the knick-knacks in his apartment; on this evening, the Chinese monkey sat on the mantelpiece and stared at Christie's two dozen roses, aghast (in Peter's stead) at their vulgarity.

'Tell me,' she said.

He took out a package of cigarettes, extracted one, lit it, drew on it. 'I got a letter — this was years after I went to live with the Kesslers — from the Air Force, a Veterans' Committee or some damn thing. They said my father was in an institution

206

in Connecticut. I was stunned – just a stupid kid – seventeen or something, wrapped up in myself the way kids are. All I could think was, he's been alive all these years and he's never come to see me. How could he do that? I set off an hour after I got the letter.'

'For Connecticut?'

He nodded. 'I thumbed my way. It was a big hospital, grass, lawn, trees. I was all the way inside before I realized it was a loony bin. Dreary halls, mile after mile of them. Bad lighting. Hospitals haven't changed much. Dreary room. Metal bedstead.' He rolled his cigarette between his fingers and lifted it to his mouth but took it away again without drawing on it. 'Everybody over twenty looks ancient to a seventeen-year-old, but this guy! Toothless, pouchy, fat in a shapeless kind of way.'

A splatter of rain hit the window followed by a gust of wind. 'He couldn't have been much older than you are now, could he?' she said. 'What was the matter with him?'

He shrugged. 'Psychiatry is a base craft. They took out his teeth when teeth were supposed to cause madness. They took out yards of intestine when auto-intoxication was the rage. They took out a kidney – God knows why. When they weren't scooping out organs, they did the usual drugging and shocking – amphetamines, cocaine, insulin, electricity. Jesus, what barbarians we are.'

He stubbed out the cigarette, not yet half-smoked, and lit another. Angela got up to shut the window; the rain started at once, as though she'd cued it, an abrupt slap against the glass, and that smell of dust and vomit that always rises from the streets when the city has one of its tropical rains.

'One day he just woke up,' Christie said.

'One of these things worked?'

He laughed. 'God, no. They left him alone for a while. Can you imagine it? To go to sleep a young man – pilot, hero, handsome, dashing – and wake up a battered old geezer. I felt responsible. I don't know why. Maybe just because he was mine. He had a small pension and no real grasp of what he could do with it, so I took him for a vacation in the mountains. I like mountains. He seemed to get a modest kind of a kick out of it — but most of the time — '

He picked up the bull from the table that separated them. 'The Kesslers: they're like — Is it dragonflies I mean? those beautiful winged things? the red and blue ones that walk on water? Or is it only skeeters that walk on water? The Kesslers wouldn't like being compared to skeeters.' He looked down at the bull in his fingers, its ears upright, its gaze clear. 'Nothing hurts them. How could it? Nothing touches them. I wish with all my heart I were like them. But my father's situation — oh, no. It was too real. Even at seventeen I knew that. Better to cause them a little distress of the sort they can deal with and keep them out of a situation they couldn't deal with at all.'

The rain gusted outside, heavy, then light, then heavy again. 'Preparing for a funeral doesn't sound to me like all that much fun,' she said.

'I know. And I'm sorry. Really sorry. But they're good at funerals. All the best families are.' He put the bull down on the table, took out another cigarette but saw that one still burned in the ashtray in front of him; he sighed and put the fresh one back.

'Is this why you've never married? Because of this?' she said.

'The hospital wrote me last June — about the time I saw you in Overton. A malignancy — that one kidney he had left. Morphine couldn't hold the pain. He was months from dying.' Christie shrugged helplessly. 'I hate pain.'

'My God,' she said. 'Are you telling me you killed your own — ?'

'Don't ask,' he interrupted. 'If you don't ask, I don't have to tell you. I'll know soon if there are going to be any consequences. I don't think there will be.'

208

The sky darkened; rain thudded against the glass and ran down it in rivulets. 'What if you're wrong? What if there *are* consequences?' she said.

'I'll act accordingly.'

'And the Kesslers?'

'They'll purse their lips whatever I do, put it down to irresponsibility and defend me to the neighbours.'

She studied him a moment. Then she leaned back in her chair and laughed. 'Well, what the hell,' she said, 'why shouldn't patricide run in the best families along with a gift for funerals? It sounds like a natural coupling to me.'

Now, I ask you, whatever could have provoked her to stay a thing like that? She must have made it up on the spot. Why else would she say it? She had many faults, but she was remarkably prescient sometimes.

'You know, Angela,' Christie said, 'I could get kind of sentimental about you.'

'Sentimental? Really? Could you? Go ahead.'

He rose, threaded his way around the table, leaned down and kissed her.

'Well, well, what d'you know?' she said, smiling up at him. 'So that's what you had in mind, is it?'

iv

They were married in Overton, an old-fashioned wedding: white veil, banks of flowers, tiered cake, local dignitaries – everything the bride of the 1950s could desire and everything Christie's first glimpse of Angela had promised. She got pregnant at once and was jubilant. She put Peter aside. She really did. The baby was born, a girl they named Mollie, and for almost two years mother and child bloomed together just as the books say mother and child should bloom.

But the pity of it is that nothing lasts, not a single, solitary thing. One morning Angela awoke to see that Mollie drooled, was fractious, whined, like any other baby. In that same moment of revelation, she saw that her hygienic suburban house on the edge of Lake Overton was indistinguishable from its neighbours and that the dinner-parties she and Christie hosted were parties where provincial burghers rubbed elbows over titbits of provincial chit-chat. Boring, boring, boring. Everything in this life she'd chosen was of a piece with Overton's wasteland stretches of supermarket and its drab, flat criss-cross of streets.

The baby's third birthday came and went. Christie, knowing Angela was not happy, suggested she talk to an obstetrician about her failure to conceive a second time. They'd both set their hearts on that large family; they'd talked about it again and again. They'd laughed and joked. Four children. No, five. Why not six? ten? an even dozen? The time had come, he said, to get some professional help. But since that morning of revelation, Angela had been working to her own agenda. She'd started writing again. Maybe she still laughed and joked about big families, but there were not going to be any more babies. Not if she had anything to do with it. She'd gone secretly on the pill.

Deception on this scale requires much concentration and much energy; it bleeds a life. The fights with Christie that had once stemmed from such erotic excitements as finance and jealousy and had once ended in glorious reunions on the dining-table or the floor or against the wall or anywhere more or less supportive and nearby, grew bitter and trivial: whether or not to buy a toaster and how much to fill the ice-tray. During the couplings that followed, Angela found herself thinking not of her own pleasure or of Christie's muscular body but of Peter and Neverland, the smell of sandalwood, the hookah, the Persian candlesticks, the Chinese monkey, even the pert little bull.

One morning, just before Mollie's fifth birthday, Angela telephoned New York.

'I can't stand it any more,' she said to Peter. 'I'm coming back.'

He was astounded. 'Is that really what you mean to say? Your letters make life in Overton sound so enviable.'

She steeled herself for what she'd decided was to come next. 'I'm not getting out of it what I went into it for.'

'I don't know what that means.'

'It's a little delicate –'

'Don't tell me anything you don't want to,' he interrupted in alarm.

She ploughed ahead. 'I'm not cut out to spend my life in a backwater like this for one child. Two children maybe. But not one. Sterility seems to run in Kessler males, doesn't it?' She paused, waiting for some protest (she had various responses prepared), but he said nothing. 'Anyhow, I'm thirty-five. It's getting late for me and God knows it's even later for Christie – which may well be the sum of the trouble. I should be able to support Mollie fairly easily by myself. I've done quite a lot of freelancing in the last year or two.' She paused again, and again he said nothing. 'Peter? Are you still there?'

'My uncle Christie is a paragon among men. You're his life and blood and marrow.'

'You don't want me to come.' She paused yet once more, and yet once more he said nothing.

Through the open window beside the telephone-table, the sounds from across Overton Lake had that hollow quality every suburban child knows: a lawn-mower in the distance, a dog barking. New York's Sunday sounds are so different. In the lull she was sure she could hear them – almost anyway – down the telephone line: hum of the highway, tinkle of music from across a courtyard, burst of shooting, siren.

'Don't let me flounder like this, damn you,' she cried. 'If you don't want to help me, just say so. I'll find somebody else.'

'I was looking for a road map last night,' Peter said, 'and my search led me into a whole pile of things, old letters, drafts of old articles – some that got written, some that didn't – several of your pieces that we worked on together, a couple of mine that could have used your help, one or two that got it, very much to their improvement. I found the notes of that musical comedy we were once going to do. Do you remember it? I've been thinking ever since that I might like to make another attempt at pulling that material into shape.'

It was the softness in his voice, not his words (Peter so rarely said anything straight out), that told Angela she had succeeded in what she'd set out to do.

A week later she was unpacking her bags in his apartment in New York. When everything was put away, she watched him cut out strings of stars from folded-up paper while Mollie laid them out; they were making a fairy village on the boldly striped carpet. It was late, one of those hot summer nights that were so often so important to Angela's life.

'Doesn't your mommy want you to go home?' Mollie asked, frightened for Peter and for the game they were playing. She'd never seen a child quite so big as he was, but she never doubted for a moment that he was a child.

'No,' he said, his face grave. 'She knows where I am.'

'It's going to be hell finding some kids for her to play with,' Angela said.

'I've already taken care of that,' he said.

'Who?' said Mollie, jumping up. 'Who? Where are they?'

Sometimes Peter understood things almost at once, as though he himself had been their architect even though he'd never encountered them before. Sometimes he was so slow that it seemed like wilful misunderstanding. This time he was slow: he didn't see that Angela had come to New York for him.

212

He'd been so afraid she'd be unhappy – having only the one child, when she'd wanted many – that he'd spent hours searching for others to fill the breach.

He laughed, as delighted as Mollie at what he'd achieved. 'I've uncovered a small social circle that operates in this very building,' he said. 'It's led by a lady of six who – I questioned her carefully – said she wouldn't mind introducing a girl of five to her friends if it were clearly understood that at five nobody knows anything.'

He'd bought smoked salmon, capers, bread, pickled herring, a bottle of champagne, strawberries. The three of them sat on the floor with the windows open and New York's night sounds filtering through. They ate off delicate white plates. Mollie fell asleep in his lap.

Towards the back of this apartment there were two small rooms that he used as an office; both had beds. Angela put Mollie to sleep in one of them, helped Peter with the dishes, and retired to the other herself. But she tossed and turned. She kicked off the sheets and dozed fitfully, dreaming of Peter's hands and the curve of his neck. She got up for a glass of water and for the feel of the cool kitchen linoleum on her feet. It was near morning; the sky was twilight already.

'What harm would it do?' she thought. 'I'll just watch him sleep – no more – just for a few minutes.'

But, oh, dear, a sleeping man is a beautiful thing, especially a man illuminated by the first light of dawn and stripped so he can sleep in the heat. If you look closely you can sometimes see a tremor move along a single muscle in his arm or his back, a nervous tension alive there, a hint of prospective danger of volatile temperament, like the flick of a cat's tail; and yet a man's so vulnerable in this exposed state, so open to attack, his trust in you and in the world so childlike and so wholly unjustified. Sometimes when Peter slept, Alice, Angela's second daughter, would watch him and wonder if anybody so beautiful could be real; and by the time she watched him, he was a middle-aged man.

When Angela watched him, he was only a little past thirty, a very young thirty, smooth-skinned, black hair curling over his forehead. The gentle rise and fall of his chest caught at her so painfully that she thought, 'What harm can it do? He won't wake.' So she crept onto the bed beside him just to feel the length of his naked body – no more than that – along the naked length of hers. Just for a few minutes. No more.

Thereafter she slept in his canopied bed, and six weeks later – the devil having come to collect his due – she wept as she bent over the toilet-bowl in the tiled bathroom. The floor was a mosaic of an old Roman design, rich, angular, clean.

'Are you crying?' Peter called in to her from the bedroom. It was early, not yet six o'clock.

'Leave me alone.'

'You *are* crying.'

'I'm sick.'

He got up from the bed and went into the bathroom. She was looking down into the bubbled sputum in the toilet-basin where tears dropped too. And this was one of the times he was so quick to understand that you'd have sworn he'd known from the very outset. Perhaps he did. Or perhaps he thought he did. But how could he? How could anybody but Angela have known?

'You came here at just the wrong time, didn't you?' he said.

'What do you know about it?'

'I know you're pregnant.'

It never crossed his mind that he himself might be responsible. He'd believed Angela's charge of sterility. It's true that when she made it, he believed it largely because it got him out of thinking about something he didn't want to think about. But he went on believing it, perhaps just because he was used to it or because he didn't much care one way or the other or

214

because nothing happened to change his view. Besides, on that morning, while Angela fought her nausea and her tears, he was so preoccupied with making sure she couldn't see how much of a shock it was to him to lose her a second time – and to the same man – that he didn't notice how deep and how destructive her own upset was.

'What are you crying for?' he said. 'This is exactly what you want, exactly what you've always wanted.' But he was afraid his voice would betray him if he said any more, so he kneeled beside her and leaned his head on her shoulder. 'Please don't cry,' he whispered. 'There's a good Wendy.'

She jerked away from him. 'Who is this Wendy? My name isn't Wendy. You've never called me Wendy in my life.'

He pulled her back. He patted her hair. 'I know,' he said, taking in a ragged breath, 'but I've always wanted to. Don't cry. I'll call Christie for you. No matter how it might seem to you, this is going to be a happiness for him beyond anything he's dreamed of. He's a wonderfully understanding fellow.'

Angela made the telephone call herself.

'How can I bear to think of your hands?' she wrote to Peter, a month or so after she'd returned to Overton, when her rage at him had died down a little – after all, this time even she had to admit that he was the innocent party in the affair – and her heart seemed so barren in her chest that she was half afraid she would die of it.

'Slender hands, long, thin fingers, dry skin: dear, dry-skinned hands. Why should dry-skinned hands be so dear?'

Christie Kessler had short, thick fingers. Mollie had short, thick fingers. Angela's were thinner but they were short too. Alice is different. She has long, thin fingers – long, slender hands. The skin is always dry.

Part Four

CHAPTER 15

i

What are you supposed to do when you find flaws in perfection? Think for yourself? Dear God, surely not. There's nothing less agreeable and less rewarding. What Alice had done, finding flaws in Peter – in this man with whom she was obsessed – well, she shut her eyes and held her breath. A good working solution, all in all, and one that serves most of us most of the time. But sometimes the spell won't hold. Sometimes circumstances get in the way. So it was with Alice, who had to grow up, a little late and way too quick, over the course of a single week-long stretch.

It began on Monday morning, a week after Tad arrived: Peter stopped eating. In England, Dr Edgecombe had said, 'When he stops eating, you've lost him.' Back went the drip. Back went the catheter, despite the risk of infection.

'Oh, Tad, you promised a solution,' Peter said wretchedly to the little boy, who stood helpless beside the bed, shifting from foot to foot, unable to bear what he saw in front of him, unable to look away, and until this moment of revelation filled with that queer faith in his own powers that only children feel – never to feel again once it's taken away.

'It isn't Parkinson's,' Charlie said, reporting the neurologist's findings to Alice in the afternoon of that same day. 'There's no drug response. None at all. It's hard to know what to make of him. His heart's all right. Lungs are all right. Kidneys okay. No disease anywhere. If he were ten or fifteen years older, I'd say it was age. As it is – '

'Do people sometimes just give up?' she said. 'Just like that? like a South Sea Islands curse? not even aware that they're doing it?'

'Not exactly a scientific diagnosis.'

'Do they though? Can something like that happen?'

Charlie's face didn't move. 'I have to leave tomorrow for a conference in Chicago,' he said. 'We can talk about it when I get back on Friday. You do know, don't you, Mrs Kessler,' he went on, 'that Dr Kessler's just been admitted?'

'Pop?' she said stupidly. 'Here? Why?'

'I think you'll find him in intensive care.'

Christie had been to visit Peter that very morning. He came every day, sometimes twice a day because sometimes he forgot he'd come in the morning and so came in the afternoon to make up for it. Sometimes he brought Tad with him – nurses from the Kessler Medical Group looked after the boy during the long hours Alice spent at the hospital – but usually he came alone. He never stayed long, and Alice always missed him when he wasn't there: he was a warming presence – a smell of mulled wine at Christmas – especially in the emotionally drained atmosphere of the psychiatric ward.

Intensive care was on the sixth floor. The charge nurse directed Alice to one of several open-ended glass cubicles, but what lay on the bed was no longer an emissary from the festive world beyond the hospital walls. Christie's face was swollen into a queer, flat soup-plate of a face, pottery-grey in colour. Inflatable cocoons tended his legs. Bottles of various vital fluids dangled from scaffolding beside him. Sleek black tubing and sleek black wires led back and forth between him and the plenipotentiaries that monitored him, regulated him, kick-started him now and again and danced out their findings in oscillations on a wallful of screens behind his head.

Alice found herself thinking: Who is this person? I've never seen him before. Is it a person at all? How can it be that I – who am so alive – bear any relation to so amorphous a husk? She reached out to touch his hand but drew back at once, her mind lurching sideways to the shapeless white dog that had licked Ahab's blood from the carpet. Cordelia had cremated Ahab in the hospital crematorium that also served the local vets; the shapeless white dog was king of the laundry-room now. But what of the other dogs? what of the dogs that had sniffed, eyed, circled: fascinated, afraid, agog? What's better about that? At least the white dog got involved. She reached out again and this time took Christie's hand in hers.

Over the next few hours he began to rally; but Alice needed him right away, the very next morning, and nothing short of a miracle could have healed him by that time. Besides, he was an old, old man, and healing wasn't really on the agenda any more, miraculous or otherwise.

ii

On the morning of the next day, Tuesday, she entered the psychiatric ward as usual and saw Charlie walking on ahead of her.

'Charlie!' she called.

He didn't turn around, so she ran after him.

'Charlie,' she said, abreast of him now, 'didn't you say you were going to a conference in Chicago?'

'I beg your pardon,' he said, detaching himself from her. 'Do I know you?'

'Of course you know me. You've dyed your hair.' But peering into his face she saw that this person might not be Charlie after all. His face had the same waxy smoothness; his teeth, the same machine-tool precision; his nose, the same regularity: but something was different. The voice was higher. The head was – well, wasn't it? – somewhat rounder. Maybe he was a bit taller too.

'I'm so sorry,' she said, tentative now. 'I thought you were Dr Peterson. You look remarkably like him.'

'Dr Peterson isn't back until Friday. I'm his partner, Dr McCorkhill. Nobody's remarked on a resemblance before. You are . . .'

'Alice Kessler. I'm surprised nobody's said how alike you are.'

'Ah, yes, Mrs Kessler. I've examined Mr Kessler. I don't really know what he's doing here in Psychiatry. His problems are basically physiological. I've arranged for a transfer to Cardiology.'

You see? What time was this for Christie to take to his bed? You stave off disaster by one wild trick, then by another, propping up this unproppable part, then that. Then suddenly – bang! – the whole structure lurches downhill at once.

'You can't do that,' Alice cried.

'I just have.'

'I don't want him moved.'

'It is perfectly clear from his records that he doesn't belong here.'

She looked down at Peter's watch on her wrist – he was no longer interested in time – and threw herself into battle. 'He doesn't belong in Cardiology either,' she said grimly. 'There's nothing wrong with his heart. Charlie said so.'

'It's the only bed available.'

'There's a bed available here. He's already in it. Have you talked to Dr Hashman about this?'

'Dr Hashman's gone.'

222

'Gone?' They must have waited for him to get out of the way, she thought suddenly. But who were 'they'? What did they want? 'Where did he go?' she demanded. 'How do you know he's gone?'

Dr McCorkhill's features registered a barely perceptible change. 'You mentioned the Chicago conference yourself. Dr Hashman delivers his paper today. It's a big day for him. Look, Mrs Kessler, there's a shortage of beds down here. There's a shortage of beds everywhere – '

'There are whole wards of beds without patients.'

'We can't open a whole ward for one patient. This bed came up in Cardiology and I grabbed it for Mr Kessler. You ought to be delighted. He's lucky to get it.'

'Where's Novali?'

'Why do you ask?'

'Have you talked to him?'

'He's getting married today.'

What came to mind was the Corn King; it had been hovering at the edge of too many of Alice's thoughts for some time now. She'd watched its construction once. That had been on her first visit to Overton, the time Peter's mother had shown her his baby pictures. Peter had taken her out to the field where the Committee were sorting the pieces; she hadn't really wanted to go. It was cold, and she hated the cold. She'd held herself irritably a little apart from Peter while he explained that by tradition, no maker of any one part of the effigy knew what the maker of any other part was doing, not even the hundreds whose contributions made up the torso and the thighs – not even the members of the Committee itself. The jumble that lay on the ground in that empty field was as chaotic as the contents of an upturned wastepaper basket.

Was it really possible, she thought, studying Dr McCorkhill in the psychiatric ward, that the disparate elements he had brought together were like that? was there a plan here, however

223

deeply buried? Could it be? or was she just adding paranoia to her troubles?

'Why can't we wait?' she said to him. She knew she was pleading and pleading, she knew, was weakness. She tried again. 'I insist we wait until tomorrow. I absolutely insist.'

'Mrs Kessler – ' Dr McCorkhill broke off, glanced up and down the hallway, then he drew her a few paces away form the bench where the waiting patients sat. He whispered into her ear. 'I'm not supposed to tell you this, but Psychiatry is closing down tomorrow. Some patients in here are getting shipped to Chicago, some to Minneapolis, some to' – his bland face shone in the neon from the ceiling – 'God knows where: the eastern seaboard, so the rumour goes. It's all done by regions. We had to move fast.' Was it true? Alice scanned the smooth cheeks. Why would he lie? Was it a trap? 'In fact, we've got less than an hour to spare,' he said. 'If Mr Kessler is in Cardiology he stays here in Overton. Otherwise, who knows?'

iii

What could she do? The transfer went ahead on schedule, and it was late afternoon on Wednesday that she got word she was to see Cardiology's social worker. She hadn't expected them to start closing in on her so soon; she really hadn't – not while she still felt scarred by that enforced retreat from the psychiatric ward. The nurses pointed her towards a disused linen-cupboard down the corridor which ran beyond their computer terminals and behind the great gondolas of revolving patient records. The door was ajar. Alice knocked on it, and to her surprise, the social worker turned out to be Mrs Carpenter.

'Oh, how good to see you again,' Alice said, and she meant it. Nobody could doubt the sincerity in that great bulk, whatever role it had to play in the devious patterns that governed Memorial Hospital. 'Have they moved you?'

'I'm one of the lucky ones.' Mrs Carpenter had a slow, melancholy smile; her lips retracted and those enormous tusk-like teeth rose up from them, then slid underground again. 'Oncology merged with Cardiology last week. You've been hiding, haven't you? Smart Mrs Kessler.'

'This place really is mad,' Alice said with a short laugh. 'How can you possibly merge Cardiology and Oncology?'

'I don't know. It's kind of sad to see Oncology all dark and deserted.' She sighed. 'Come in. Do sit down. I'm afraid it's very cramped in here – and no window. I did like my little window.' Alice squeezed herself into a chair beside the desk that Mrs Carpenter's blubbery body flowed around, engulfing it rather than sitting at it. 'Are you comfortable there? Oh, dear, there's hardly room for you, and you're so nice and thin.'

Then without even changing her tone, Mrs Carpenter added, 'I'm afraid hospice has rejected Mr Kessler.'

That fall years ago, in the field outside Overton, Peter had explained to Alice that the first job in building a Corn King was to lay out the pieces. Since the many contributors knew only the height of the figure – and since people are amazingly stupid when it comes to making sense of such information – the pieces were a wild disarray of shapes, sizes and materials. The laying-out process which Alice had watched took at least an hour. When it was finished, there was an evenness to the distribution on the ground, a sort of entropy, like flotsam on the sea after a ship has gone down; but as far as she could tell, coherence was as elusive as ever.

'If you're getting ready to throw Peter out,' she said to Mrs Carpenter, 'what does hospice have to do with it? I didn't know you had a hospice in Overton.'

'It's one of the places he might go when he leaves here – or might have gone. It's a pity they – '

225

'When you change wards you get extra days,' Alice interrupted. This had been the White Knight's parting shot to her.

'Of course you do. We've got a little leeway this – '

'You have to tell people who go to hospice that they're dying, don't you?' Alice interrupted again. Mrs Carpenter nodded. 'Peter couldn't take that. I know he couldn't.'

'Mrs Kessler, the simple fact of the matter is that he can't stay here. He's a care patient, and Cardiology hasn't the right kind of staff to handle care patients.'

'Who says Peter's a care patient?' Alice demanded, flinging herself into battle again. 'He hasn't even seen a doctor yet. What is a care patient anyhow?'

Mrs Carpenter smiled her melancholy smile again. 'I've tried all three facilities for him.'

'Three facilities?' Alice said. 'What three? I don't even know what "three facilities" means.' Mrs Carpenter looked at her blankly. 'Go on then. Tell me.'

'Tell you what?'

'Why they rejected him. I might as well know.'

Mrs Carpenter flipped through the papers on her desk. 'Rehabilitation said, well, essentially they said he isn't strong enough for rehabilitation. I've told you about hospice. And the Fourth Floor: they said he isn't sick enough for them.'

Even the Corn King's torso made more sense than this. The time Alice had watched, the Committee cemented together hundreds of chunks – paper, wood, cloth: anything that would burn – and strapped them into shape with iron rods and metal bands; what emerged was a huge, ramshackle barrel with stumps on one end – not very meaningful maybe, but at least *something* had taken shape on the ground.

'Too sick for Rehabilitation,' Alice said, 'wrong sick for Cardiology, not sick enough for the Fourth Floor, rejected by hospice. Am I supposed to understand this? What is this Fourth Floor?'

'You don't know about the Fourth Floor? Everybody knows about the Fourth Floor.'

'I don't know anything about anything.'

'It's one of Memorial's innovations. We're very proud of it. You're sure you don't know?' Alice shook her head. 'It's a special facility for people who are too sick for rehabilitation but not sick enough for hospice.'

'A special facility – I must be missing something,' Alice said. She tried again to concentrate. 'It sounds like a place set up precisely for the purpose of taking care of patients like Peter.'

Mrs Carpenter gnawed at the end of her pencil. 'Well, in fact, there's a slight gap between being too sick for Rehabilitation and not being quite sick enough for the Fourth Floor – a very slight gap – but it just so happens that Mr Kessler falls into it.'

'A gap?'

'Yes.'

'Too sick for the one, not sick enough for the other?'

'I'm afraid so.'

'So what am I supposed to do?'

'We're just going to have to locate a bed for him outside the hospital network.'

'I don't know what that means.'

'Mrs Kessler, you're going to have to find him a bed in a nursing-home.'

Alice shook her head. 'Forget the nursing-home,' she said. 'I'm sure there are other possibilities.'

iv

On Thursday morning Alice paced the cardiology ward hallways until Dr McCorkhill arrived on his rounds; she caught him as he emerged from the elevator.

'I knew this would happen,' she said angrily. 'The social

worker here says Peter's got to – ' She broke off. 'Charlie?' She peered into his face. 'Is it you?'

'Of course it's me.'

'I thought you might be – Weren't you supposed to be in Chicago until tomorrow? You and Dr McCorkhill are as alike as Tweedledee and Tweedledum. I can hardly tell you apart. How amazing.' She detected a flicker of annoyance in him. 'Cordelia tells me you got Schpiegal a bed in a small hospital,' she rushed on. 'Is this a place that might work for Peter? Could he go there from here?'

The annoyance died at once. 'I was going to propose it myself. It's an excellent facility – the best of the nursing-homes in Overton. I think you've made an excellent – '

'A nursing-home won't do,' Alice interrupted. 'So Schpiegal's in a nursing-home, is he?' She hadn't approved Cordelia's snuffling Ahab, either – nor had the vet.

'You know, Mrs Kessler, the last ten years have seen a lot of changes in the kind of care nursing-homes provide. Your prejudices are out of date. They keep their patients very, very clean. If a patient needs changing twenty-four times a day, they do it.'

In fact, now that she came to think of it, Charlie's no-face face reminded her a little of the Corn King's. The effigy's limbs, like the torso, were hodgepodge, but the head was different. It was the one piece made as a whole; and the Kesslers, who made it, had standards no one else in town even tried to reach. In that field, years ago, the neatly made head had floated beside the chaos of the body on the ground like God's face over the waters; Alice had watched the Committee attach it, and as she watched her feeling changed from irritation to dread. She'd taken Peter's arm in both of hers for reassurance, she'd held her body next to his, seeking out the completeness of him there beside her, the indestructibility of him, the harmony and certainty that were so very much a part of him.

228

'Oh, Charlie,' she cried suddenly desolate, 'why does dying have to be so terrible?'

'Who says anything about dying?' Charlie drew himself up. 'Mr Kessler's not dying. What gave you that idea?'

'Dutch said so,' she faltered.

'He's not sufficiently up on modern developments to render an opinion.'

'The English doctors said the same thing.'

'The training of English doctors is several years shorter than the training of American doctors. The fact is, people like your husband can live for years. Very little can sustain life. Four hundred calories is ample. That's why I prescribed it. Look at it this way. He's never going to run the marathon again, is he? But he'll be comfortable. With modern techniques, you can have your husband around for – oh, I don't know – maybe two years, maybe even three.'

'I don't want him put in a nursing-home,' she said doggedly. 'There must be some other solution.'

'We'll talk about it later.' Charlie started off down the corridor, then walked back to her. 'What would they do with a case like this in England?'

Alice didn't know. She didn't have any idea. 'They might be merciful enough to give him an overdose of something,' she said.

There was a sudden stillness in Charlie. 'Do you think that's right?' he said.

'If what you suggest is all that lies in front of him' – she shook her head wearily – 'I'd kill him myself if I knew how.'

v

On Friday, the last day of Alice's week of growing up, she had to pay for this bit of ill-considered thought.

She woke early with her mind made up. No bed in the

229

hospital proper. No bed in any of various hospital facilities. Nursing-homes out of the question. Where did that leave her? Simple: she'd take care of Peter herself. She'd done it before; she could do it again. She set about the task with her customary dispatch. By noon she'd put Tad on a plane for Switzerland. From the airport she went to the hospital, carrying with her details of electrical supply and storage space in Cordelia's apartment as well as a floor plan that showed where hospital bed and equipment would go. The nights were going to be tough; for that reason she half expected the hospital to resist her plan.

But the nurses at the desk were reassuring; several offered advice. Mrs Carpenter was delighted, enchanted. She promised help. She said the hospital would draw up a programme; she said there was a network of support; she brought glossy brochures out of her desk drawer. She was still talking when a call from Charlie came through.

'Taking Mr Kessler home is out of the question,' he said to Alice. 'I didn't really think you were serious yesterday.'

'Everybody else seems happy with the idea,' she said, wondering how he came to know about it all. 'I'm much stronger than I look, you know.'

'Now you listen to me, Mrs Kessler. The hospital has four shifts a day, two nurses a shift, and all of them together are hard pressed to manage your husband. It's more than you can handle alone – far more.'

'Nurses have other patients. When I get too tired, I'll bring him back.'

Charlie's voice went cold. 'Readmit him?'

'Of course.'

'It's illegal.' His voice was colder than before.

'Nonsense,' Alice laughed.

'I will not be a party to it.'

'It can't be illegal. What are hospitals for?'

230

'A hospital treats patients. It does not provide care. The two are entirely different.'

'Well, then,' said Alice, losing patience, 'all I'm proposing is to care for him at home. You can't really object to my giving it a try, can you? What is there to lose?'

'This is more than you can possibly take on. It's more than *anybody* can take on alone.'

Alice drew in her breath. 'I appreciate your concern, Charlie. Really I do. But as far as I'm concerned, I have no choice.'

Throughout the day she went on busily about her arrangements, but that night Cordelia was waiting for her when she got back from the hospital.

'You can't bring Peter here,' Cordelia said at once. 'This is my house.'

Alice set down the bag of groceries she was carrying on what used to be Cordelia's desk and now served as a dining-table. 'Of course it's your house. What are you talking about?' Alice opened the bag on the table and took out butter and eggs. Why had she bought more eggs? She had a dozen in the refrigerator, and she'd decided only a few days before that she had no longer liked eggs.

Cordelia held her hands clasped together across her chest; the little withered hand clutched at the healthy one for reassurance and support. 'I'm not getting involved in a court case.'

'Court case?' Alice said. 'What court case?'

'I've talked to Charlie.'

'Oh?'

'You told him you were going to kill Peter.'

Alice burst out laughing. 'Oh, Cordelia, don't be silly. Look, are you ever going to cough up some paper for the Corn King's hand?' The chicken-wire skeleton lay on the table beside the bag of groceries. Alice was pleased with it; huge as it was, it had an airy grace.

'I'm not here to discuss an effigy,' Cordelia said.

'We don't have to discuss it. I just need some of those old bills so I can finish it – that is, if you still want to use old bills. Can't you find me something out of all those piles?'

'Don't you try stonewalling me, Alice Kessler.' Cordelia's two hands sprang apart; the healthy one snatched at the withered one, trapped it, soothed it. 'I'd be an accessory.'

'To what? Are you still on about – '

'This conversation is quite enough. And there's the conversation with Charlie.'

'Look, Cordelia, Charlie wants to put Peter in Sunny Acres with Schpiegal, but I am not you and Peter is not Schpiegal. It's out of the question.'

'Charlie knows other good nursing-homes.'

'There is no such thing as a good nursing-home, certainly not for somebody as sick as Peter is. Besides, you said it was a hospital.'

'Schpiegal is very comfortable there. Charlie visits every day. He told me so.'

It was something in Cordelia's voice, almost more than the words, that caught Alice's attention. 'Haven't you visited him yourself?'

'I will not have murder in my house.' Cordelia's voice rose abruptly to a screech, and Alice thought of the seagulls that wheeled in the air above the ancient house in Devon when the tide was in. She sat down and reached out to the huge hand in the middle of the table.

'You flatter me,' Alice said.

'I don't think so.'

'Look, Cordelia, people often say things they don't mean when they're upset. It was just one of those' – Alice groped for a word that made some sense and finished lamely – 'foolish things.'

'I will not get myself involved in a court case. Even as the landlady. That's final.'

232

Alice got up from her chair. 'Suppose – Suppose I swear to you I won't – oh, this is so ridiculous –' When Cordelia said nothing Alice went on. 'Suppose I swear I won't murder him. Will that satisfy you? I swear to you as a friend that I won't murder him – or anybody else – on *your* property? Now let's get back to the Corn King's hand. When I've got Peter here, I'm not going to have time to work on it.'

Cordelia walked around the table and put her healthy arm on Alice's shoulders. 'Since we're doing this supposing, Allie,' she said, 'suppose you could have it any way you want.'

'I wouldn't be in Overton at all.'

'I know that. But you are in Overton. Suppose there were alternatives to taking care of Peter on your own.'

'There aren't.'

'Listen to me,' Cordelia said. 'If there were an alternative, something that would satisfy you, would bringing him here be your first choice?'

'I don't know. Probably.'

'Come on. Be honest with me – with yourself.'

'Oh, of course it wouldn't, Cordelia.' Alice sagged a little. 'I'd keep him in the hospital if I could. Obviously I would. That's what I've been trying to do, and I still don't really understand why I can't. It's going to be awful work. I don't know how long I'll last, either. I figure I might hold out two weeks if I'm lucky.'

'You don't want to do it at all.'

'Of course I don't. Who would willingly undertake such a thing?'

'Well, look at it this way, Allie. I'm the one who's keeping you from it. It's not your responsibility. You tried. You failed. Now you don't have to do it. Whatever happens now, you have nothing to reproach yourself with.' The trap was sprung and shut so quickly – Cordelia's shrewdness appearing with such unexpected force – that Alice wasn't even aware of it until her breath froze in her lungs. 'I'm giving you a way to excuse it to yourself,' Cordelia went on. 'Much easier for both of us, don't you think? Now I'll go and see if I can dig up a couple of bills so you can flesh out the Corn King's hand tomorrow morning. That's soon enough for you, isn't it?'

vi

After Cordelia left, the frozen feeling in Alice's chest only got worse. She took measured breaths in and out, in and out. She tried lying down; she tried brandy. There seemed to be some sort of Arctic waste inside her. She said to herself, 'I saw that trap of Cordelia's coming. Well, didn't I? Of course I did. Who could fail to have seen it? Is *this* why Judas hanged himself?'

Late as it was, she went back to the hospital and talked softly to Peter. He was too tired to listen. She read out loud. He turned his head away. By midnight, she was just sitting slumped beside the bed. What good is a vigil? Why do people do it? The collapse of hope is as obvious to the trained eye as heart failure. The night–nurse, a small round woman with pendulous lips, poked her head through the door.

'Do you knit?' she asked Alice.

Alice shook her head.

'Crochet?'

Alice shook her head again.

'What's that in your lap?'

Somewhat shamefacedly, Alice held up the book.

'Ah, crossword-puzzles,' the nurse said. 'Good. You need something at a time like this.'

Alice sat there beside Peter for an hour longer, trying to concentrate on the puzzles but swaying instead between betrayal and anxiety. It didn't make sense. It just didn't. There had to be some piece hidden somewhere, something critical, the Corn

234

King's heart perhaps or perhaps his liver, some part buried deep in the chaos of that torso.

There is terror in the workings of bureaucracy. All you have to do is think of the Corn King, strapped to a metal frame and winched upright. Alice would never forget her first sight of it as it rose from the ground: crooked, huge, hideous, skewed, inept, a Frankenstein's joke of a thing with that incongruous, tidy head on its shoulders. At the time, she knew she should have laughed at it as the aldermen who'd made it laughed – those myriad disconnected parts amalgamated into a grotesque whole for which no individual could possibly bear any responsibility – but what she'd felt instead was panic.

She'd thought back then, even all those years ago: this is the Beast of the Apocalypse. Burn it and it fertilizes the ground only to rise again next year, bigger, uglier, more incoherent. No wonder there was silence in heaven for the space of half an hour. Who could possibly battle a monster like this? Who would have even half a chance?

And so it was that murder first occurred to her as a viable alternative to whatever it was that the boneyard of Sunny Acres represented – and towards which she and Peter were being forced inch by inch.

Which is to say, this is the moment – this frozen culmination of this belated week of growing up – when Alice Kessler at long last realized that her illusions, all of them, had deserted her.

CHAPTER 16

i

Now I will be honest with you. If you take care of a man as sick as Peter — and you do it day in and day out, week after week, month after month — you are no stranger to thoughts of killing him. Love him or don't love him: it makes no difference to the fact of the thoughts, however much difference it might make to their frequency. Oddly enough, such thoughts come to be somewhat reassuring, pleasant almost, clean and orderly, certainly more agreeable than pretending you don't hear that tenth call for help in ten minutes. That's low-grade, that is, and it's your hourly fodder. Through it you watch yourself sink in your own esteem to depths you never dreamed anybody could sink — not anybody at all. This is the reality. Thoughts of murder are game-playing; you know perfectly well you're not going to do it.

So Alice sat there with her crossword puzzles on her lap, not playing the game for the first time. She was above all a rationalist. Peter always said so. She'd thought it was his joke (a funny way to characterize an obsessive), but you could never tell with Peter. The sequence of ideas in her head certainly seemed to support him.

The next Monday she waited for Mrs Carpenter with an anxiety she'd never known before; she demanded help in finding another place to live. Mrs Carpenter said that social workers in hospitals don't deal with housing; she called Overton's central Social Services Department. They couldn't help either. 'Your client will have to go to the private sector,' they told her. 'Tell her to try the Yellow Pages.'

Alice changed ten dollars into quarters and took over the telephone booth in the corridor. She called Felicity's friend, who had offered her an apartment out of town; the apartment was taken. The first estate agent she talked to said that Overton was too dull a town for tourist apartments. He was chatty, kind. With the Corn Scorch coming up, the season for long-term rentals was over, he said, and besides – no offence, he said – he didn't think he could in good conscience recommend tenants who lived abroad, especially if those tenants might be staying only a few months. The second agency told her much the same thing. In two hours she'd called every listing in the book. She bought the local newspapers; during the afternoon she tried all the numbers she found in them.

The next day she set off around town. She stopped at large apartment complexes to inquire. She looked for signs in windows and notices in supermarkets. Then she started on hotels and motels, but hotels and motels do not rent rooms to hospital cases. Only one small place was willing to bend the rules, a kitchenless stop-off in a sleazy neighbourhood. Alice took two rooms at once and called Mrs Carpenter in great excitement – only to find out that Memorial would not send its nursing staff or equipment to such a dangerous area.

Alice went in despair to see Felicity, but Felicity was outfitting the one extra room in the house for Christie, who was going to need full-time nursing himself for at least a month. Back at the hospital, Alice pestered nurses, doctors, porters, people who worked in the cafeteria and the gift shop – anybody

237

who would stop long enough to listen to her. She got another handful of quarters and began calling family friends, people who'd known Peter when he was small, people who knew Christie and the other Kesslers. She'd been on the telephone for over an hour without break when Mrs Carpenter sent for her and told her that the hospital did not feel she was making an effort to place Peter.

'Not making an effort!' Alice cried. 'What more do they want? I haven't done anything else for forty-eight hours.'

'Sit down, Mrs Kessler,' Mrs Carpenter said.

'I don't want to sit down. I want to find a place to live.'

'There are ways of doing these things, and – '

'I've tried everything I can think of. How can I take care of Peter if I can't find a place to do it in?'

'If you are seen to be doing things the right way, the hospital will take a more lenient view. In a hospital you must do things the hospital's way. Look at a few nursing-homes.'

'I'm not putting Peter in a nursing-home. I don't think he could bear it. I don't know that I could bear it either.'

'All you've got to do is look. The hospital will see you're co-operating, and meantime – '

Alice studied those magnificent tusks of teeth, and she had to admit that Mrs Carpenter had a point. After all, if she was exploring all the options, she had to explore them. She nodded.

' – and meantime, I'll contact Memorial's Fourth Floor again.'

'The Fourth Floor.' Alice sat down abruptly. 'I don't see – What do you mean? They rejected him.'

'That was days ago.' Mrs Carpenter riffled through the papers on her desk. 'His condition has deteriorated markedly since then. Anybody can see that. It's time for a second assessment.'

'Why didn't you say so?' The weight lifted off Alice so suddenly that she felt giddy. 'I didn't know he'd get a second chance.'

238

'But I'll do it only on the condition that you go and look at nursing-homes.'

So after lunch Alice set out to visit Schpiegal Macher–Daly at Happy Acres.

Happy Acres stood half-way down a tree-shaded street about a mile or so from the hospital complex. It wasn't a bad-looking building, ochre-coloured brick, purpose-built, no frills but well kept with a small sward of lawn in front of it and a plaque that said:

* * * * * * * * * *
Happy Acres
Residential Home
Nursing-Home
* * * * * * * * * *

Glass double-doors opened into a large, motel-like anteroom and a smell of canned succotash; three old women faded into the patterns of the easy chairs they sat in. The floor was carpeted, and the plastic trim on the walls was in good repair. Pastel seascapes hung slightly askew on stucco walls. Alice could see a dining-room beyond, darkened for the foodless stretch of the American afternoon. To one side she found a door that said:

RECEPTION
Please Enter

She turned the knob. Inside was a desk, a display of framed certificates and a minuscule sign that Alice peered down to read:

Please ring and be seated

She rang and turned to study the certificates. Happy Acres was licensed by the state to run a nursing-home; it was licensed to accept Medicare patients; Morris Morris Darby, MD, was licensed to practise medicine.

The door behind the desk opened and a young man appeared. He had a face almost as bland as Charlie's and Dr McCorkhill's, but he was young; so far only his teeth had been restructured. Alice figured that with a chin implant and a year of weight training, he'd be virtually indistinguishable from the other two. 'Good afternoon, ma'am,' he said.

'I've come to visit a patient called Schpiegal Macher-Daly,' Alice said.

'May I ask you who gave you this information?'

'What information?'

'We cannot give out information to unauthorized persons.'

'I don't want any information,' Alice said. 'I want to see Schpiegal Macher-Daly.'

'Who told you he was a guest here?'

'He's not a guest. He's a patient.'

The boy pursed his lips. 'Do you perhaps mean that he is a Medicare guest?' he said.

'I don't know. I suppose so. *Is* that what I mean?'

'He's just settling in. Why don't you give me a message? I will take it to him myself.'

'He's been here over a week.' Alice was puzzled. Resistance was the last thing she'd expected. 'Besides, I'm not sure he's up to a message. I think he's pretty sick.'

'Then perhaps you should come back another day.'

'Are you saying he's worse?'

'He is comfortable. All our guests are comfortable. We pride ourselves on that.'

There was an awkward pause. Alice glanced at the certificates again, then she went on in a rush. 'I want to see him because I have to find a bed for my husband. I don't think a nursing-home is right – for my husband, I mean – but I promised I'd take a look, and the hospital says – ' She broke off.

240

'Oh, I see,' said the young man, bowing a little in her direction and turning to bow, as he spoke, towards the hallway behind. 'That makes all the difference, doesn't it? We like to protect our guests from unnecessary intrusion. You understand, don't you? I'll take you to Dr Darby. He'll be delighted – delighted. Follow me. It's right this way. This side of the desk. Take care. There's a slight step here.'

Alice followed him. He led her down a short corridor and stopped at a door with gold lettering on it that said:

Dr M. Morris Darby
Director

He tapped and beckoned for her to enter. It was one of those curiously American rooms, disinfected of charm as well as germs: an extruded, pre-packaged, pure place, untouched by human hands. Wood-panelled. Or was it wood? Of course not, Alice said to herself. What wood is this uniform in cut and sheen? It's plastic. All of it. Dr Morris Morris Darby was as plastic as the room, an older mannequin in the department-store window that featured Charlie and Dr McCorkhill and would soon feature the young assistant: perfectly tall, perfectly greying at the temples, smooth-skinned, tanned, grey-suited, the hairs of his eyebrows as ordered as the barbs of a feather.

He rose from behind his desk as she entered. 'How may I help you, dear lady?' he said.

'I'd like to visit Mr Macher-Daly,' Alice said, a little startled to hear a warm voice emerge from such a figure. 'And I guess I want to talk about finding a bed for my husband.'

'Do sit down. And you are Mrs – ?'

'Kessler. Is there some difficulty about my seeing Mr Macher-Daly?'

'Of course not, although it *is* unusual for an outsider to take an interest. These are sad times, Mrs Kessler. People are afraid of sickness. Why don't you tell me a little about your husband?'

241

'I'm afraid he's dying.'

'Oh, surely not.'

'Not everybody agrees, but most do.'

Dr Darby drew his pinnate eyebrows together, looked down at his desk, then back up at her. He spoke very gently. 'Opinions in such matters are only opinions, and doctors are only people.'

'I'm afraid it *is* true.'

'I doubt if I'd agree.'

'How can you agree or disagree? You haven't seen him.'

'We at Happy Acres rarely agree with hospital diagnoses.'

A ray of sun shone through Dr Darby's window and lit the panels behind him, and Alice realized suddenly that the panelling was wood after all – not plastic, but wood carefully disguised to look like plastic. How very odd, she thought. 'Is Mr Macher-Daly conscious?' she said then.

Dr Darby leaned back in his chair. 'He's not very alert, I must confess, Mrs Kessler. And this does make me a little reluctant to take you to see him.' When Alice said nothing, he went on. 'In fact, I'm afraid a visit would only distress you both.'

'I certainly don't want to distress him.'

'Of course you don't.'

Alice looked down at her hands. 'But I'd like to see the room anyway – for my husband's sake if not for Schpiegal's. Besides, if he's not all that alert, am I really going to distress him?'

Dr Darby shook his head. 'You must think of yourself too. The guests on our Medicare floor are very sick.'

'I've seen sick patients before.'

Dr Darby waited a moment. Alice waited too. Then he picked up the receiver of the telephone on his desk, considered it a moment and replaced it. 'These are interesting institutions, you know,' he said. 'Our Medicare floors are basically government facilities. Very strictly regulated.' Dr Darby picked up a sheaf of papers from his desk. 'Do you realize that every milligram of skin cream we put on a guest – every ounce of feed – goes into a record that has to be made out in twelve copies? one copy to each of ten different authorities and two for our own files?'

'What's feed? It sounds like something for farm animals.'

'Our Medicare guests cannot eat on their own.'

Alice was not sure what this might mean, so she said again, 'I'd like to see the room.'

'Come back during visiting hours, and I'll take you around myself. Meantime, why don't you tell me a little about Mr Kessler? Where is he now? At Memorial?'

'Your prospectus doesn't say anything about visiting hours,' Alice persisted.

'Doesn't it?' he said vaguely. 'Gabriel,' he said into the telephone, 'get me a file for Mr Kessler, will you?' He put his hand over the receiver and said to Alice, 'Visiting hours are between ten and twelve in the morning.'

'It's only a quarter past twelve right now.'

'The cleaning shift comes on at twelve.'

'I don't mind,' Alice said. 'If you're busy, perhaps Gabriel can show me the way.'

Dr Darby sighed, pushed his chair away from his desk and got up. 'Don't say I didn't warn you.' He led her out into the entrance-hall again.

'The elevator's over there,' he said. Alice walked over to it and pushed the UP button. Nothing happened. 'It's because of the cleaning shift,' he said. 'We might have quite a wait. Why don't you consider – '

'Stairs?' Alice suggested.

He turned irresolutely towards a pair of heavy doors, and just then the elevator rumbled in its shaft. When it arrived, Alice and Dr Darby got in. They rode up. The doors slid open.

What I tell you now is not honesty. It is truth. No satire. No farce. No exaggeration. It's the smell that hits you first. The urine is easy to identify. The other smell is nothing Alice had ever encountered before: an amalgam of musk and rot, heavy, oppressive, faintly sweet, animal rather than vegetable.

'This way,' said Dr Darby.

There was a central desk with rooms off a short corridor behind it. Nobody stood behind the desk or in the corridor. No nurses. No patients. No visitors. It wasn't until later that Alice realized she hadn't seen any cleaning staff either. Dr Darby led her down the corridor. He paused outside an open door.

'Are you sure you want to go in?' he said.

Alice nodded.

'This is Mr Macher-Daly's room.'

Alice nodded again.

Three metal beds stood close together, sides up to make them into cribs; in each lay a figure. From the far reach of the room there issued a single, faint mewing sound. Then silence.

'Schpiegal?' Alice said timidly.

Dr Darby led her to the middle bed.

She stared down at the person who had been her Sunday lunch companion a month before. He lay on his side, curled into a foetal position except for the head, which was arched back on his neck, mouth wide open, face as grey and as anonymous as a paving-stone; if she hadn't known who he was – if Dr Darby hadn't pointed him out to her – she would not have known even what his sex was.

'What's the' – she cleared her throat – 'tube in his nose for?'

'He became oedematous on an intravenous line,' Dr Darby said.

'What does that mean?'

'Sometimes cancer patients swell if you feed them through

244

their veins. We never use veins. We feed straight into the stomach.'

'Those tubes, they look – ' Alice couldn't finish her sentence.

Dr Darby's perfect face crumpled a little at the edges. 'I know what you mean. They're awful, aren't they? Some of our guests tear them out. I can't say I blame them. I certainly wouldn't want one.'

Alice let him take her by the elbow and lead her away.

iii

By the time she got to the car, there were spots in front of her eyes. She lowered herself sideways onto the seat. The speedometer of this shiny rented car went up to 140 miles per hour. She'd noticed it on the way out to Happy Acres. Was it possible? she thought. Could she really go that fast? Could anybody?

She turned the key in the ignition and drove. It was only a fluke that she happened to notice the street sign of the road she turned into some ten minutes later: Willow Lane. She knew Willow Lane. That's where Dutch Hashman lived. She remembered the number of his house because 1331 is eleven cubed. She drove slowly down the street. The house was somewhat larger than most, no hedge, sweeping lawn, path, a couple of trees, leaves deep on the ground – white-painted, two-storyed, fluted pillars flanking the door. Number 1331 Willow Lane. She parked in front and walked up the path. The bell ding-donged. She heard a scramble of heavy feet, and the door flung open, banging against the wall inside.

Two giants jockeyed for position on the threshold, which was barely large enough for one of them – men in their thirties. She stared at the blank, dully happy faces, skin pulled tight around the eyes.

'Dr Hashman?' she ventured.

The giants gaped. One was bearded, one clean-shaven.

'Is he here?' she asked.

The bearded one frowned. 'Daddy?' he said. 'Does she want Daddy, Luke?' It was a goatee of sorts, grey flecked, neatly trimmed.

Luke leaned forward to examine her more closely. 'Dunno. Maybe we should ask.'

The scene was so bizarre that she blinked, half expecting it to disappear altogether. 'Is your daddy at home?'

'We haven't asked you yet. It isn't – '

'Hey, you guys, is that for me?' Dutch Hashman shouldered them aside, both of them a head taller than he. 'What is this?' he said, irritated at seeing her. 'You should've called. I'd have come to the hospital. What is it?'

'I've just been to Happy – ' The constriction around her heart tightened with an abrupt jerk, and she stumbled on the step. Dutch reached out to help her. She backed away from him.

'You need a cup of coffee or something, don't you? These are my sons.' He cocked his head at the men. 'Luke, Larry, say hello to Mrs Kessler.'

'Don't want to,' Luke said.

'Then go find mommy. Mrs Kessler and I gotta talk.'

'Dunno where she is.'

'Out back. Burning leaves.'

The two turned and galumphed away down the corridor.

'Come into the living-room,' Dutch said, steering her into a large, untidy room with overstuffed chairs in floral prints.

She held the arms of the chair she sat in while he busied himself in the kitchen beyond. There were child-like drawings in crayon on the walls, round faces, dots for eyes, electric hair. The coffee Dutch came back with was strong, hot, milkless. Alice screwed up her face in distaste.

'Drink it,' he said.

246

She nodded. 'I saw them,' she said,.

'Drink the coffee.'

'That's where they want to send Peter, isn't it?'

'Where?'

'Happy Acres. What a name! Happy – ' She broke off, then started again. 'Ten rooms maybe. Doors all open. They lie on blue mattresses. All of them – blue. The mattresses are blue. Why blue? They're puffy, sort of – the mattresses, I mean.'

'Air mattresses.'

'What?'

'To lessen the effect of bedsores.'

'Oh, I hadn't – Why are they blue? What's the smell?'

'Catabolism.'

'Cata-what?'

'The reverse of metabolism: the breakdown of bodily structures.'

'What sort of – uh – bodily structures?'

'You're smelling bedsores mainly.'

'You know these places?'

Dutch spread his hands. 'Nobody'd claim a nursing-home is fun. They're dog farms, every one of 'em.'

She put down the cup. 'You don't know what I'm talking about, do you?'

'Alice, I go to these places every day. I got patients in all of them – most of them anyhow.'

'On the Medicare floors?'

'Medicare floors? You mean hospice-type care? not those, no. The resident physician takes care of them.'

'Then you don't know what I'm talking about.'

Alice studied the cup with the dregs of coffee in it, a floral pattern, small chip out of the rim. 'Every one had a tube in the nose.'

'Tube?'

'Like this. In the nose'.

'An NG tube? Oh, come on, now.'

'Is that what they're called? NG tubes? What do they do?'

'NG: nasogastric: nose to stomach. That don't make sense. You didn't see right. They're too uncomfortable. They got their uses, but – '

'Usually when you bastards say "uncomfortable" you mean agonizing.'

'They ulcerate the skin that touches them.'

'In the mouth?'

'You don't want to hear this.'

'Tell me.'

He sighed. 'And the throat.'

There was a sudden gust of wind beyond the window. Smoke leapt and swirled around the fire that burned in the garden.

'They're not going to get Peter,' she shouted at him. 'Do you hear me?'

A second gust of wind blew the smoke out of the way; Alice could see the two giants and their mother, her hair caught up in the breeze, as they played around the fire together.

Alice leaned back in the overstuffed chair. 'Is it going to snow?' she said then.

Dutch studied her a moment. 'Probably,' he said.

'Best to get the leaves burned before it snows, isn't it?'

'Yeah.'

'Have you always kept your sons at home?'

He nodded. 'I like children.'

'Not an easy life.'

He glanced toward the window. 'When Luke was born – Well, you know what they say: "No reason why the next one won't be perfectly normal." ' He shrugged. 'They were wrong. It just happens.' A tongue of flame shot up through the billows of smoke outside. The giants roared with delight.

'I'm sorry I shouted at you,' Alice said.

'That happens sometimes, too.'

248

'There wasn't anybody around. Not even any nurses.'

'Listen to me, Alice. If patient conditions you describe really existed, they'd have every regulatory agency in the state down on them. Happy Acres is run by some multinational. They couldn't afford that sort of scandal.'

She took in her breath. 'Will you go and see Schpiegal?'

'Schpiegal Macher-Daly?'

'So you can see what I saw.'

'They got a doctor over at Happy Acres. Schpiegal don't need another one.'

'He needs a friend.'

'I never knew him much.'

Alice stared out the window. 'Please,' she said.

'Okay. Okay. If it'll put your mind at rest.'

'When?'

'Tomorrow. But I'm telling you you're imagining this.'

'Promise?'

'I promise.'

iv

The earth switches its magnetic poles back and forth, North to South, South to North. It trembles and shakes inside. It boils. We don't stand here; we only float like scum on oatmeal, ready to be sucked under at any moment. Do I accept this? Of course I don't. Who can accept such things? But you get used to them. You can get used to anything.

Alice swallowed back her nausea and set out to visit another nursing-home. She had to be sure. Before the afternoon was over she'd looked at three of them; when she left the last one, no spots appeared in front of her yes. She had had to be sure: now she was. Tomorrow Dutch would see what she had seen. Tomorrow she would have an ally.

But that night, when she got back to Cordelia's, Cordelia wept and told her that Schpiegal was dead.

Alice couldn't sleep. She was afraid to sleep. She lay in bed and stared out at the dark, got up, found a bottle of scent, put a dab on her upper lip. How could anybody bear that reek? The only thing she must have missed at Happy Acres was the empty beds.

She rearranged her pillows – and rearranged them again. She pulled the covers over her head. She pulled them off. The sheets slid to the floor in a heap. This was no time for numbers. And yet – Four rooms on the smallest Medicare floor she saw, ten on the largest, maybe as much as half the beds empty: an average of, say, ten patients per home. Four homes together made forty people. Assume each patient lives two months (assume Schpiegal died quickly); assume she'd seen all the beds available to Overton's hundred thousand inhabitants, and you've got something on the order of two hundred and fifty deaths a year. On average one percent of the population dies every year. Which is to say, something like a quarter of all deaths in Overton were happening in these places.

The prospectuses said the charge for Medicare patients was $72.53 a day. The amount never varied, which meant it had to be some sort of government-approved figure. Alice puzzled over it. $72.53 a day: barely the price of a good motel room. Memorial took in some $600 a day. So where was the profit margin? Dutch said Happy Acres was owned by a multinational, and Dr Darby didn't look like a man who worked for a charitable wage.

There just had to be money somewhere. Lots of it. Here was the missing piece. Here was the Corn King's heart.

Now what she felt was something well beyond fear.

The next morning she was at the hospital by seven, waiting for Mrs Carpenter.

'What about the Fourth Floor?' she demanded as soon as Mrs Carpenter got out of the elevator. It was quarter to nine. 'Have they come through with an answer? Will they take him?'

'Why don't we go to my office to discuss this?'

'Why haven't they taken him? There must be a reason. What went wrong?'

'I haven't said they wouldn't take him.'

'Yes, you have.'

'It isn't final. Let's go to my – '

'What isn't final?'

'Their decision. Come with me, Mrs Kessler.' She took Alice by the arm and led her to the linen-closet office. 'Sit down,' she said.

'Why do you always want me to sit down? Why won't they take him?'

Mrs Carpenter sighed and sat down herself. 'You see' – her eyes slid away from Alice to the scatter of papers on her desk – 'he doesn't, um, quite – '

Alice held her breath.

' – quite qualify for just exactly what they want.' Mrs Carpenter jerked her glance up to Alice and back down again. 'But as I say, it's not final. You shouldn't – '

'What makes them think he isn't exactly what they want? Have they actually looked at him? Or did all this happen on paper? Or between a couple of computers somewhere? They're never going to take him, are they?'

'Who?'

'The Fourth Floor! The Fourth Floor!'

'You mustn't anticipate. They may. It's just that – '

'What does that mean?'

'What does what mean? I don't think you're getting quite enough sleep, Mrs Kessler. You must look after – '

'How come they always make their assessments when I'm not around?' Alice cried. 'I'm practically always around. How do they manage it? When did they do this skulking about? At midnight? By candlelight? Who are they? Has anybody ever seen them? Have you?'

'Listen to me, Mrs Kessler. They won't even have a bed available for three or four days – '

Alice sat down abruptly. 'Three or four days? Does that mean I've got three or four days left?'

'I'll call them in for the final assessment in a day or two. Now, tell me, how did your investigations go yesterday? Are you reassured?'

Those three children in Mickey Mouse ears: were they boys? girls? Alice suddenly realized she couldn't tell. She squinted at them. No sex to begin with. No sex at the end. No wonder everybody's so preoccupied with it in between.

'I want you to call in hospice again too,' Alice said, swinging back to Mrs Carpenter. 'If the Fourth Floor can make a second assessment, so can hospice. I'll tell Peter everything they want me to tell him. I'll tell everybody everything. I'll do whatever they require. We have to have an alternative in case the Fourth Floor falls through again. At least the place is clean.' She was assailed by sudden doubt. 'It is clean, isn't it? hospice?'

'Of course it's clean. But I'm not sure – '

'What about the Fourth Floor?'

'They're both part of the hospital, Mrs Kessler.'

'You've seen them yourself?'

'I go there every day.'

'You've actually seen the patients?'

'Yes, I – '

'That's all right then.' Alice shut her eyes. 'Yes, I am reassured. Thank you.'

252

'I just don't want to push the Fourth Floor into making their assessment too early. When there's another change – and there will be soon – I'll call them in. He's a very sick man.'

'What about hospice?'

'Well, um, I think our best chance is with the Fourth Floor.'

'What's wrong with hospice? Peter's not sick. He's dying. Isn't that what hospice is for? the dying?'

'I think you'd better talk to Dr Pederson about that,' Mrs Carpenter said.

'What's the point? He believes in eternal life.'

Mrs Carpenter's large black eyes slid away from Alice; she picked up a sheet of paper from the pile in front of her. She bent forward. She frowned. 'It says here that Mr Kessler's on morphine.' She looked up at Alice. 'When did that happen?'

'I don't know. Day before yesterday, I think,' Alice said.

'Why didn't you say anything to me about this? You did it yourself, didn't you?' Mrs Carpenter was conspiratorial, agiggle. 'How wonderful. Aren't you smart! Now listen, before I call the Fourth Floor in, you've got to get that morphine into him at least twice a day. Do you understand? It can't be just once. It's got to be regular.'

'Twice doesn't seem very regular to –' Alice began. 'It's some sort of requirement, isn't it? for the Fourth Floor? Is twice enough? Does he need anything else?'

Mrs Carpenter bit her lip. 'I really shouldn't be talking about this kind of thing, you know.'

'Oh, please. Please tell me.'

Mrs Carpenter beckoned her closer and whispered in her ear. 'All he needs is two doses of morphine a day and the eighty-two ounces of water he's already getting. Morphine's what I've been waiting for – or, well, I don't know, maybe antibiotics. It's just what we need.'

'Eighty-two ounces?'

'It's two litres or something.'

'No it isn't. Why are these guidelines kept secret?' But Alice could see at once that she had gone too far. 'I'm so sorry,' she went on hurriedly. 'It's none of my business, is it? But will it work? Will it get Peter to the Fourth Floor?'

'I'm almost certain it will.'

'Only "almost"? Is that all?'

'The decision isn't mine. I just fill out the forms, but I can tell you – in the strictest confidence (you do understand that, don't you?) – that you've really got nothing more to worry about as long as you get that morphine into him.'

Peter had not spoken in days – not a single word – but that morning, after Alice had been sitting by his bed for an hour or so, he half-waked from the twilight slumber that had become his way of being. With his face to the wall he said, 'I was thinking' – there was fear in his voice – 'It's just make-believe, isn't it?'

'What is?'

He said nothing for a minute or two. 'That I'm somebody's father.'

Alice didn't know how to answer. 'You do remember' – she paused, unsure again – 'you do remember Tad, don't you?'

'It would make me so old if I were a real father.'

She drew back, then bent over him again. 'Tad is ours, Peter, yours and mine. You are his father.'

'But not really?'

'Not if you don't wish it,' she said.

He shuddered. Then he closed his eyes and slept.

CHAPTER 17

i

Myself I agree with Peter. Who wants to be somebody's father? or somebody's mother? Reproduce, they say. Oh, what a cute little thing, they say. Why do we fall for it? A lousy, exhausting, boring job. Thankless too. Whatever we do the kids hate us for it. Why do we never learn?

Pity poor Angela. She was smarter than most, and yet there she was in the year 1962 with a second daughter, when in her heart she knew even the first was a mistake. She tried to love Alice the way she loved Mollie; she believed – and believed strongly – that parents shouldn't favour one child over the other. She just couldn't do it. She resented Alice, who had got herself conceived when she shouldn't have. Except for Alice, the plan had worked so well. Angela had recaptured Peter, a New York job, and the moral high ground. She could have kept them all too. Except for Alice.

Pity poor Angela. The pill is supposed to be infallible. Well, all right, perhaps she hadn't taken is as regularly as she should have during the first weeks in New York, but you can't think of everything. Besides, she'd more than half-persuaded herself that Peter couldn't have children. Was she to be condemned to

Christie and the stultifying role of doctor's wife for such minor oversights? As for abortion, forget it. Abortion would have revealed her hand to Peter – and to Christie as well. How could she *not* resent this child?

Pity poor Angela. Because of Alice, she couldn't sleep at night; she could no longer concentrate; her body ached. Because of Alice, she found herself in the hands of shrinks. Most shrinks are good enough people. The trouble is, they don't know anything. They can't help anybody by design, although sometimes – rarely – they succeed by accident. As one of them said to me a few years ago (an honest, high-ranking shrink this was), 'A patient comes to us: we drug him; we shock him. Until something happens. Until he has a heart attack or something.' A base craft, as Christie said. Angela raged at her shrink, who was a friend of Christie's and – as happens more often in the closed profession of medicine than patients would like to think – all was revealed, at least to Christie and the Overton Kesslers. They said nothing to Peter. Of course they didn't. (You could never be sure what Peter might do.)

But a secret like this is such a delicious secret in a Midwest town. You couldn't possibly cage it – not while its principals lived in the neighbourhood. Besides, even today a scandal like this could easily ruin a family practice; Overton is in the Bible Belt. So it was that before Alice was born, Christie embarked on the career of peripatetic medical consultant to the Swiss-based drug conglomorate, Gertsch International; he left his beloved family practice, all he'd ever wanted in life. It was not a good foundation for a marriage.

The family travelled together. Sometimes Mollie and Alice went to school in the United States; in Chicago, in Portland, in Dallas; sometimes they went abroad, mainly to England, although they did spend a few months in South America, a year in India and the occasional winter in Switzerland. They were never long enough in any of these places to develop

256

friendships or good study habits or, in the foreign-speaking countries, a firm grasp of the language. But if nothing else, both girls learned the detachment from their own kind that men value so deeply in themselves, although not in their wives. Besides, Mollie played the piano well; when she was eighteen, she auditioned for and was accepted by the Mannes School in Manhattan. Alice had that facility with numbers; the year Mollie graduated from Mannes, Alice took US college entrance exams in Basel (this was her final winter in Switzerland), and in the spring, Barnard College came through with an offer for her.

Her plane flew in from Geneva. Her cousin Peter was to meet her after customs, carrying a sign saying 'Alice Kessler' on it. She didn't need the sign. She recognized him immediately, although she'd seen him only twice before, and she'd been very little both times.

'Hello, Alice Kessler,' he said.

Bed, she decided at once, standing there looking at him, flight bag in hand, people milling about.

She herself was taken aback by the speed and force of her reaction. She'd never lusted after grown men before. In fact, she'd never lusted after anybody before. Sex wasn't a matter she'd bothered with much; she'd had her opportunities, but none of them had caught her fancy.

During the ride from Kennedy to Manhattan she watched Peter's hands on the wheel (those long, slender fingers, so very like her own) and pondered with that hard-won detachment of hers: why this man and not another? It wasn't just his looks. At least she didn't think it was. Men are so much alike: two eyes, a nose, a mouth, arms, legs. The only real mystery, she said to herself – denying the mystery even as she stated it – is how you can tell one from the next.

He took her to a restaurant on the Upper West Side, an Italian restaurant with tables out on the street. It was beyond the call of duty; his brief was only to make sure she got to the Barnard dormitory and to be available in case of need. But his first wife Lilith was dying in hospital on the Lower East Side (Lilith, like her namesake, plays no part in the central story), and he was bereft. Besides, the weather was surprisingly good for late September, soft and warm, rather than hot and sticky; the girl had Angela's blonde hair and almond-shaped eyes. Her skin glowed the way only young skin does, lush and rosy, lustrous and innocent. And her hands – what was it about them? He'd never seen hands that appealed to him more. They were so graceful and so strong – both at once.

'I'd have known you anywhere,' he said to her. 'What do you want to eat on your first night in New York?'

'Whatever you eat,' she said.

He ordered Fettucine Alfredo and a bottle of Spumante. The waiter winked at her, knowing she wasn't yet eighteen – a magnificent young waiter with dreadlocks and a brooding profile. She barely noticed him. A good Spumante, say the experts, is crisp and lemony; you can taste the sunshine in it. She drank; she toasted Peter; she laughed at what he said and the way he said it – and wanted only for him to laugh with her.

Ten days before this, he'd come back from Hollywood; he'd spent a month there as a consultant on the filming of his latest novel – that's the famous one, *The Burial of God*, the second volume of the quartet that was to be his *magnum opus*. The great Dysan, the guy whose pictures routinely grossed in a league with *Gone with the Wind* – remember him? – he's the one who bought the rights. Dysan told Peter that *Burial* was going to be the biggest ever – as long as they could come up with a suitably upbeat title, that is. A pity he was wrong. Anyhow, Alice was as impressed as you'd expect by this glamorous adventure of Peter's. She knew Lilith hadn't been strong enough to make the trip west; she knew Peter probably would have stayed longer if Lilith hadn't taken a turn for the worse.

258

Lilith had always been delicate, and he loved delicate things. How could he laugh? Even so, that's what Alice wanted. I will make him laugh, she said to herself. Then he'll see in me what I see in him. But she was not at all sure just what this was; she watched his every move, seeking clues in the devil's arch of his eyebrows and the sheen of evening light on the planes of his cheeks.

'What's Hollywood like?' Alice said. 'Is it really different from other places?'

'It's not like any city I know – and it hasn't fired me with a passion to know it better. I'm not sure it's a city anybody *could* know, no matter how hard the try or how passionate the trier. I rented a house up in the hills – '

'What about it?' she interrupted, seeing a faint smile on his face and knowing that whatever had caused it was about to escape.

He kept his glance averted, as he usually did, but the faint smile reappeared. 'They had an exercycle between the beds.'

'*Between* the beds?' she laughed. 'You rode the thing?'

There was a ripple of half-embarrassed assent. 'But you don't want to hear about this,' he said, 'not on your first night in the big city.'

'Yes, I do!' she cried.

'Wouldn't you rather – ?'

'No. Tell me about this house.'

'But – '

'Tell me. Tell me.'

She leaned forward on her elbows, a delighted anticipation on her face. Who could resist her? Peter's faint smile appeared once more. 'They'd built a noble balcony outside – fine proportions in unfinished teak and weathered like an old wooden boat – that stretched across the entire front of the house. It was at just the right height so that if I stood up, my head was in the smog, but if I stooped down, I could see below it: the buildings, the streets and the glitter of the ocean beyond.'

'Does smog really end like that?'

'I went out there every day, and it was always the same.'

'Always as clear-cut?'

He nodded. 'A grey nothing when I was upright. (The best people in Hollywood never sit down: chairs put you at a disadvantage.) There was perfect clarity only when I was almost on my knees, and I hate kneeling.'

Alice found it hard to look away from him, even to fork pasta into her mouth; so it was that she saw bafflement on his face for the first time – and barely kept herself from reaching out to take hold of the hands that were so like her own, to comfort, to reassure, to say, 'everything's going to be all right,' even though she knew everything wasn't going to be all right, couldn't be all right, not this evening, not tomorrow, perhaps not for months to come. In the midst of all this, she caught his glance, and in the bright, black pupils of his eyes – in that split second before he looked away – she saw herself reflected. 'Is that really me?' she thought. 'Am I really as pretty as that?'

The thought shocked her; it had come wholly unbidden – unwelcome too: she disliked what she could not control. So she said, aiming for the firm ground of her best behaviour, 'It sounds like such a wonderful adventure – to be a consultant on a movie – what does it mean?'

He gave a helpless shrug. 'I don't know.'

'You mustn't tease me. What do consultants do?'

'The only thing I know about them is that they are paid very well.' His cheeks reddened a little. Was it self-deprecation? She didn't know. Come to think of it, why didn't he talk about the movie stars he'd met? the parties he'd gone to? Dysan kept the biggest names in Hollywood in his stable. So it was that Peter showed her that other unexpected quality of his:

260

she'd read a long story about him and Dysan in a Swiss news-paper (the project was that big) and yet – Was it true? Book, movie, Hollywood? Any of it? Had Peter made it up, all of it, and fooled everybody?

Of course, if he'd felt more himself – if Lilith hadn't been weighing so heavily on his spirits – he might well have told her some fanciful tale (or at least a fancified tale) just for the fun of it, just to watch her reaction. But then again, he might not have. He'd gone to California expecting to dazzle and be dazzled. Instead, he'd just been bored – which embarrassed him. It seemed so meagre a response to the glitter: bored by the people, bored by the process, bored by the money, bored even by what Dysan proposed to do with his book.

'So you went to the land of movies to watch smog on a balcony,' she said.

He started to answer, but the sound of the street welled up and drowned him, as New York sounds often do – raucous, harsh; traffic, sirens, conversation, scraps of music in the dis-tance. She could see his mouth form words – a sensuous mouth, somewhat askew as the best mouths are, nose flared a little at the nostrils – but she couldn't hear him. The shoulders, the way he sat: why did he never relax?

'What?' she cried. 'Can you say it again?'

The din quietened.

' – like zabaglione,' she heard him say.

'Zaba what? Is it a movie? I never saw it.'

At last his smile was the sudden, quick smile – deep, full – that took her by surprise throughout their lives together, just as it took her by surprise this night. 'Zabaglione is *not* a movie, little Alice Kessler. Where have you been all these years?'

'Isn't it? What is it then?'

Despite himself he looked directly at her. 'It's a glorious froth. You eat it.'

'When?'

'Now.'

'Oh, I thought – ' What had she thought? Something – surely something – but she'd caught her reflection in his eyes again. Why couldn't she tell what colour they were? They had green flecks in them, and yet they were dark. Was it possible? Light and dark in the same eyes? She tried with all her strength to withdraw her gaze from this strange mirror – but could not. Was the elegant forehead she saw there really her own? Why had she never realized how fine her cheekbones were?

'I've never seen a man as beautiful as you,' she blurted out.

And he laughed.

She was enchanted. At once she forgot what had caused this sound that was as warm and light as the zabaglione itself turned out to be; but the enchantment stayed with her – wavering less (in all the years that followed) than any man has a right to expect. They sat outside until the night was dark. When Peter went to the till to pay, the dreadlocked waiter came to collect their coffee-cups and stood beside her a moment. She was watching Peter dreamily, wondering (only half realizing it) what the musculature of his back was like, when the waiter said to her, 'That guy could practically be your father. You sure you know what you're doing?'

She turned her glowing face to him. 'Father, mother, brother, sisters – aunts, uncles, nieces, nephews – all rolled in one. Whatever it is, he's it. You just wait, he'll be my husband and the father of my child as well.'

Later, in the dormitory, she lay awake and struggled to work out the details.

First things first – which presented her with a problem in logistics. She was going to have to assault Peter in his own bed, and the assault itself was going to take all the aplomb she could muster. How could she deal with bloodying the sheets as well? Mollie had bled all over the place. Alice decided she'd have to get rid of her virginity first. Virgins are boring as well as messy. Everybody said so.

ii

But she wasn't about to offer her body to the first guy she ran across; she wouldn't know how to put the question to him. She thought and thought and in the end, she decided to consult Peter himself. She telephoned him; she invited herself to his apartment. After all, she assumed he could explain anything she needed explained, no matter what the subject, and also – because she knew so little about such matters – she assumed he wouldn't know what was really in her mind. It was November. She'd been in New York six weeks; he'd taken her out to dinner twice in that time, no more than his role in the family called for.

'Just precisely what are you asking me, Alice Kessler?' he said, alarmed and flattered both, intrigued – more than intrigued. She was so fresh he could practically see dew-drops on her, and by now poor Lilith was dead and buried.

The problem so absorbed Alice – had so absorbed her for these past six weeks – that she didn't catch the complexity of his response. 'You're not going to make me repeat it, are you?' she said.

'What about Columbia? It's just across the street.'

'I don't know any boys there.'

'Do you have to know them?'

She considered a moment. 'I think it would help.'

'What about Giles?'

'Who?'

'Mollie's guy. You told me about him. Giles Frigamajig. From your description he doesn't put me in mind of the giants of history, but I don't imagine a giant of history is necessary.'

'That's not his name. Did I say that was his name?'

'Won't he do? If you can find him, that is?'

Alice scanned Peter's face, her own alight with the pleasure his gave her, and said, 'I don't like the way he looks.'

'Perhaps there's some magic in him that the eye can't detect.'

'What, for example?'

'If worst comes to worst, you could toss a bag over his head.'

'You're not taking me seriously,' she said.

About this she was wrong. He took her seriously now and had done so from that first day. She was stable where her mother had not been, and yet she had the intensity that he'd so admired in Angela – that he could not find in himself. If you are given a second chance in life, you are a fool not to take it. Even so, he was not sure, and he did not like being unsure. He always favoured the weaker side: he did not like the thought that he might be taking advantage of it. For this reason alone, he'd kept rigidly to his designated family role. On the other hand, the more he looked at her, the more he saw strength, not weakness.

This apartment had three rooms all looking through the top branches of the trees in Riverside Park, across the Hudson and onto the New Jersey Palisades beyond. It was dark outside, but the louvres on the shutters were not wholly closed; through them, Alice could see the glow of the river and a flickering line of lights from the opposite shore. Inside the rooms, the secret, Neverland feel was as strong as it had been in Angela's day. The bull and the Chinese monkey dominated the mantel-piece again, face to face again, another confrontation.

'Why do you see the need to rush yourself like this?' Peter said. His voice was very gentle. 'Why not wait for opportunity to present itself?'

'Oh, no. I can't do that.'

'Why not?'

'Because – ' She looked into his eyes then (the eyes that were light and dark all at once, that she could not even now give a colour to), and they seemed to her to catch the deep, patterned flow of the river as well as the glittering secret of Neverland (whatever that is). Despite herself she said, 'If I wait too long somebody else will come along and claim you.'

He did not know how to answer. 'Are you so sure somebody hasn't done just that already?' he said, evading her, teasing her.

'No.'

He turned away. 'I'm old enough to be your father.' He actually said these words, so you can see that he was as innocent of the truth as she was.

Peter was forty-nine years old on that November night. Most men of forty-nine have the quality of the butcher's shop to them: pork bellies with pink meat showing through button gaps in shirts; plucked chickens with tight wrinkles and pin-feathers; slabs of beef with beef face, beef jowl, purple scrotal sack like offal on the quick-sale counter. Not Peter. To begin with he didn't look forty-nine. You'd probably have guessed his age at thirty-five, but the way he held himself, the tension in him, that childlike delight in things: he seemed younger than that.

They slept in each other's arms (no blood: after all, it doesn't always happen), and she woke just as the first light appeared in the sky. It was a cold morning, pristine, as the best mornings are in New York. He slept on. Gently she drew back the sheet to study him. His muscled back was muscled just as she'd imagined it, almost as though the intensity of her imaginings alone had created it for her. The shapes of his body – chest, hips, neck, arms, legs – were the geometric shapes of Euclid's conic sections that had always been her favourite area of mathematics: those sensuous, elegant, sweeping curves that the greatest Greeks had studied in the age of Pericles, that was the greatest age of them all.

Looking down on him, it wasn't Greece she thought of, though, but Switzerland. She thought of winter high up in the

Alps: the ice-covered pine trees in the early-morning sun and the sound the ice made when it fell as the morning warmed up. The Bernese Oberland can be springlike even this late in the year; when it's overcast in the valley down below, you're up above the fog-line in the mountains, and if the snow clears in patches – which it does more often than you might expect – tiny spring flowers, buttercups and anemones, come up through the grass. Everything is so clean.

That was it. That's what it was about him. Wherever he was, was clean.

iii

Later on, in May, while Alice finished her Freshman year at Barnard College, Mollie got married in the leafiest suburb in Washington, where Christie and Angela had gone when the Swiss appointment ended. Angela herself turned fifty-four on the day of Mollie's wedding, which is to say, her job as mother was finished. The time had come for her to claim her reward for the weary years as duenna to growing girls and wife to a peripatetic medical consultant. Besides, Lilith had been dead for several months by this time, and Angela knew Peter well enough to know she couldn't wait too long. So she packed her bags. She told Christie it was over. Finished. She left him slumped in an outdoor chair on the porch of their house, tears rolling down his cheeks and a month of dinners in the freezer. She took the train to New York, where she hadn't been since she'd discovered she was pregnant with Alice.

She half ran to Peter's apartment on Riverside Drive, could hardly bear the suspense of the ride up in the elevator: an ancient, elegant device, filled with mirrors that showed her nothing even though she looked in them, and operated by an ancient, tired man whom she pitied in a passing sort of way for being so tired and so ancient when her own life was about to begin again. She rang Peter's bell. She heard his steps approach.

The door flung open and there he was, as beautiful as ever. 'Peter!' she cried, throwing her arms around his neck.

He drew back. 'My God,' he whispered aghast, 'Angela? Is it you?'

Angela had retained her first blush longer than most women. In her late forties she was still very, very pretty, far prettier – in the simplest sense of the word – than she had any right to be. Perhaps it was only justice (helped on by tobacco) that when she turned fifty and the years took their revenge, they took it so mercilessly. Yet because they were merciless across the board and robbed her of her close vision, she did not realize how extensive the damage was: just how pouchy her face had become, just how shapeless her body and how swollen her ankles. And she'd despaired so long over an empty life that she'd acquired a workhouse slump of the shoulders and a forward carriage of the head.

Nothing had prepared Peter for what he saw, no letter, no photograph, nothing Alice had said. He was deeply shaken; he took in his breath and put his arm through Angela's as he put his arm through his own mother's, with that exaggerated civility the young sometimes use when confronted with elderly flesh. And Angela, who had as sharp an eye as any reporter ever had – she, who had seen him with his mother and had stored away his civilities in her reporter's mind (to say nothing of her lover's mind) – she let him lead her to the living-room and to a chair, a bentwood rocker, elegant, lovely, uncomfortable, like all his chairs. She followed his touch unresisting, unable to resist.

'Let me get you a drink,' he said. He glanced quickly at his watch. Surely he had an appointment somewhere. If only he tried hard enough, he'd remember it. His mind, agile as ever, scrambled this way and that – but found nothing, no way to escape this situation, no way to turn it to his own advantage.

Besides, he felt guilty about Alice in front of her mother, and he hated feeling guilty. He felt he owed explanations, and he hated owing explanations. He felt beholden somehow, and he hated feeling beholden. Also Peter was not quite like other men; the sight of Angela grown old stirred an alien, half-forgotten unease in him. He had no idea what it was (his own mother would have seen at once that he was afraid), but he knew enough to hate it most of all.

'What would you like? Scotch? Bourbon?' he said. He turned away before she could answer and looked out of the window at the green shoots of the oak tree, just the tips of them, where they reached up into view. 'Do you realize it's been nearly twenty years since we last saw each other? Wait, I know.' He smiled out at the oak tree. 'Plainly,' he said, 'the only proper drink is a martini.'

He didn't know it – of course he didn't – but he could have said nothing that would have hurt her more. She half-coughed and half-laughed. 'Sure. Why not? For old time's sake. After all, what am I here for, if not for old times' sake?'

He went to the kitchen for ice; the unease in him refused to let up, and he dropped the tray, which wasn't like him. He mixed too much vermouth in the gin, which wasn't like him either. He cut his finger while he was peeling lemon zest for the glasses. Back in the living-room, he handed her a drink; a drop of blood from his cut finger smeared the glass, but she swallowed the drink in a single gulp before he could reclaim the glass and wipe it clean.

All he wanted was for her to go away. 'Time runs on so fast it leaves me spinning,' he said, trying to lighten the air for himself as much as for her.

She gave a short, harsh laugh. 'Does it indeed?'

He tried again (nobody can say he didn't). 'I hardly know where to begin. Tell me about life in Washington and the cherry trees in bloom. It's the right month for blooming, isn't it? I've always thought that flowers are at their prettiest when they're on the very littlest trees.'

'You don't care about that.'

'How do you know?'

'How do I know? Jesus, I'm the world expert on what Peter Kessler cares about and what he doesn't.'

He took in an unsteady breath. 'You're not making this very easy for me, Angela.'

'For you! Don't you ever think of anybody but yourself? What about me? I came here – ' But what could she say? 'Is there something left in that pitcher?' She stuck out her glass. 'Or are you limiting your guests to one drink per session? How old was Lilith when she died?'

He got up without a word, angry now (with justice too, dammit), and poured what remained of the martinis into Angela's glass. 'She was forty-five,' he said.

'Younger than I am.'

'Yes.'

'I never liked her much. Christ, this is a stingy drink. So what about one of my daughters instead?'

Conversations with Angela often went askew in ways conversations with other people never did; he knew she didn't yet know what she was saying. 'Instead of what?' he said. 'Is there some conjunction here I've missed?'

'One of my daughters.'

'Instead of a drink?'

'Why did you put so much vermouth in this damn thing?'

He went to the kitchen again, happy only at the respite that making a second pitcherful of martinis gave him. When he'd refilled her glass, he fastened his gaze on the window and took a sip of his own drink.

She watched him suspiciously. He was plainly mad as hell, and yet – Why was he letting her talk to him like this? 'Peter?'

He didn't shift his glance.

She'd never trusted him. What's he ashamed of? she thought suddenly. Years ago he'd driven through a red light and clipped an old man's car fender. Hardly any damage, but it could have been much more serious. The old man got out of his car, leaned into Peter's window and delivered a tirade – more than justified, as Angela, who saw it all, could testify. Peter said nothing. Not a word. Not even a nod of acknowledgement, much less apology. He just sat there, angry-faced, turned aside, while the words poured over him. Just as he sat now. Was it something they'd talked about? But what? She cast that retentive mind of hers over the last few exchanges.

'You haven't – ?' She broke off.

The look of bafflement crossed his face, only a ripple across the surface, but bafflement still. He did not turn.

'God-damn you, Peter Kessler. Have you taken one of my daughters to bed?'

'I don't want to talk about this.'

She laughed bitterly. 'Mollie's been nipping at your pants, has she? Sensible girl, Mollie. She likes men. She really took to you when she was five. Remember? Of course she's newly married and pregnant – quick off the mark, Mollie: two weeks married and six months pregnant. Not that that would get in your way.'

He said nothing.

'You are as heartless as a child,' she said.

This time he had no idea how to reply. Angry as he was, he feared what she said was true.

'She's not happy,' Angela said.

'Who's not happy?'

'She's married a fool.'

'Perhaps she sees something in him you don't.'

'So it's not Mollie?' she said.

He twisted his shoulders toward the window.

'That's a relief,' she said. 'Who then?'

270

The muscles of his cheek stiffened.

'But not Mollie?' She frowned, studying him. 'Alice is too young.'

I was in the eye of a storm once. The air in the room went still in a way I've never known air to go still before or since – an ocean-depth stillness, an underwater stillness that muffled sound and did something queer to the light. When the thunderclaps began again, they were so abrupt and so powerful that I was afraid the building would collapse under them.

'Oh, God. Not Alice!' Angela cried. 'Oh, Jesus, Peter. You don't mean that. You can't. Not Alice. Why am I talking to you at all? How can I bear it?' Her words came out in gasps. 'I ought to – Why don't I get a knife and kill you? I've always wanted to. Did I ever tell you that? It's a secret passion. I used to dream about it night after night. I even knew what knife I'd use. There was one with a serrated edge. Remember it? Maybe it's the very one you cut your finger with just now. We got it in Chicago – you and I – it was French. I could see your blood on it as real as the blood you got on my glass. I saw it there – your blood – on the glass a moment ago. I tasted it. I wanted to. Did you know that? I could – If you want Alice, she's yours. She'll do anything you want. Or she'll seem to. But you can't win with Alice. Not even you.'

Now was the time for Peter to say, 'I know what I've done is wrong.' But he didn't say it. He didn't even say, 'The woman, she tempted me' – which, in all fairness, he had every right to say. Instead, his hand trembling with a mix of emotions (some of which he recognized, some of which he didn't), he reached out and scraped at a bubble of paint on the radiator beside him.

Angela watched until she could bear it no longer. 'She'll beat you. You just wait. She'll dance on your grave. She'll have no mercy.'

271

'I know she'll beat me,' he said in the cold voice of battle. 'She's so young.'

'I don't mean that, you fool. You're not – You haven't decided to get married, have you?'

'If she'll have me.'

'Oh, Jesus. She'll want children.'

He found a pencil in his pocket, took it out and scraped at the paint bubble with it. It made a raspy sound.

'Besides, you don't understand. Alice is – She's sneaky. You don't know her. She's not what she seems. She does things she won't tell you about. She says things she doesn't mean.'

'Don't we all?'

'Not like Alice.'

'She seems painfully honest to me. Overly straightforward if anything.' Scrape, scrape.

'Overly straightforward – ?' Angela's lungs seemed to be fail her. She couldn't get old air out of them; she couldn't get new air in. 'When Alice was little – ' she began. 'No, you wouldn't care about that, would you? What *do* you care about? You! The innocent bystander. You live this wonderful life in New York, and what happens to me? I live the life of an exile. Acres of provincial emptiness in a dozen different countries, each one duller than the one before. How do you think I spent those seventeen years? Seventeen *years*. I spent them taking tranquillizers and looking for a parking-space. There's a testament for you.'

He kept his eyes rigidly averted; beyond the window the day was serene and sun-dappled. 'It's the life you chose,' he said. His efforts with the pencil brought no more paint off the radiator, so he turned his attention to the shutter adjustment. He fiddled with it. He jiggled it.

'Look at me, damn you!' she cried. She got to her feet, took a jerky step towards him, then stopped, took a jerky step back and fell into the chair again. 'When Alice was about twelve, she said once – we were in the kitchen and she had an *Unabridged Webster's* open on the table – she said, "Wouldn't it be wonderful to know all the words in this book?" I said – I don't know why (I'd never say such a thing to Mollie) – I said – '

Tears ran down Angela's face and into her mouth; she drew them in with what little air she could draw in, and choked. 'I didn't mean it,' she went on. 'It's just one of those things you say to kids. I said, "*I* know them all." And she – All right, all right! So I don't know them all. Of course I don't. Who does? But she didn't say anything. She just looked at me. Twelve years old! What right does that little bitch have to judge me? And now she's got her talons into you. It serves you right, you bastard.'

Angela lifted her hands to the crêpe-like skin on her face. 'Oh, please, Peter' – her voice ricocheted from high to low and back again – 'Please. Not Alice. Anybody but Alice.'

She got up and stumbled out of the room, out of the apartment, down the stairs, not waiting for the elevator, out of the building.

Nobody knows precisely what happened after that; the next day she was found dead in a hotel not far from Grand Central Station. Peter could never bring himself to think of her as she was that day – or as dead either. He often managed to forget things he didn't like. For the rest of his life he kept her in his mind as she'd been when he first saw her, when she was young: that hot day in the *Postscript* offices with her stocking seams crooked, her slip showing, her dress ill-chosen and ill-fitting, and all that uncontrolled emotion, wild, strong and as random as the trail of hairpins she left in her wake.

All things considered, it wasn't such a bad way to remember her. It certainly caught the essence of her. Even the job she did on herself in that hotel room near Grand Central was messy and violent in just that way, although it had a major virtue and a redeeming grace: it was quick.

CHAPTER 18

i

In this, if in nothing else, Angela was luckier than Peter. At Memorial Hospital there was only the tiniest hiccough in the bureaucratic machinations that channelled Peter through his slow, drawn-out, un-Angela-like death. Mrs Carpenter ran to Alice with the good news.

'The Fourth Floor has come through at last,' she said. 'Your worries are over.' It was Thursday morning.

'You're sure?' Alice said. 'There's not going to be some other hitch?'

'I have the papers right here. It's all settled. You can relax.'

But nobody came for Peter that afternoon. Nobody came on Friday, either, not in the morning, not in the afternoon. Nobody over the weekend. Nobody on Monday. On Tuesday Mrs Carpenter called her in.

'I'm afraid I have some disappointing news,' she said. 'The Fourth Floor has rejected Mr Kessler.'

'You told me' – Alice's voice quavered – 'that it was final. You said so.'

'I'm so sorry – so very sorry. Sometimes this sort of thing happens. It just does.'

'But the morphine and the eighty-two ounces: what about them?'

Mrs Carpenter furrowed the brow over her large, blunt nose. 'During the weekend, he became – well, he's now what we call a "total care" patient.'

'Not total care on Friday?'

'No.'

'But total care on Sunday.'

'Yes.'

Alice knew what Mrs Carpenter was talking about. She'd watched it happen. By Sunday, none of Peter's internal machinery functioned on its own. By Sunday, he couldn't even turn his own body in his own bed. Nurses in pairs had to turn him every two hours, day and night.

But never once did Alice imagine this terrible metamorphosis could bring about these terrible consequences.

'Why don't they take total care patients?' she said. 'What's so bad about them?'

'Oh, dear, there's nothing bad about them. Nothing at all. It's just that, well, you see, there's a gap.'

'He's got past the gap. You said so. You told me so yourself. Right here in this room. Don't you remember?'

'Yes, yes, he did. You're quite right. But that was only the *first* gap. This is the *second* gap.'

Alice stared at her blankly. 'Another gap?'

Mrs Carpenter nodded. 'There is one, let me see' – she glanced up at the children in Mickey Mouse ears that guarded her desk – 'this one divides people who are sick enough for the Fourth Floor from the ones who are *too* sick for it.'

'I thought – ' Alice stopped short. She didn't know what she thought.

'The Fourth Floor doesn't have the funding that total care patients need. Only hospice has that.'

'But you – ' Alice stopped short again.

Mrs Carpenter bent toward her earnestly. 'Medicare doesn't pay enough for the Fourth Floor to nurse them at the standard that the hospital requires.'

'Then he has to stay in the hospital,' Alice said, forging ahead.

Mrs Carpenter shook her head. 'The hospital doesn't have the funds, either.'

'Then he'll have to go to hospice.'

'Oh, no, they've rejected him too.'

'Again? When did they come again? I've been here day and night. I never saw anybody. When did you call them in? They can't reject him now. Not now.'

'I'm afraid they can. They are entirely independent.'

When the emotion is strong enough, things glow at the edges. 'How could they?' Alice cried. 'No, no, don't tell me.' She laughed abruptly. 'There's a *third* gap, isn't there?'

Mrs Carpenter nodded. 'There's a gap that divides the people who are sick enough for hospice from those that are sick in just exactly the right *way* for hospice. Hospice must be very careful to get patients who are sick in just exactly the right way. They have to – '

'Hospice are the only ones who have the money to care for people like him? Is that right?' Alice rushed on. 'At least those private hell-holes won't want him. The hospital gets $600 a day. Hospice must get more. It doesn't? No? But I – ' She broke off, then rushed on again. 'Well, anyway, the nursing-homes get only $72.53. Plainly that's not enough. Plainly they can't take him. So what are you going to do? Are you going to throw him out on the street?'

'No, no,' Mrs Carpenter said. 'Oh, no. Of course not. We wouldn't do a thing like that. The nursing-homes are entirely willing to take such cases. In fact, Happy Acres has agreed to pick him up the day after tomorrow. All you have to do is sign the papers.'

In a way, it's a giggle: the sheer unexpectedness of it − the pie in the face, the unseen banana skin. That complacent old tyrant, Karl Marx, says somewhere that all great events in history repeat themselves, the first time as tragedy, the second time as farce. Trust an intellectual to screw it up. It's farce the first time around − and farce the second. In fact, it's not even farce. It's slapstick: more Groucho Marx than Karl Marx. And sometimes it goes on and on, pratfall after pratfall in an endless afternoon of summer television reruns.

But really to kill? To kill Peter? Was it possible?

If you sprinkle iron filings on a piece of paper − kids do this in school physics − there's just scatter. No pattern at all. But bring a magnet up from the underside, and there's this whoosh, this rustle of sound − soft, delicate: the filings swoop together in graceful sunburst arches. There is a time before; then polariz-ation; then comes afterwards. Afterwards, everything is dif-ferent.

Alice didn't remember leaving Mrs Carpenter's cubby-hole of an office. Back in Peter's room, she sat down beside the bed, reached out to touch him, drew back, reached out again and again drew back. She couldn't bear the thought of his blood.

That meant no knives.

She had no gun. She didn't know how to shoot one.

An American who can't shoot a gun? Living in Europe weakens the blood. She hadn't learned to drive until she was thirty-two either. How can you be American if you can't drive a car or shoot a man?

What about smothering?

Peter was too weak to resist her, and the sleep he slept − he slept most of the time now − was so deep that it was almost coma. But hospital pillows are hard and unyielding. Not to be able to breathe − oh, no, it would never do.

278

She got up and paced back and forth in the room. Why are hospital rooms so ugly? Is it some trick of the insurance trade? some subtle form of rationing? Make the place so unpleasant that patients are in a frenzy to get out? Ugly proportions in a window that looked out on the ugly parking-lot beyond. Ugly stucco on ugly walls. Ugly, squat, inescapable television set dominating everything. This sort of thing can't be good for the sick.

What about a plastic bag?

Those warnings to keep them away from children: if it hurt to die with a plastic bag over your head – if it was frightening – you wouldn't need all those warnings. Well, would you? If a plastic bag over the head is painful or scary, the child is going to take it off. Alice was not sentimental about children. She thought of Tad, and thinking about him, decided that the same child, all asnivel for himself, would delight in suffocating his friend. The matter called for experiment.

Plastic bags near the vegetables and the soft fruit in Overton's Piggly Wiggly aren't any good; they're too small to go over a head. The potato display is more promising. Alice pulled three large bags off the roll, put oranges in one, a lettuce in the second, some zucchini in the third. Back at Cordelia's she unpacked the groceries and went upstairs to the bedroom that was so darkened by trees even in full daylight that sleeping in it at night was like nesting.

She sat down at the vanity-table with its glass cover and its flowered ruffles. Things begin. They end. The corners of her eyes showed signs of crows' feet. How could little Alice get old? She leaned forward to examine the skin more closely. There was a crease in the cheek where her dimples were. What about the streak of grey in her hair? The real mystery, she thought, was how she could bear to look so calmly at these hints of what was to come. Why didn't she run screaming from the room?

She opened one of the bags and put it over her head.

A moment later she took it off. Too much air. In Cordelia's study lay boxes of manuscript-sized rubber bands, enough rubber bands to last several lifetimes. Alice fetched a handful. Back at the vanity table, she tried again. Bag first, then rubber band: hook the rubber band under the chin and slip it over the top of the head. A sense of wet heat is almost immediate but not terrifying. She looked at her watch, waited a minute, two. So far so good. Only sweat and heat. No sense of suffocation. She took off the bag and turned it inside out to dry. There were hitches, though. A rubber band's okay for suicide. But you'd need three hands to do it to somebody else: one hand to hold the somebody's head above the pillow and two to manoeuvre the bag and the rubber band into place. Otherwise he might wake.

If he waked – you see what a joke this is – if he waked, he'd be scared to death.

Use a piece of string instead. Get the day's morphine into him. Get the nurses to turn him at the same time. Then she'd have two hours alone with him. Wait twenty minutes. He'd be groggy on top of that sleep of his – almost anaesthetized. He'd never know what was happening. How could she fail? The man was more than half-dead already.

iii

The next morning, as soon as she could see he was in pain after the doctors had made their morning visits – Dutch and Charlie had both looked in – she fetched his nurse, who slipped the needle under his skin, smiled sympathy and left.

Alice checked her watch – Peter's watch really (she didn't want to wear her own) – large, with a second hand that moved in nervous, shy, undecided jumps. She was watching it mark off the allotted twenty minutes when she looked up to find

Dutch standing in front of her; the lines on his face were as deep as divisions in a stained glass window.

'What are you doing here?' she gasped, asweat with the shock of seeing him.

'I came back.'

'I can see that. Why?'

He jerked his head towards the door.

'You want to talk to me?' she said.

'Yeah.'

She got up reluctantly and followed him out into the hall. He wore his knitted cap in Christmas colours and his leather jacket with *I Love Arabella* on it.

'You look awful,' he said, leading her down the corridor as he talked. 'Don't you never brush your hair?'

'Is it bad?' She touched it absently.

'Hideous. Ain't you got a comb or something?'

'I'll brush it tomorrow. You didn't come all the way back here just to tell me that, did you?'

'Listen, I know how rattled you gotta be about this Fourth-Floor business.'

'Yes,' she said.

'We'd better put a DNR on him, don't you think?'

'What's that?'

'Do not resuscitate.'

'My God, isn't there one already?'

He stopped and studied her in the fluorescent light of the corridor, then turned and walked on, motioning her to follow. 'Now you look here, Mrs Alice Kessler, I'm gonna get that DNR on the books – take me maybe ten minutes – then I'm coming back. Understand me? I'm gonna take a look at that catheter, then I'm gonna examine the man, talk to him a bit.'

'He's just had a shot of morphine.'

'Okay, I'll sit with him. I got nothing better to do this morning.'

They reached the end of the corridor where the big window looked out over the nursing-homes and the poorer sections of town to the distant highway beyond. There was fog everywhere. The ground below was only intermittently visible; thick, grey air shifted in waves like sea water in a storm, revealing sudden glimpses of ramshackle housing and litter-strewn streets.

'No other patients to see?' she said.

'Nope. Got the rest of the day off.'

'What about Arabella?'

'Wednesdays she does the books. You got to keep careful books on a string of fifteen girls.'

'Do you?'

'The IRS gets tetchy.'

'I've always liked the fog,' Alice said.

'Why don't you go home?' He reached out and touched her arm. 'Brush your hair? Do something? Get outta here?'

Alice went back to Cordelia's. She went for the sake of her hair. That was careless: to overlook her own hair.

She was back at the hospital for the evening. Again, she got Peter turned. Again, she got the morphine into him. Again, she sat beside the bed to watch the second hand mark off the time. Repetition is a trick of the comic's trade – the second pie in the face that hits just as the laughter from the first eases off – and it was laughter that Alice choked back when she looked up from her mesmerized study of the watch to find Dr Novali standing in front of her, his sharp insect-face atwitch.

'Dutch thought maybe I ought to come and have a talk to you,' he said.

'Did he indeed?' she said.

'There's one last thing we haven't yet gone into.'

The sudden hope was so strong she was afraid her voice wouldn't work. 'Oh?' she whispered. 'What is it?'

His features slid into an angular smile. 'Come out into the

282

hallway. I'll tell you about it.' They walked slowly down the corridor just as she'd walked that morning with Dutch. 'Have you thought about ECT?' he said.

'ECT? Shock therapy? For Peter?'

'I've got a video about it in my office. You could – '

'He'd go back to the psychiatric wing?'

'Well, yes, that's another advantage.'

Those fluorescent lights are harsh, especially when it's dark outside. Alice had to bend half backward to see up into Dr Novali's face. 'Couldn't he have drug treatment there?'

'He's already had drug treatment. I couldn't justify it.'

'There must be all kinds of other drugs – new drugs, ones you haven't tried.'

They reached the window at the end of the corridor. The day's fog had cleared, and the window looked out over a night sky stained with that orange glow that city lights throw up. Dr Novali took a seat on the window-sill and dandled his legs, which were so long that even from the height of the sill they were half acrouch. He stared down at them.

She said tentatively, 'There are regulations?'

He nodded.

'Would he be unconscious when you did it?'

'Oh, yes.'

'It wouldn't hurt him?'

Dr Novali shook his head. 'We always give an anaesthetic.'

'What would – ' she began and stopped short. He twisted his long body to look out of the window and twisted it back, a queer gesture like a cricket rubbing its wings together. 'What might the treatments do to him?' she said then.

Dr Novali kept his eyes on the dark night. 'Well, they might kill him,' he said. Who says God doesn't have a sense of humour?

But something in Dr Novali's voice nagged at her. 'Suppose it didn't kill him,' she said. 'What then?'

283

'It might break his back.'

'Jesus, then I refuse.'

'But who knows?' he said. 'It might even work. That's always a possibility. You wouldn't want to deny him that, would you?'

Alice watched him carefully. Never trust anybody in a hospital, especially not a doctor. 'How *much* might it help? Suppose it worked the best you can imagine. What then?'

Dr Novali turned back to the window. 'Well, um, he'd be better.'

'Better? How much better?'

The pity that ruffled his face told her the answer before he said it. 'Maybe he could get to the chair from the bed on his own – maybe even get back again.'

'What about the pot?'

'Pot?'

'John. Bog. Water closet. Toilet. Lavatory. Could he get up and pee by himself?'

'Oh, no, nothing so dramatic as that.'

Through the windows, car headlights twinkled at the edge of that orange-black night like a row of sequins on Arabella's G-string.

'In short, if everything works perfectly,' Alice said, 'you can put him back to where he was three weeks ago.' Dr Novali said nothing. 'Is that it?'

The shoulders of his tall, thin body slumped. 'What are you going to do?'

She reached out and took his hand. 'Thanks,' she said. 'It was good of you. I really appreciate it.'

Back in Peter's room, Alice paced back and forth to calm her breathing. Third time lucky. That's what they say. She sat down, opened her purse –

And the telephone rang. Tweedle, tweedle. What kind of a sound is that for the sound of fate? Peter stirred, opened his eyes. Tweedle, tweedle. He sighed and stared emptily at her.

284

She answered the phone.

'Alice?'

'Yes.'

'It's Dutch.'

'I know.'

'Is Peter all right?'

'Yes.'

'I got good news.'

'Good what?'

'Hospice has accepted him.'

The body of the telephone clattered to the floor. A long time ago, going under an anaesthetic – she was only a little girl then, six or seven (tonsils probably) – she'd heard a terrible buzzing in her ears and seen a squadron of insects flying straight at her, as vicious as dive bombers.

'Alice?'

The receiver shook in her hands. 'I just – I just dropped the telephone. I'm sorry. You were saying – ?'

'Is the man all right?'

'Of course he's all right. Why have they changed their minds?'

'Who cares? The important thing – '

'I care. They were so damn definite. I don't trust them.'

'You ask too many questions.'

'I just want to know the catch. Are they going to pull out tomorrow?'

'Just accept it. Sometimes God smiles.'

'Only when He's joking. Tell me why all of a sudden they've decided to take Peter.'

'Ah, come on – '

'I have to know.'

He harrumphed. 'They got certain criteria for hospice, and basically Peter don't qualify, so – '

'That's what I figure. That's what scares me. Not that I know

285

what these – what do you call them? criteria? – not that I know what they are. I only know that whatever they are, he doesn't qualify.'

'Look, we made a compromise, which they were kind enough to do.'

She said nothing.

'This is for real, Alice. Believe me.'

'I don't believe anybody.'

He laughed then. 'Well, think of it this way, Kessler's an important name in this town. Understand me?'

'No.'

'So you make them kind of nervous. What the hell, you make *me* nervous.'

Just before eight o'clock the following morning Peter Kessler was moved from Memorial Hospital to hospice in the annexe nearby.

CHAPTER 19

i

Dr Briggle, who ran Overton's hospice, paid a visit on Peter's first afternoon there. He was old – fearfully old, maybe twenty-five years older than Peter. The skin on his face hung loose from the bones, but the body beneath his suit was solid enough, almost athletic, not stooped, no creaking to be seen or heard, no timidity in the step.

He went directly to the bed, reached down and took Peter's hand. 'How are you this afternoon?' he said. There was no tremor in the voice either.

Peter turned his head aside.

'Mr Kessler?'

Peter had this room to himself. The wall behind his bed was bare except for a crucifix. The window looked out on the single tall brick-red chimney of the dog crematorium, which puffed smoke into the winter sky. Alice could not look at it without thinking of Ahab and the tattoo of his front paws that had shared her optimism – and the missing back paw.

Dr Briggle raised his voice. 'Mr Kessler? Can you hear me?'

Peter kept his head where it was.

Dr Briggle leaned down close enough to put his mouth next

to Peter's ear. 'Tell me something, do you know what day it is?'

No reaction.

'I think the transfer tired him,' said Dr Briggle. He straightened up. 'Let's let him get a little rest. Why don't you come with me, Mrs Kessler? I'll show you around – tell you something about what we do here.'

He led her to the day-room at the front of the building, just around the corner from the nurses' desk – a large, airy, gently Edwardian place with cane furniture and flowered upholstery, whorls of lilac and leaves in blue, pink and green. A few plants stood guard, and a bank of windows looked out into the sprinkling of snow. He escorted her to a sofa and – courtly – ushered her onto it with a bow of his head.

'The hospice movement dates from the Middle Ages,' he said. 'Did you know that?'

Alice shook her head.

'Hospices used to be way-stations for travellers to the Holy Land.'

She couldn't see why he was telling her this. 'I thought they were always places to die in.'

'Only for the poor in those days. Then later – a few hundred years on – Catholic ladies ran hospices in France and Ireland. That was in the mid-nineteenth century. Would you like some coffee? We have a very good machine just around the corner. Can I get you a cup?'

Alice shook her head.

'The idea is that we don't interfere except to make a hard phase of life a little less hard. We'll use whatever seems to help: pain-killers, moral support and family involvement. We like to think that hospice is to death what modern childbirth is to the beginning of life – just the easing of a natural process.'

'I'm glad about – ' Alice began and then stopped. 'I think Peter needs more morphine. He isn't getting enough.'

288

'Isn't he? What makes you say that?'

'He's so afraid.'

'He doesn't have to be afraid here.'

'The pain frightens him.'

Large snowflakes fell beyond the window; the air on the short trip from hospital to annexe had been cold and wet. 'We like to strike a balance between alertness and morphine. This sometimes takes a little experimentation.'

'Why would he want to be alert? Who wouldn't rather drowse through it all?'

'Trust me, Mrs Kessler.'

'I'll try.'

'We have, in fact, increased the dose a little. Let's see how he gets on with that, shall we?' Alice wasn't sure whether she was being dismissed or not; she half rose. Then – when he didn't rise with her – she sat again. 'There must be questions you want to ask,' he said.

'Well, yes.' She was a little embarrassed, although she was not sure why. 'Can we forget the tray?'

At noon a nurse had brought Peter a plate of macaroni and cheese; Alice had asked her to take it away, but she'd said she was bound by the rules to leave it.

'It is important to put meals in front of him,' Dr Briggle said.

'Nobody forced him to eat at the hospital.'

'Nobody's forcing him here.'

'The smell of food makes him feel sick. His sense of smell is so much more acute than it used to be.'

'These are matters of conscience, Mrs Kessler.'

'Lunch?' Alice said, taken aback. 'That's got something to do with conscience?'

'All human activity has to do with conscience.'

'Even macaroni and cheese?'

'He must have food brought to him, and we must put water in his veins.'

'Why?'

The sudden irritation in Dr Briggle's frown heaped layers of crêpe on top of his eyebrows. 'Because that is how my conscience dictates it, Mrs Kessler – to say nothing of the laws of this state. I do not believe in letting people starve to death.'

'I thought you said – ' Alice began, then lost courage.

'Now I must ask you a question,' Dr Briggle said. 'You haven't given up your search for a nursing-home, have you?' This time the terror that flooded through her was so abrupt that it literally took her breath away. 'The increase in morphine may make your husband feel better,' Dr Briggle went on. 'In that case, we just might persuade him to take something by mouth. If he eats, his condition will stabilize, and if his condition stabilizes, he cannot stay here.'

'He's not safe here?' she whispered. 'Not even here?'

'We are subject to regulations like all other hospital bodies. After all, people sometimes go home from hospice.'

'Even Medicare patients?'

'Well, not often, I have to – '

'Do they ever? Have you *ever* known one to go home?'

Dr Briggle sighed angrily. 'The point, Mrs Kessler, is that if your husband's condition stabilizes, he cannot stay here.'

Alice punched Dutch's telephone number with fingers so clumsy they slipped on the buttons. 'Dr Briggle says,' she said, barely able to get the words out, 'that if Peter refuses to die at a proper, government-regulated pace – if he rallies – he's going to end up in the filth and stench of a nursing-home.'

'He ain't gonna rally for more than an hour, Alice. You're going to be lucky if you get more than five minutes at a stretch.'

'Charlie thinks it's possible. More than possible.'

'They gave me their word. I told you that. They're just

290

covering themselves. Besides, Charlie's a young man. What's he know about dying?'

'How to make money out of it.'

Dutch laughed. 'Well, yeah, we all got our price. His is lower than some. Nobody's going to move Peter while I'm around. You got nothing to worry about. Understand me?'

'As long as you're around.'

'Yeah. Right. Trust me.'

'That's what Briggle says and Briggle lies. I trust nobody. Not you. Not him. Nobody.'

'Everything's gonna be all right. Hear me? Now cheer up.'

ii

The first grown-up joke Alice learned was one that Angela had pasted on the larder door of one of the many houses the family stayed in. A little stick figure labelled A is miserable. He mopes. He whines. Life is tough. Another stick figure B says, 'Cheer up. Things could get worse.' So A cheers up. 'And sure enough,' says the final bubble, 'things got worse.' It took Alice years to figure out how such a thing could be funny.

Dutch said, 'Cheer up. Everything's gonna be all right.' She cheered up. What did she expect? Dutch got hit by a truck.

It was a Ford Diesel, a Semi carrying canned peaches from Newark to Portland. The question on everybody's lips was, 'What was such a behemoth doing in the centre of Overton?' Well, the driver was looking for Arabella's Go-Go Joint (famous among truckers on this otherwise barren transcontinental stretch); he'd taken a wrong turning on that cloverleaf Alice had monitored day and night from corridor windows in Memorial Hospital but could monitor no longer from the windows of hospice, which overlooked only the crematorium. The hit was broadside. A sizeable chunk of Dutch got spread over the road

291

just outside Memorial Hospital. The rest of him went into intensive care.

The foreboding that hung over Alice was so heavy that Peter, even in his extremity, sensed it and drew himself back half an inch from the abyss.

'I wish I – ' he began, but the strength ran out and he could say no more.

'How is it that – ?'

Alice didn't know what he wanted. The Bach Prelude on the tape recorder? A shift of his shoulders in bed? 'Forget the phrasing,' she pleaded with him. 'Just tell me the word that counts. What can phrasing matter now?'

Dr Briggle visited every morning. Every morning he said, 'Tell me, Mr Kessler, do you know what day it is?'

Peter had never responded, but on the morning after Dutch's accident, there was a faint twitch of the head, a spark of anger, a public display of solidarity with Alice.

A smile hitched the drapery of Dr Briggle's face. 'You know,' he said, turning away from the bed to face her, 'I think Mr Kessler is a little stronger this morning.'

Alice was filled with dread.

The next morning Peter opened his mouth and shaped the beginning of a word.

The morning Dutch died, Peter made the supreme effort. He said, 'I want – '

'He wants to talk to me,' Dr Briggle said, turning in delight to Alice, who sat beside the bed with her book of crossword puzzles squashed into a clump in her hands. He turned back and leaned over Peter's bed. 'What is it? Tell me.'

' – want to ask – '

'Yes?'

' – ask you a question.'

Dr Briggle turned to Alice again. 'He wants to ask me a

question,' he said happily. 'That's good. Wonderful. What question? Ask me anything. I'll do my best.'

'What – '

'Yes?'

' – day is it?'

'What day is it? That's your question? You want to know what day it is?' Dr Briggle turned to Alice once more, his face puzzled and grave by turns. 'He doesn't know what day it is,' he said.

Sweat had broken out on the palms of her hands. Are there no end of jokes for the dying? Peter's sense of humour was at its best in contempt. Here in his contempt for Dr Briggle was the culmination of the energy he'd been drawing on for days.

iii

The morning of Dutch's funeral, Dr Briggle called her into his office, which was on the ground floor of the annexe and had those vertical Venetian blinds over the windows to hide the acres of black tarmac outside – not a large room, old furniture, pictures on the walls, books, an ancient typewriter and a very modern computer side by side, not unpleasant. Dr Briggle sat behind the green baize of his desk and smelled of cologne.

'Mr Kessler has stabilized,' he said.

'Where?' she said.

'Where what?'

'What place are you sending him to?'

'We've located a bed for him at Happy Acres. You've met Dr Darby, haven't you? I've known Dr Darby for years. His Medicare floor is the best-run hospice-like institution in Overton.'

'When?'

'Dr Pederson and I have arranged for the transfer to take place tomorrow morning.'

She had to go back to Cordelia's first. Who carries an executioner's equipment around *all* the time? The dogs were half-asleep as she passed them going in through the laundry-room. The washing-machine hummed. Charlie was greedy; she was sure he'd auctioned Peter. Not that she had any way of knowing. But she could just see Charlie on the telephone, taking bids for his kickback. How do you arrange payment for a dying man? Cash on delivery?

In all this time – the years of Peter's illness, the weeks of hospitalization – Alice had not wept. Not once. Maybe now, she thought: maybe now. She'd cried before Peter got so sick, but it seemed to her, thinking back on it, that she'd cried only to change his mind or to make him feel guilty or simply to irritate him. Not a bad device, all in all – an occasional victory accompanied by a tender, tearful reconciliation. But what victory could there be now?

She got up, walked around Cordelia's glass-walled room, sat, stared, got up once more, walked, sat and stared again. The Corn King's hand no longer lay on the table. This morning, still just a skeleton (Cordelia hadn't been able to part with a single old receipt), it went out to the burning field to go on the effigy as it was, unfleshed and unburnable, to be burned this very night. Frightened people scream. Women in movies are forever screaming. She'd passed Cordelia's car going out as she came in. She was alone. A house hidden away in its own inner-city park is a good place for screaming.

She opened her mouth and threw out a sound.

It wasn't a success: more of strangulated gurgle than scream – not even enough to upset the dogs.

She wondered if Charlie and Briggle split the kickback. There had to be a standard procedure for this sort of thing. There are standard procedures for everything. Briggle had to get something for it. Fifty-fifty? Seventeen and a half percent? Like VAT?

How can you be so self-conscious that you can't scream even when you're all by yourself? She took in her breath and tried again.

This time the sound was shrill enough to startle her and make her ears ring. The dogs started yapping. That was good. She tried again. The dogs yowled. Just as she thought she might be getting the hang of it — she and the dogs together — her voice cut off mid-scream. Some control seemed to have slipped somewhere in her neck. The dogs went on alone.

She coughed gently. No blood or anything — nothing serious — but her throat was very sore. She slumped in her chair.

The dogs were quiet by the time she went upstairs and packed plastic bag and piece of string in her purse. She opened the door to the laundry-room. They lay still, but their eyes swivelled in their sockets, marking her progress as she went.

Part Five

CHAPTER 20

The first time Alice watched Peter sleep she was only eight years old, only a little girl in puff sleeves and a sash. He'd given up magazines by that time; he'd given up editing, pasting up, all that had once seemed to him more important than anything else in life – just dropped them, forgotten them, the way he did with people sometimes. He'd got the idea for the quartet that he was never to finish, and he was enchanted, abubble with enthusiasm – enchanted with himself as well as with the idea, which had come to him full-blown as his best ideas always did. In a single week, he'd quit his job (not a simple matter: he was editorial director of a major news magazine called *Science*), and worked out the plot and titles for all four books. Not that he was rigid about it. He loved changing things.

The first book was to be titled *Night*; it was set in New Mexico. At the beginning of his second week as a novelist, he drove west from New York. He wandered around mesas and pueblo sites; he went to Los Alamos, which appealed to him because it was a secret city on a secret mountain, an ordinary-looking place and yet the nursery for the most terrible power the world has ever known. He'd filled several hundred pages with notes. Then he drove to Texas to visit Christie and Angela in Houston, where Gertsch International had stationed them for that year.

The evening he arrived, he talked at the dinner-table over roast lamb and a baked Alaska about what he'd seen and what he planned to do. Alice didn't understand much of what he was saying – she was too small – but even now, all these years later, she could remember the descriptive parts, the cadence of his voice as he spoke and the look of him as he sat there. There were candles on the table; the light from them flickered in the pupils of his eyes.

'New Mexico is a landscape without people,' he'd said. 'It's a brown landscape – baked brown – all the way out to the timber shades of the mountain ranges. There's a little green too, very faint, as though the living green of a dozen trees had been drained to colour a hundred square miles.'

How could anybody speak so beautifully? She kicked and screamed when Angela took her to bed that night, away from the cadence of that voice. To placate her, Angela said she could be the one to wake Peter in the morning for breakfast. So it was that at eight years old, Alice Kessler stood in the doorway to the guest-room in her best dress, watching a naked man sleep, monitoring his intake of air and the letting go. He slept on his back, silently. His bare shoulders showed above the sheet, strong shoulders, smooth – one arm above his head, across his brow and the dark of his hair. She remembered it all.

He slept as silently in Overton's hospice on this last night of his life as he'd slept all those years ago. The similarity should have stopped there. That Peter had been young – black hair and smooth, naked shoulders. This Peter was grey through and through, grey eyelids over eyeballs as slippery white as lychee nuts. But the magic was still inside somewhere; she couldn't touch it or see it anymore but she knew it was there. Well,

300

didn't she? If it wasn't there, where was it? It had to be somewhere.

She climbed up into the high hospital bed, lay beside him and pulled his frail, distorted body against hers.

'Mommy?' he said.

'I'm here,' she said.

He sighed, and within moments she felt a deep relaxation come over him. Why had she not got up on the bed before? It seemed to give him more peace than anything else. A little later she opened up the plastic bag, slipped it over his head and tied the string around his neck. She checked her watch. Ten minutes to eight. His breathing grew shallow. Then it stopped altogether.

At eight o'clock she untied the string and removed the bag.

She'd never seen a dead person before. In the movies – on television – the mouths aren't open. She shut Peter's tentatively. They lie to us about everything. Why not about dead men's mouths? That bandage Ichabod Crane wore around his chin: she'd always wondered about it, although never enough to ask. The mouth dropped open.

'It's because he's so relaxed.'

Alice's heart lurched in her chest.

The blonde, pregnant nurse stood opposite her. 'It's always like that,' she said.

Peter's eyes were closed. Alice knew she must have closed them herself, but she couldn't remember doing it.

'Myself, I'd say he was one of the lucky ones,' the nurse said. Her voice was very gentle.

Alice nodded.

'The man across the hall – he died in the ambulance on the way to Happy Acres. That was just last week. He was one of the lucky ones, too.'

'Was his wife with him?'

'Oh, yes.' The nurse smiled. 'He had family. My grand-mother always said you can't be lucky without a family.'

Alice nodded again.

'It would probably be a good idea to put that away,' the nurse said then.

'What?'

'That.' The nurse pointed at the plastic bag, which had fallen off the bed and lay half-hidden beneath it. 'The string, too. That was a good idea – string. Rubber bands are more compli-cated than they seem.'

Alice got up from the bed. 'What are you going to do?' she said, leaning down to gather up the bag and the string.

'I'll get you a taxi as soon as the formalities are over. There are papers to sign. You shouldn't drive yourself home. Not tonight.'

'May I sit with him a while?'

'I'll come back in a few minutes.'

Alice leaned her body against the bed and took Peter's hands in hers. They were cold already, an unexpected kind of cold for somebody who'd never felt it before, except in meat from the butcher.

The nurse reappeared. 'Would prayer help?' she said. She carried an ice-bag in her hand.

Alice shook her head. 'I just want to be with him a little longer. Is that all right? Just a little longer?'

'Really?' the nurse said, disconcerted. 'I mean, it's – '

'It's not customary?'

'His eyes are going for research. Remember? You signed the papers. That was – let me think – when you first admitted him. Eyes don't keep very well.'

'Oh, just a minute longer,' Alice pleaded. 'Just one minute. Please.' She put her head down on his shoulder, and the cold crept its way past her cheek while ice clunk-chinked impatiently at the doorway.

302

CHAPTER 21

That sound — the hollow clunk-chink of ice — was the very
first sound Alice associated with Peter as well as the very last.
The very first time she met him, she was only three years old.
She couldn't remember anything else from that far back. Only
Peter. She was sitting on the kitchen floor (the linoleum had
one of those swishing patterns, tan and white: she hadn't liked
it then; she didn't like the memory of it now), playing with
some toy, a doll most likely, her legs splayed out with that
marvellous flexibility tiny children have, head bent down,
wholly preoccupied, wholly unaware.

Then she heard the ice, and she heard this voice say — this
voice with cadences unlike the cadences of any other voice —
'If somebody comes up for to do you good, you'd better run
for your life.'

She looked up out of her game and saw Peter.

He was standing beside Angela, who was stirring the gravy;
she tended to oversalt if she talked when she cooked, especially
if she was talking to an attractive man. Most children of three
wouldn't have cared how much salt got stirred into the adults'

food, but the little Kessler girls sat at the dinner-table with the guests and so were sophisticated in such matters.

Alice had never seen anything like Peter. He was tall enough so that from her seat on the floor, the parallax gave him something of the proportions of an El Greco Christ. Not that she knew anything about El Greco. Not that Peter looked Christ-like, either. He must have been thirty-five at the time, but his skin was clear and unlined. Amusement flickered in his face, caught back here and there by a boyish uncertainty, a mercurial creature, phosphorescence on water, each characteristic at odds with the rest. He stood by Angela's stove, one leg in front of the other, weight on the back leg, front leg straight and balanced out on the foot behind. He was tense. He was always tense.

Alice decided there and then, staring up at him from her squat on the floor, that she would grow big as fast as she could and marry this beautiful creature. She'd marry him and live with him forever after.

And, oh, how tenderly she would care for him when he got to be an old man.

AFTERWORD

I would like to emphasize two things.

First, the setting, the characters and the human entanglements in this book are pure fairy-tale.

Second, the medical part of the story, I'm sorry to say, is no fairy-tale. It's all too real. I based it on a case-history, backed up by hefty research into Medicare, America's national medical program for the elderly. I knew right from the beginning – from late in 1988 – that I'd stumbled onto a huge scandal. I could hardly believe it myself. It's the sort of thing you might catch in a screaming newspaper headline, one of those horrors from some Third World backwater; yet here it was, thriving – expanding – in the most powerful and technologically advanced nation on earth.

I turned myself into a machine for getting it all down on paper. I worked harder than I've ever worked and produced a thoroughly documented, non-fiction study in just over two years. What an innocent. I was really taken aback when no US publisher would touch it – not as it was, not with a view to a rewrite, not under any circumstances – and, as several people in publishing here in the UK pointed out, a non-fiction treatment of an internal American affair, one that deals with intricacies of US law and administration, isn't likely to attract readers abroad. I didn't know quite what to make of my position. I'd uncovered

306

a savage, wide-scale, institutionalized violation of human rights, and I couldn't make anybody listen to me.

So I began work on this novel.

Don't think I've exaggerated anything, either. Quite the contrary. Literally millions of gravely ill Americans end up in the dying-rooms I describe, and for precisely the Kafkaesque reasons I give. Such rooms constitute a fate so terrible that one California state inspector, seeing them for the first time – he was a survivor of the Auschwitz death-camp half a century ago – cried out in shock, 'This is America! You can't do this here.'[1]

The US government foots the bill for these places, claiming they provide 'hospice-type care'. In the nursing-home trade, they're called 'produce departments'.[2] This is a *double entendre*. A produce department is where a supermarket keeps its vegetables. Also, these patients 'produce' something: money.

How? I discovered four ways; there are doubtless many more.

1) Saving on staff. Nobody wants to work on Medicare floors; the only people willing to do so come from the lowest rungs of the labour pool. Training is minimal; understaffing routine; overwork the rule. Turnover often exceeds 100% a year. No workers are effectively banned, no matter what their records – and these can (and all too often do) include theft and criminal assault carried out in nursing-homes themselves.[3]

2) Minimizing care. Government criteria require nasogastric tubes, and for reasons nobody understands, patients with such tubes become almost as passive as vegetative patients[4] – hence the real joke in that *double entendre*. On top of this, they are grossly overmedicated.[5] Such people are cheap to tend. Besides, not even the best homes have money enough for wholly adequate care; the others pare to the bone. Four-

[1] Quoted by F. Smith, 'No Place to Die', Part 4, *San Jose Mercury News*, Nov. 12, 1986.

[2] J. L. Yates, journalist and hospice aide, who worked as manager of a nursing-home in Texas, interview Dec. 1988.

[3] M. Freudenheim, 'Nursing-Homes Face Pressures that Imperil Care for Elderly', *New York Times*, May 28, 1985.

[4] F. Rowse, attorney for Society for the Right to Die, New York, interview Feb. 1989.

[5] D. Eastman, 'America's Other Drug Problem', *AARP News*, Apr. 1989.

fifths of the work – including insertion of feeding tubes and catheters – is done by the untrained staff.[6]

3) Padding bills. Medicare pays separately for extras such as dressings, drugs, medical procedures, transfusions, etc. With a little ingenuity, a nursing-home can inflate bills for these by as much as 2000%.[7]

4) A host of miscellaneous petty fiddles. Theft from patients is a perk of the job. Falsification of records – to show care or medication given or withheld – is standard. Many of these patients are prescribed morphine as well as other drugs: morphine is the one they often don't get. Addiction rates among staff are high; if staff or management don't want the morphine for themselves, there's a ready market on the street. This is a US pharmacopoeia drug; cut it ten times – which is about the usual street dose – and you've got a small fortune. There's even a going street price for keys to nursing-home drug-cabinets.[8]

How does a nursing-home get away with it?

Patients don't complain because they are physically incapable of complaining, and families rarely object on their behalf. Americans are afraid of death; as one nurse said to me, 'Usually I can't get relatives as near as the door to the room.' It doesn't take much to keep them away altogether.

Doctors are no better; they hate the places. As many as nine out of ten of them refuse to go in the front door, much less as far as a patient's room. Most write prescriptions, sign charts and death certificates without examining patients – sometimes just sitting in their cars outside.[9] Their only regulator is the home's medical director, whose salary is paid by whatever body profits from what goes on in the home.

As for regulation of this – of what goes on in the homes themselves – state agencies are inadequate at best and, more often than not, corrupt. Jobs in them are almost as undesirable as jobs in nursing-homes, and again the staff comes from the bottom rung. Again training is inadequate, understaffing and overwork routine; turnover is higher than in the homes – up to 250% a year.[10] As for corruption, nursing-home

---

[6] E. Kiester, 'Stand Up and Fight', *50 Plus*, Jun. 1988.
[7] J. L. Yates; F. Smith, loc. cit.
[8] J. L. Yates.
[9] Ibid.
[10] J. Petchel, 'Group-home regulation inadequate, officials say', *Miami Herald*, Apr. 14, 1988.

inspections are often signalled in advance.[11] If a 'deficiency' comes to light even so, all the home's operator has to do is show compliance the next time around – and the matter goes no further. The pattern, as a New York State Health Department memo put it, is 'noncompliance, correction, noncompliance'.[12]

Here in the UK, it remains cheaper to let the dying die. But there are signs of a change.

Take two newspaper stories that I just happened to catch in my daily reading while I was working on this novel. The first appeared in the *Guardian*[13] – a discussion of ways to combat the organs-for-transplant shortage. It goes into proposals for a programme of 'elective ventilation', whereby potential organ-donors may be transferred to a special unit when they are on the point of death and there warehoused, American style, until 'their organs can be retrieved'. And where do we find the donors? In hospital geriatric wards, among other places.

The second article[14] – more frightening than the first – describes how UK government guidelines, published on 12 August 1994, allow hospitals to evict patients to nursing-homes in precisely the same way and on precisely the same grounds – a largely meaningless and easily manipulated distinction between 'treatment' and 'care' – that lead to evictions such as I describe in the US.

Now put these articles together with the endless NHS cuts, the acceleration towards private medicine – the very nature of which enforces a profit motive – and the fact that US corporations are moving into the nursing-home industry here. What emerges is a route to profit, and a very nasty one at that: not only an excellent price for warehousing the should-be-dead, but a bonus in organs for sale on top of it.

Remember, too, that Britain is even less well regulated than the poorly regulated United States; it's already a petri dish for American researchers who want to experiment with patients in ways the US government won't allow. So who's to say there are obstacles to US corporations providing the British with the same cheap – and

[11] J. Anderson & R. Spear, 'Nursing-Home Inspections: A Sham?', *Washington Post*, Mar. 29, 1988.
[12] W. Barrett, 'A Case of Medical Neglect', *Village Voice*, May 14, 1985.
[13] P. Kent, 'Life After Death', Jul. 27, 1994.
[14] D. Fletcher, 'Aged forced to quit hospital', *Daily Telegraph*, Aug. 13, 1994.

wonderfully profitable – 'hospice-type care' they provide at home? All that's missing is that famous Yankee know-how.

Myself, I'd bet plans are well under way.